The Doom Tha
Weird mysteries of the Cthulhu Mythos

Richard A. Lupoff

Table of Contents

INTRODUCTION

The central conceit of the famous "mythos" stories of H.P. Lovecraft was concerned with the idea that Earth had been colonized by malign aliens in the remote past, long before mankind arose and became civilized, who eventually became worshipped and feared as evil Gods by their human servitors. Eventually these aliens had been "banished" to another dimensional limbo by a benign Elder Race, but might one day return to reclaim the Earth "when the stars are right."

During his lifetime, Lovecraft encouraged other authors to write their own stories based on these precepts, and to develop his ideas. Countless authors accepted his invitation, including, inter alia, Robert Bloch, August Derlerth, Robert E. Howard, Henry Kuttner, Frank Belknap Long, and Clark Ashton Smith. The parade of other writers has continued, unabated, to the present day, and they include Richard A. Lupoff.

Lupoff has written his own interpretation of Lovecraft's vision:

We are told that humans — or creatures that could reasonably be defined as humans — have walked the earth for 2,000,000 years at the least, and perhaps for as long as 5,000,000 years. And yet civilization, in any form that we would recognize and acknowledge, has existed for a mere 10,000 to 15,000 years. We are thus asked to believe that Gug and her mate Ug led a primitive existence, hunting and gathering or perhaps scratching a few crude holes in the ground and dropping seeds into them each spring, and made little more progress than that for a minimum of 1,985,000 years. Following this there sprang into being virtually simultaneously the miracles of Angkor Wat, Babylon, Thebes, Kukulcan, Yucatan, and Cuzco.

We are also told that life has existed on the earth for at least 2,000,000,000 years, and perhaps as long as 6,000,000,000. Uncounted millions of species have evolved and disappeared. Whole orders of life have emerged and departed. Creatures as tiny as a virus and so huge as to dwarf the mammoth or the whale, creatures of infinite variety and endless complexity, have lived and died on this world. And yet we are told that of all these species, only one, our own, and at that, only in a relative flicker of an eyelash, has developed true consciousness and intelligence.

What nonsense! What arrogance! What blind, ignorant balderdash!

Richard A. Lupoff lives in Berkeley, California with his wife Patricia, and has enjoyed successful careers in several mediums. Beginning in his student days in New York (he was born in Brooklyn) he first worked as a print journalist, then in the emerging computer industry with IBM. His first book (non-fiction) was *Master of Adventure : The Worlds of Edgar Rice Burroughs* (1965). Earlier, he and Patricia had won a Hugo Award for their fanzine *Xero* in 1963, and from its pages he compiled (with Don Thompson) *All in Color for a Dime* (1970), another non-fiction book, about the history of American comics. His first SF novel was *One Million Centuries* (1967) and parallel with his writing was a 50 year career interviewing famous (and not so famous) writers on his own show on local radio station KPFA.

After he started appearing regularly in the fantasy and SF magazines, and anthologies, Lupoff became recognized as the "go to" man for anthologists wanting to commission original short fiction. They knew they could rely on him to deliver a quality story on a huge range of diverse themes, and spanning all genres. Prominent in these works were Lupoff's stories exploring the "mythos" created by H.P. Lovecraft.

Writing a background note in 2005 for anthologist Stephen Jones, the astute editor who first published his Lovecraftian short story "Brackish Waters", Lupoff revealed how he had first encountered the stories of H.P. Lovecraft as a youngster:

"One week I stumbled across a little paperback anthology called The Avon Ghost Reader. As I remember, it had a deliriously lurid cover painting — a green, claw-like hand rising menacingly in the foreground, a spooky-looking old mansion in the distance — and a marvellous selection of frightening stories, including 'The Dunwich Horror' by H.P. Lovecraft. At age eleven I had no understanding of the publishing industry, and didn't realise that this story was a reprint and that its author had been dead for nearly a decade.

"What I did understand was that I'd stumbled across an author of unusual merit. I vowed to watch for his byline. My next reward was a copy of another little paperback, Weird Shadow Over Innsmouth, and I

6

was totally hooked. I've been a Lovecraft fan for most of my life, and I am delighted to see the Old Gentleman finally getting his due. I'm equally gratified to have made my own small contribution to the traditions of his work."

One has to raise a wry smile at the words "small contribution", which is typical of Lupoff's modesty and self-effacement. It is manifestly inadequate when one considers his many Lovecraftian stories, culminating in his astonishing tome *Marblehead: A novel of H .P . Lovecraft* (2006) aka *"Lovecraft's Book"* (abridged, 1976) which is a dazzling blending of fact and fiction that transcends genre writing.

And yet there is something paradoxical in the fact that Lupoff should have become such a fan of Lovecraft, because their approach to writing was actually very dissimilar. Most likely it was because Lupoff encountered his stories at a very young, impressionable age. Lovecraft entered his psyche, and became submerged along with myriad other writers.

In his essay "Some Notes on Interplanetary Fiction" (included in the collection of his writings titled *Marginalia* (Arkham House 1944) H.P. Lovecraft wrote:

"Inconceivable events and conditions form a class apart from all other story elements, and cannot be made convincing by any mere process of casual narration. They have the handicap of incredibility to overcome; and this can be accomplished only through a careful realism in every other phase of the story, plus a gradual atmospheric or emotional building-up of the utmost subtlety. The emphasis, too must be kept right — hovering always over the wonder of the central abnormality itself. It must be remembered that any violation of what we know as natural law is in itself a far more tremendous thing than any other event or feeling which could possibly affect a human being. Therefore in a story dealing with such a thing we cannot expect to create any sense of life or illusion of reality if we treat the wonder casually and have the characters moving about under ordinary motivations. The characters, though they must be natural, should be subordinated to the central marvel around which they are grouped. The true "hero" of a marvel tale is not any human being, but simply a set of phenomena."

In complete contrast to Lovecraft's thesis, Lupoff's own approach to writing is to *put human beings centre stage*. This was to eventually contribute to his drifting away from science fiction into other fields, most notably that of the murder mystery novel. A detailed and fascinating exploration of Lupoff's writing career and his motivations can be found in his latest book, *Where Memory Hides: A Writer's Life* (Bold Venture Press, 2016) and so does not need to be detailed here.

Over five decades, Lupoff has experimented, writing stories in the "style" of many popular writers, but in all cases they are never mere pastiches, because Lupoff seeks to invest them with his own evolving voice. He has never ceased to develop as a writer, and is clearly utterly enamoured of the *craft* of writing — in particular what has been labelled as "popular fiction" (though in *Where Memory Hides* Lupoff has convincingly argued that there should be no real distinction between what he has termed "Hi Lit" and "Low Lit".) Lupoff has an almost eidetic memory for the myriad stories he has read, and an abiding admiration for authors who thrilled him as a teenager with so-called popular fiction, and even when he became older and his tastes wider and more sophisticated, he sought to analyse and understand the appeal of his earlier pulp idols, *as well as* the emerging and recognised giants of the mainstream.

Lupoff's "take" on Lovecraft is an important contribution to fantastic literature, and after reading and enjoying his stories over many years, I recently suggested to him that it was high time that the best of them were collected into one book. To which he replied: "I like your idea of assembling my Lovecraft stories into one book. In fact an editor at Chaosium made the same suggestion some years ago, but nothing ever came of it... I'll scout around my files (both "e" and paper) and bookshelves and see what I can put together."

Shortly thereafter I had the great pleasure of reading all his Lovecraftian stories (including many I had never read before) and then agreeing a generous selection of the best of them, with the author, and assembling them for publication.

It is an honour and a privilege to present them to you now, collected into single book form for the very first time!

Philip Harbottle,
Wallsend,
Tyne and Wear

February 2017

Acknowledgments

THE DOOM THAT CAME TO DUNWICH
Return to Lovecraft Country, edited by Scott David Aniolowski, Triad Publications, 1997

THE SECRET OF THE SAHARA
The Mammoth Book of New Jules Verne Adventures, edited by Mike Ashley, Robinson, 2005

THE TURRET
Made in Goatswood, edited by Scott David Aniolowski, Chaosium Publications, 1995

THE PELTONVILLE HORROR
It's That Time Again 2, edited by Jim Harmon, BearManor Media, 2001

THE DEVIL'S HOP YARD
Chrysalis 2, edited by Roy Torgenson, Zebra Books, 1978

DOCUMENTS IN THE CASE OF ELIZABETH AKELEY
Magazine of Fantasy and Science Fiction, May 1962

BRACKISH WATERS
Weird Shadows Over Innsmouth, edited by Stephen Jones, Fedogan & Bremer, 2005

ADVENTURE OF THE VOORISH SIGN
Shadows Over Baker Street, edited by Michael Reeves and John Pelan, Del Rey, 2005

NOTHING PERSONAL
Cthulhu's Reign, edited by Darrell Schweitzer, DAW, 2010

THE DOOM THAT CAME TO DUNWICH

When a traveler in north central Massachusetts takes the wrong fork at the junction of the Aylesbury Pike just beyond Dean's Corners he may feel that he has fallen through a crack in time and emerged into an earlier era in New England. The countryside is marked by rolling hills and meadows, spotted here and there with stands of woodland that, at first glance, appear lush and healthy, but that, upon closer examination, seem to emit an almost palpable miasma of *wrongness*. The grasses are oddly yellow. The tree trunks seem to be writhing in pain, while their leaves appear oddly *fat* and to give off an unpleasantly oily exudation.

If one arrives in what has become known as Dunwich Country at night, the sense of temporal alienation is especially strong. The few advertising billboards that were erected along the Pike in earlier decades have fallen into wrack and ruin, but no one has bothered either to rehabilitate or to remove them. The few tatters of once-colorful posters that remain attached to their frameworks, flapping in every errant gust of wind, remind the traveler of products long removed from the market: Graham-Paige automobiles, Atwater-Kent superheterodyne radio sets, Junius Brutus Cigars.

Even tuning the radio to stations in Boston, Providence or Worcester does little good, for the particular conformation of the terrain, or perhaps the presence of deposits of as yet undetected ores beneath the ground or of unexplained atmospheric conditions, makes it impossible to receive more than an unpleasant mélange of sound, interspersed with indecipherable whisperings and gurglings.

Rounding the base of Sentinel Hill on the outskirts of Dunwich, the site of the infamous "horror" of 1928, the traveler beholds an incongruous sight: a modern laboratory and office building of mirrored glass construction. Activity in the building proceeds uninterrupted, day and night. A wire-mesh fence surrounds the facility, and a single rolling gateway is guarded at all times by stern-faced young men and women. These individuals are clad in dark uniforms of unfamiliar cut and tint, identifiable neither as military nor police in nature. Each uniform jacket carries a shoulder patch and each uniform cap a metal device, but the spiraling helix into which these insignia are formed is also unique to the Dunwich facility. This ensign, it may be noted, is laminated as well on the stock of the dull-black, frightening sidearm which each uniformed guard carries.

A small wooden plaque is mounted beside the rolling gate, in sparse letters identifying the facility as the property of the Dunwich Research Project. No newspaper files or directories of government organizations make mention of the Dunwich Research Project, and neither the directory issued by the Dunwich Telephone Company, nor that company's Directory Assistance operators are able to furnish a number by means of which the facility may be contacted.

However, careful study of federal appropriations documents of past years may reveal "black" items in the budgets of major agencies which, a selected few Washington insiders are willing to concede, may indeed have been directed through back channels to the Project. Further study of federal records will show that these covert appropriations for the Dunwich Research Project began in 1929.

The initial appropriation was extremely small, but in later years the funding for the Dunwich Research Project increased despite crisis, Depression, or war. The names of every President from Herbert Hoover to the present time will be found attached to these "black" items.

It was to this region that young Cordelia Whateley, a graduate student of anthropology at McGill University in Montreal, Quebec, drove her conservative gray four-door sedan in the late spring of the year. Her examinations over for the semester, she had determined to spend the next several months researching her master's dissertation on the events of 1928. It was Miss Whateley's belief that an encounter with one or more alien beings had provided the basis for those horrific happenings. Because she was herself a member of a distant (and undecayed) branch of the Whateley family, she had been inculcated from infancy with a revulsion for her (decayed) kith and kin. This she wished to resolve once and for all: to prove that her distant cousin Wilbur Whateley had been not so much a menace to be feared and loathed as he was a sport of nature deserving of the sympathy and aid which he failed to receive from those around him.

Miss Whateley brought her automobile to a stop outside the rolling gate of the Dunwich Research Project. The guard on duty, a young man with a square jaw and muscular build, approached her and courteously asked her business at the Project. She showed him a letter from her faculty adviser at McGill, addressed to the Director of the Dunwich Institute, and a response, on Institute letterhead, welcoming her inquiry and authorizing all concerned to offer the bearer every possible courtesy and assistance.

The merest suggestion of a smile played around the lips of the guard as he handed the documents back to Miss Whateley. "You'll want the Dunwich Institute, miss," the guard explained. "This is the Dunwich Research Project. The Institute is in Dunwich Town. On South Water Street. Dr. Armitage is the Director. That's his signature on the bottom of your letter. You want the Institute, miss. The Research Project is off limits."

He gestured courteously, suggesting but not exactly duplicating, a military salute. Then, with a series of clear and vigorous hand gestures (he was wearing white gloves) he directed Miss Whateley to depart and return to town.

Cordelia Whateley complied, swinging her automobile around and pointing its nose back toward Dunwich proper. As she circled Sentinel Hill she could not help noticing that an array of radar dishes dotted the top of the hill. To her, they looked like a recrudescence of white, puffy toadstools.

The town of Dunwich had neither grown nor changed noticeably from the illustrations and descriptions Cordelia Whateley had studied in preparation for her visit to the region. Authorities in the United States had been reluctant to send materials dealing with Dunwich out of the country, even to so friendly a neighbor as that to the north, but a friend of Miss Whateley's at the University of Massachusetts had managed to borrow many such documents and share them with the researcher by means of electronic transmission.

As Cordelia Whateley motored down Winthrop Street toward South Water, she noticed that Osborne's Store still stood at the corner of Winthrop and Blindford. Beside it, a grimy-windowed establishment advertised EATS and ALE. No other name identified the establishment, but after a lifetime in which her world had become increasingly dominated by malls and franchise enterprises, Cordelia Whateley found the survival of Osborne's Store and of an establishment identified solely as EATS and ALE oddly comforting.

Opposite Osborne's Store stood a steepled, greystone building. Cordelia tried to make out the device that topped the steeple. In the darkness she could not be certain, but she thought it was the same ensign she had seen on the uniforms of the guards at the Dunwich Research Project. Lights flickered inside the building, and the sound of chanting could be heard.

She located the Dunwich Institute and stood before its Spartan exterior, searching for a means of admittance. The Institute was located in a building of Colonial architecture, but rather than serving as a source of elegance and charm, the frame construction with its chipped and faded whitewash and its black front door surmounted by a dust-shrouded fanlight, caused a shudder to pass through her body.

Beside the door a rectangular brass plate, once gleaming but now covered with a patina of dullness, still bore the legend, *Dunwich Institute — founded 1928 — Henry Armitage, Ph.D. President.* Cordelia Whateley searched for a doorbell, and, failing to locate one, instead reached for the brass knocker bolted to the wooden door. The knocker, covered with the same dull patina as the plate, was shaped like a creature differing from any Cordelia Whateley had ever before seen. It bore many tentacles, and great staring eyes, and from it there seemed to seep a miasma of pure evil such as she had never in her life encountered.

Cordelia Whateley had taken her large, well-filled purse with her when she left her automobile. Now, having retrieved the purse and clutching it with one hand, she drew a breath, grasped the brass creature, raised it and let it fall. It struck with a loud, metallic sound of unpleasant nature. Cordelia Whateley found herself staring from her hand to the knocker, and then to her hand once again. Surely the knocker was of brass: of old, tarnished brass. Why, then, did her hand feel as if her fingers had grasped the rubbery, slimy, moist tentacles of a living creature? And why, when she released the door-knocker, had it seemed to cling stubbornly to her fingers so that she had to pull them away to gain her release?

She had not long to ponder the problem, for the door drew back noisily on rusted hinges and she stood face to face with an aged individual who blinked at her with faded, rheumy eyes. He stood well over six feet in height. His sparse hair was pure white and his face bore an expression of despair overlaid with chronic fear.

"I am Henry Armitage," the old man said. "Who are you, young woman, and what do you want of me?"

Cordelia Whateley was taken aback by the old man's appearance but she had rehearsed for this moment and she delivered the lines she had prepared. "I — I am Cordelia Whateley. From McGill University. I — I wrote to you about my work, and you sent me this reply." She held Armitage's own letter so he could see it in the yellow light filtering from behind him. Was it possible? Yes, the Institute building was illuminated by oil-lamp and candle. With a chilling shock she realized that she had not seen an electric appliance or even a gaslight in Dunwich.

Although Cordelia Whateley had arrived in Dunwich Country at an hour when the afternoon sunlight was still fairly bright, here in the narrow streets of the town itself a darkness had descended that was not the comforting, pleasant darkness of a New England evening. Involuntarily, Cordelia Whateley looked behind her. The streets of Dunwich seemed abnormally empty of pedestrian traffic, and the few canvas-covered vehicles that moved on the old streets seemed almost to huddle within themselves as they passed.

Armitage extended a thin hand covered with pale, wrinkled skin. "Come in. You are late. Almost too late. I receive very few visitors. I expected you earlier in the day."

Cordelia Whateley followed Armitage into the ancient building. An almost palpable miasma of age and decay seemed to arise from the heavy furnishings and threadbare carpet. Armitage indicated an overstuffed chair covered in faded velvet. Cordelia Whateley lowered herself carefully into it.

"I would have been here earlier," she tried to explain, "but — "

"But you went to Sentinel Hill, didn't you?" Armitage cut her off.

"Yes, I — "

"You tried to get into the Project. The Dunwich Research Project. I was afraid of that. You're very lucky indeed."

"Lucky? I don't understand. I — " Cordelia Whateley put her hand to her forehead. "I'm so sorry. Could I have a glass of water? I'm afraid I'm feeling faint."

While Armitage was out of the room, Cordelia Whateley studied its contents as best she could without leaving her chair. The walls were covered with glass-fronted bookcases, all of them filled to their limits. Many were locked. The books themselves, for the most part, looked ancient. The bindings were tattered; such lettering as Cordelia Whateley could make out was faded. In size, the volumes ranged from huge tomes that would cover a desktop if opened, to tiny items little larger than a common postage stamp.

Her eye was caught in particular by a small book, little more than a pamphlet, in fact, with an illustration on its cover. The illustration, barely visible in the yellow light of the dark, musty room, seemed a crude representation of the door-knocker that Cordelia Whateley had handled at this very building. The slim book was bound in black leather, and its title, embossed in gold lettering in an obsolete typeface, read simply, *De Obéissance à les Maîtres Vieux* .

Henry Armitage's hand on her shoulder startled Cordelia Whateley. She gasped and turned. He extended a glass toward her. It might once have been part of a set of fine crystal but its rim now showed a jagged chip, its sides were streaked and the water it contained was of a vaguely unpleasant color and odor. Cordelia Whateley accepted the vessel and took one reluctant sip of its contents before placing it on a dust-coated table.

"You asked why I thought you lucky," Armitage said. "Visitors to the Project sometimes disappear. Young Selena Bishop went up there last spring and hasn't been heard of since. In Dunwich Town, people don't like to receive an invitation to visit the Project."

"But then," Cordelia Whateley frowned, "why do they go? Why don't they just refuse to go?"

"When you're summoned to the Project, you go. That's the way it is in Dunwich Town."

"But people could just move away, couldn't they? Don't the buses run? And the Aylesbury Pike is nearby. It's only an hour or two to Boston by automobile."

"You don't leave Dunwich Country as easily as you might think, young miss. No, not if *they* want you to stay here. Rice and Morgan thought they could leave. They learned better. I'm the only one left now, of the three of us. I was the oldest, and you'd think I'd be long gone by now. But Rice was buried at sea and Morgan was cremated. They'd both left instructions that, whatever happened, *they were not to be interred in Dunwich Country.*"

He clapped his hands, and the sound was like an exclamation mark at the end of his sentence. Then he resumed. "The undertaker, Hopkins, respected their wishes. I made him do that. He wanted to bury 'em, he wanted to bury 'em in the town graveyard out near Jacob's Pond, but I wouldn't let him. We had a terrible battle, believe me, young miss. But if I ever see Rice and Morgan again — I don't expect to, I don't think we get to go on once our flesh is finished, but I could be wrong, and if I am, and if I ever see Rice and Morgan again, I'm sure they'll thank me for making that fool Hopkins do what they wanted him to do."

He stopped, short of breath after his long statement. But before Cordelia Whateley could speak, he put a question to her. "How old do you think I am, young miss?"

She looked at him appraisingly. Her own great-grandfather, Cain Whateley, had lived to 109, and Armitage looked every bit as old as Cain had in his last days. "I've read what I can find about the horror, and it says that you had a white beard in 1928. If you are the same Dr. Armitage ..."

He gave her a sly grin. "You've done your homework. I'd expect as much of an undecayed Whateley. I think I see a tinge of the Wizard himself in your face. Yes, I'm the same Henry Armitage. Shaved off my beard in '42. Hoped to get into the army then, and get out of Dunwich Country. *They* were onto me, though. Said I was too old, but I'd shaved it off by then so I kept it off."

"But if you're the same Henry Armitage — " Cordelia Whateley looked longingly at the chipped goblet of water but could not bring herself to take another sip. "You were an old man in 1928, and that was nearly seventy years ago. That's impossible. You'd have to be — "

"Yes," he nodded, "I was almost eighty in 1928. I'm afraid I've given up on ever leaving Dunwich, but if the town is still here in a few years, I hope you'll come to my 150th birthday party."

He stood over her, reached down and patted her on the knee. Could this incredibly old man be — Cordelia Whateley shook her head. She must have misread the look in his eye. What she thought for a moment she had seen there was impossible.

She said, "I don't mean to keep you up. I could come back in the morning. I mean," she made a show of looking at the battery-powered watch on her wrist. She frowned and held it closer to the nearest oil-lamp. "I just put a new battery in," she muttered.

Armitage smiled. "Electrical implements don't always work well in Dunwich. You did drive here, did you not, young miss?"

Cordelia Whateley nodded.

"You may have trouble starting your car in the morning."

"But —"

"Never mind. We can dine at the inn. Then we can return here and I will assist you with your work as best I can. I have always felt a certain sense of — well, obligation is not exactly the word, but it will do — toward the Whateleys."

Cordelia Whateley was flustered. "You're very kind, Professor. But you need your sleep. A man your age —"

"I do not sleep," Armitage replied. "Come, let us go to the inn. We can walk from here."

They walked from the Dunwich Institute back past Osborne's Store. The inn to which Armitage referred was not the restaurant Cordelia Whateley had seen, but another, located in a building that must have existed since the days of King George III and Governor Winthrop. They were waited on by a young woman — she could hardly have been into her teens, Cordelia Whateley realized — who seemed terrified of Henry Armitage. Armitage whispered a few words to the waitress, who nodded and disappeared into the kitchen, her long skirts brushing the floor behind her. Apparently Armitage had ordered for both of them, a custom that had gone out of fashion in Cordelia Whateley's world long ago.

Cordelia Whateley looked around the room. Dour New Englanders of past centuries frowned down from framed canvases that lined the old wood-paneled walls. A small fire struggled fitfully to survive on a gray stone hearth. The only other illumination was furnished by oil-lamps. Beside the hearth a musician sat upon a high stool, picking out a tune on a stringed instrument that Cordelia Whateley did not recognize. The tune, however, seemed vaguely familiar: it was a transcription of a piano composition by the mad Russian composer Alexander Nikolayevich Scriabin.

The musician was a woman. At first glance she appeared to be aged, perhaps as much so as Henry Armitage himself, but as Cordelia Whateley studied the woman she realized that her hair was that of the albino rather than the crone. In her features, Cordelia Whateley suspected that she could detect a hint of the legendary Lavinia Whateley or — perhaps — of herself.

Without ceasing to play, the woman raised her eyes from the fingerboard of her instrument and focused them upon Cordelia Whateley. Even in the faint light of wood flame and oil-lamp, it was clear that those eyes were hopelessly clouded by milk-white cataracts, cataracts the color of the woman's wild albino hair.

The only customers aside from Cordelia Whateley and Henry Armitage were a group of dark-clad persons wearing the uniform and insignia of the Dunwich Research Project.

After a few minutes one of them, a gray-haired, severe-visaged woman, approached their table. "Professor Armitage," she said sharply, "I didn't know that you had invited a guest to visit you."

Armitage said, "I didn't invite her. She wrote and said she was coming from Canada. I couldn't prevent."

I couldn't prevent, Cordelia mused. What an odd expression.

The uniformed woman nodded angrily and returned to her own table. Henry Armitage had not introduced Cordelia Whateley to her.

The waitress reappeared with a tray of dishes and glasses. A dust-coated bottle stood on the tray as well. The waitress set the dishes and bottle on the table. Cordelia Whateley's dish held a slab of very rare meat — she assumed that it was beef. It was set off by a portion of broccoli and several very small roasted potatoes. Henry Armitage's dish was empty save for a sprig of parsley.

"Is that all you're going to eat?" Cordelia Whateley asked.

Armitage shook his head. "I have had my nourishment."

"But — I could have come here alone for dinner. You didn't need to — "

"It is not good to be alone on the streets of Dunwich after dark, young miss." Armitage reached across the table and took Cordelia Whateley by the wrist. He held her briefly, then dropped his own hand to his lap. He wore a threadbare black suit, a white shirt with a frayed collar, and a bow tie in an abstract print that Cordelia Whateley found almost hypnotic in the flickering yellow light of the oil-lamp on their table.

"Why not? Is Dunwich unsafe? We have muggers in Montreal, too, you know. I think I can protect myself."

"Muggers?" A tiny laugh escaped Armitage's lips, but even so Cordelia Whateley noticed a reaction among the uniformed men and women at the other table. "There are no muggers in Dunwich," Armitage said. "No, young miss. There are no muggers."

After a long day's journey from her home in Montreal, Cordelia Whateley experienced a combination of hunger and fatigue. She lifted her knife and fork and prepared to slice the rare meat on her plate. Her usual preference was for meat more thoroughly roasted than this, but appetite and reluctance to provoke any disagreement in the inn caused her to plunge the tines of her fork into the roast, and then the sharp point of her knife.

Perhaps it was the dim and unsteady illumination in the inn coupled with the effects of fatigue and several sips of wine that created an illusion, but the meat appeared to *writhe* away from Cordelia Whateley's implements. An involuntary gasp escaped her. The uniformed diners and even the blind musician turned their eyes toward her. She whispered, "Doctor Armitage, I'm — I'm afraid I've lost my appetite. If we could leave now, and we'll start our work in the morning …"

The ancient man shook his head negatingly. "You must not put off. We will return to the Institute."

Half fainting from fatigue and wine, yet equally eager to be at her work, Cordelia Whateley agreed. Upon returning to the Institute, Professor Armitage produced a ring of keys from the pocket of his shabby black suit and unlocked the glass-fronted bookcase containing the largest of the volumes Cordelia Whateley had previously seen.

He selected one and carried it to a heavy deal table beside which a wooden reading-chair had already been placed, and laid it carefully upon the table. "You will find useful information here, young miss." Having said this he retired to a far corner and folded himself into a chair. To Cordelia Whateley he seemed to disappear.

She examined the volume Armitage had laid out. It was a bound collection of large news pages, the paper yellowing and flaking away at the edges. "I thought everybody was transferring newspaper files to microfilm," Cordelia Whateley said.

From his darkened corner, Henry Armitage replied, "Many in Dunwich Town like things as they were."

Cordelia Whateley, examining the masthead of the bound newspaper, read aloud, "The Dunwich Daily Dispatch."

"Only called it a daily," Armitage commented. "You could never tell when there'd be an issue. The editor, Ephraim Clay, used to say it was a daily, came out once a day, just not every day. I think that was some kind of joke. Never understood Ephraim very well. A strange man. But look at those issues for 1928. You'll learn all you need to know."

Cordelia Whateley fumbled in her large purse and brought out a small tape recorder. She pressed a switch and began dictating segments from various 1928 issues of the *Dunwich Daily Dispatch* .

One of them, reprinted from a Boston newspaper, reported the death of Cordelia's distant cousin, Wilbur Whateley. The article bore no byline, but it described the youthful, dying giant in shuddersome detail. Cordelia's voice quavered and shook as she spoke, but she managed to continue to the end of the article.

Above the waist it was semi-anthropomorphic (the dispatch ran) though its chest, where the dog's rending paws still rested watchfully, had the leathery, reticulated hide of a crocodile or alligator. The back was piebald with yellow and black, and dimly suggested the squamous covering of certain snakes. Below the waist, though, it was the worst; for here all human resemblance left off and sheer phantasy began. The skin was thickly covered with coarse black fur, and from the abdomen a score of long greenish-grey tentacles with red sucking mouths protruded limply. Their arrangement was odd, and seemed to follow the symmetries of some cosmic geometry unknown to earth or the solar system. On each of the hips, deep set in a kind of pinkish, ciliated orbit, was what seemed to be a rudimentary eye; whilst in lieu of a tail there depended a kind of trunk or feeler with purple annular markings, and with many evidences of being an undeveloped mouth or throat. The limbs, save for their black fur, roughly resembled the hind legs of prehistoric earth's giant saurians; and terminated in ridgy-veined pads that were neither hooves nor claws. When the thing breathed, its tail and tentacles rhythmically changed colour, as if from some circulatory cause normal to the non-

human side of its ancestry. In the tentacles this was observable as a deepening of the greenish tinge, whilst in the tail it was manifest as a yellowish appearance which alternated with a sickly greyish-white in the spaces between the purple rings. Of genuine blood there was none; only the foetid greenish-yellow ichor which trickled along the painted floor beyond the radius of the stickiness, and left a curious discolouration behind it.

Cordelia Whateley collapsed into the wooden reading-chair. She pressed her hands to her chest, trying to steady her breathing. After a while she managed to raise her face and peer into the darkened corner where Armitage sat, patiently waiting for her to speak.

Finally she managed to mumble, "It's impossible. Impossible. I know my Cousin Wilbur was — not normal. Not like other men, even other Whateleys. But this — how could such a being exist?"

Armitage did not respond directly. Instead, he asked, "Did you know that Wilbur was a twin?"

"No. My parents and grandparents would never speak of the Dunwich branch of the family. Only my great-grandfather, Cain Whateley, told me stories. I remember my parents were furious with him. I used to ask them about the Whateleys, but they would never tell me anything, and when I asked about things that Great-grandfather Cain told me, they said it was all nonsense. They said he'd seen too many horror movies when he was a boy, and read too many cheap magazines, that he was so old he couldn't distinguish what he'd read about or seen in the movies from what was real."

Armitage made a soft sound but spoke no words.

"Even Great-grandfather Cain never mentioned Wilbur's being a twin."

"But still he was," Armitage told her. "Read on."

Cordelia Whateley felt a painful thirst, the wine she had sipped at the inn had left a dry aftertaste in her mouth and throat. But recollection of the malodoriferous water Armitage had offered her earlier militated against her renewing the request. Instead, she continued leafing through old *Dunwich Daily Dispatches*, pausing frequently to dictate excerpts into her miniature tape recorder.

A gasp of horror and revulsion escaped her when she came to the description of another creature, but she read the words aloud from the

24

yellowing page, first attributing them accurately to still another cousin, Curtis Whateley. The reporter, once more anonymous, seemingly had seen fit to record Curtis Whateley's degenerate Miskatonic Valley speech in its full phonetic peculiarity:

Bigger'n a barn... all made o' squirmin' ropes... hull thing sort o' shaped like a hen's egg bigger'n anything with dozens o' legs like hogsheads that haff shut up when they step... nothin' solid abaout it — all like jelly, an' made o' sep'rit wrigglin' ropes pushed close together... great bulgin' eyes all over it... ten or twenty maouths or trunks a-stickin' aout all along the sides, big as stove-pipes, an' all a-tossin' an' openin' an' shuttin'... all grey, with kinder blue or purple rings...ban' Gawd in Heaven — that haff face on top!

And another quotation, from another news page, attributed to the same Curtis Whateley.

Oh, oh, my Gawd, that haff face — that haff face on top of it... that face with the red eyes an' crinkly albino hair, an' no chin, like the Whateleys... It was an octopus, centipede, spider kind o' thing, but they was a haff-shaped man's face on top of it, and it looked like Wizard Whateley's, only it was yards and yards acrost...

Cordelia Whateley collapsed, sobbing.

"That was Wilbur's brother." Henry Armitage spoke in an ancient, papery voice. "He never had a name, or if he did, no one in all the Valley ever knew it. Save, perhaps, Wilbur, or his mother, Lavinia." Armitage's breath rasped. "Or mebbe his step-father, old Wizard Whateley."

Cordelia Whateley managed to raise her eyes. She ran her fingers through her hair. She had heard superstitious tales of men or women whose hair had turned white in a single night, from sheer terror. She wondered if that was happening to her. She wondered if she was going mad.

"What do you mean, step-father?" she croaked. "Wasn't Lavinia's husband the real father? Who was, then?"

"Not old Wizard Whateley, you can be sartin.'" Armitage was lapsing into the local argot.

"Who was the father?" Cordelia Whateley demanded.

Armitage uttered a frightening chuckle. He rose, an elongated, shadowy figure still obscured by darkness. To Cordelia Whateley he seemed unnaturally tall, perhaps as tall as her Cousin Wilbur's legendary stature. But maybe all was illusion, maybe all was the effect of the dim, flickering illumination of fireplace and oil-lamp.

"Wizard Whateley was not the father of the twins. Not any more than Joseph the Carpenter was the father of Jesus of Nazareth." He paused. "That is, ef you b'lieve that Christian balderdash, o' course. Ef you do, then the father was God, wa'nt he? An' Joseph merely the foster-father of the infant Jesus? Ef you believe that Christian balderdash, o' course."

"Well, I — I've never thought about it very much, Professor."

"Wilbur Whateley and his giant brother, his daemon brother, were star-spawn, young miss. Their father was a bein' from the vaults of space, a member of a civilization old beyawnd human comprehension an' distant be'awnd human imagination. An' he come here to earth — Gawd alone knows why — an' he fathered two sons awn the blessed Lavinia Whateley. An' the good people o' Dunwich Town kilt 'em. Yes, the good people o' Dunwich Town refused t' understand, refused t' care, refused t' give the slightest sympathy or assistance to them two innocent children of an alien father and an earthly mother. We kilt 'em. The Romans had nothin' on us. They kilt themselves one Son o' Gawd. We kilt us two. An' our punishment will be terrible, young miss. The stars are right, know it, young miss, the stars are right and our punishment will be terrible."

A low moan escaped Cordelia Whateley. She had come to Professor Armitage in hopes of learning the truth about her cursed relatives, and instead had been subjected to the ravings of this madman. "It's impossible," she managed, "an alien and a human could never interbreed. It's a biological impossibility."

"You think so?" Armitage challenged. He was growing calmer, and reverting from his Dunwich dialect into the cultured academic pronunciation he had used at first. "A mere few years ago it might have seemed impossible, but we are learning better. Most of the people of Dunwich know little of such things, and such things have been wisely kept from them. But a few of us — those ones at the Project and I alone here at the Institute — we keep abreast of modern science. And we know that genetic material from one creature can be implanted within the ovum of another, even a creature of another species. Did you know that DNA extracted from a laboratory mouse and injected into the cells of a common fruit fly has produced eyes on the legs of that fly? Eyes, young miss, eyes. Think of what you've just read."

"But — but its horrid. It's blasphemous! How can you countenance such wickedness in the name of science?"

"Ah." Armitage seemed pleased. He advanced toward Cordelia Whateley and stood with his back to the fireplace. His dark suit now longer seemed threadbare, his white hair appeared to stand out from his scalp like a hydra's snakes. He seemed to tower nearly to the high, echoing ceiling. He seemed simultaneously as young as an infant and as old as the continents. "Ah," he repeated, "I suspect that you do believe in that religious nonsense. You use words like wickedness. Like blasphemy. Next you'll accuse use of sinning."

"Yes," she almost shouted. "Yes. It is sinful!"

She thought she caught the flash of firelight glinting off Henry Armitage's teeth as he grinned down at her. "He's coming, you know."

"Nobody is coming." She felt a growing desperation in the pit of her belly.

"But he is. He is. He's on his way now. You'll see."

Cordelia Whateley pushed herself to her feet. "I have to leave now." She scrambled toward the door, clutching her purse in one hand and her small tape recorder in the other. "Don't — don't help me — don't see me out — I'll find my own way."

Armitage seemed to loom even taller. She couldn't understand how he managed to stay in the building without his head colliding with the rafters and beams overhead. But he did not pursue her. He merely stood with his back to the fireplace, hands balled in fists, resting on his hips.

And he laughed. He laughed, and he roared in a voice like the voice of a blaspheming godlet, "The father is coming. He's coming to Sentinel Hill, young miss. And he's mad. You know what the students like to say? The few students we have left in this demon-damned town? He's coming back, young miss, and he's mad as hell!"

Cordelia Whateley plunged through the door and stood panting on the portico of the Dunwich Institute.

Behind her, through the open door, the voice of Henry Armitage boomed out, "He'll come to Sentinel Hill. Trust me. See if you can get in. He's coming to Sentinel Hill."

Cordelia Whateley managed to fumble the keys to her conservative sedan from her oversized purse. She unlocked the automobile's door, plunged inside, started the engine after several tantalizing false attempts and switched on the lights and tore madly through deserted Dunwich streets, heading finally for the outskirts of town and the installation at Sentinel Hill.

The grounds of the Dunwich Research Project were illuminated as glaringly as if it had been noontime on a brilliant day. Vaguely military-looking vehicles crowded the roads inside the gates and were parked helter-skelter around the buildings. The rolling gate itself had been left wide open and utterly untended, and Cordelia had no trouble driving her car onto the grounds and finding an opening near a cluster of military vehicles. They were parked halfway up Sentinel Hill, and Cordelia had to swing her sedan around the end of a row and leave it pointing downhill.

The giant radar dishes atop Sentinel Hill swung slowly in unison as if following a single object that approached from far overhead, invisible to the naked eye. Great searchlights like props from a monochromatic motion picture about a long-concluded war sped beams of vivid white light into the black night sky.

Men and women in the distinctive garb of the Dunwich Research Project raced past Cordelia Whateley, ignoring her utterly in their concentration on their assigned tasks.

Now a tiny speck appeared fleetingly in a searchlight beam. A woman near Cordelia Whateley pointed at it and shouted, "He's coming, he's almost here!"

Cordelia Whateley watched until the black dot was picked up by another searchlight, and another. Near her a corpulent man in dark uniform fell to his knees on the oddly-colored New England grass. He held a book in his hands, and on its cover Cordelia Whateley recognized the illustration and the title as those she had seen in a locked bookcase at the Dunwich Institute.

Strangely, as the man knelt and opened the leather-bound volume, his costume seemed less to reflect a military origin than an ecclesiastical one. He began to read aloud, but in a language utterly unlike any that Cordelia Whateley had ever heard.

The speck in the sky was growing perceptibly larger. Cordelia Whateley had half-expected the Dunwich Research Project to be a branch of the American military establishment, most likely a refined version of the controversial Strategic Defense Initiative of former years. She half-expected to see missile-launchers rising from Sentinel Hill, and deadly rockets rising from them to destroy the thing that was growing larger with each passing moment.

But to her shock she realized that the open meadow beside Sentinel Hill was spread as a gigantic altar. It was covered with tapestries into which were woven depictions of blasphemous beings performing unspeakable acts upon writhing humans, their mouths open in silent screams of anguish and terror. And standing in the middle of the huge altar, naked, motionless, seemingly drugged, were men and women, boys and girls, clearly every missing person whose disappearance from the Miskatonic Valley and all of Dunwich Country for years past had gone unexplained.

And all around Cordelia Whateley dark-clad men and women were kneeling in adoration, singing and gesturing to that which drew closer and closer to them.

The thing was unbelievably huge. Cordelia Whateley revised her estimate of its size again and again, expecting it to land at any moment, but instead it grew, and it grew, filling the sky, blotting out the stars.

And in the illumination of the searchlights Cordelia Whateley could make out the shape of the thing. It was like a gargantuan jellyfish, literally miles in breadth. Thousands — no, millions — of tentacles dangled from its underside, writhing and squirming, stretching eagerly toward the hapless, naked victims who awaited them below.

The tentacles were greenish at their base, and white along their expanse, and deep crimson at their tips. And as they approached the altar those tips opened to reveal rows of glittering, triangular teeth that snapped and gnashed in anticipation of their coming feast.

And among the tentacles, on thicker, longer stalks, were large, round, rolling eyeballs that flashed and shifted from victim to victim, from altar to sycophant. And around the edges of the being rows upon rows of ciliated, transluscent, gelatinous extensions rippled in repulsive rhythmic sequence.

Cordelia Whateley snapped to awareness as if awakening from a hypnotic trance. She raced across the meadow to her automobile and turned the key in the ignition. Nothing happened. But the car stood at the end of a row of vehicles halfway up Sentinel Hill, and she set the gear lever in neutral and released the parking brake, struggling with sheer will power to make the sedan roll downhill.

It did!

Just before the ground leveled out she shoved the gear lever into low, whispering a prayer. The engine caught and she sped through the open gate of the Dunwich Research Project. She kept the accelerator pressed to the floor, ignoring laws and obstacles equally, tears streaming down her cheeks and screams emerging from her mouth, until she reached the Aylesbury Pike.

Here she drew up and climbed from the car. She clambered onto its hood and from there onto its roof and turned her gaze back toward Dunwich. The distinctive shape of Sentinel Hill was silhouetted against distant clouds and stars.

The giant, jellyfish-thing was still settling. Cordelia Whateley realized now that even her greatest estimate of its size was grossly insufficient. It was larger than the altar, larger than Sentinel Hill, larger than the entire Dunwich Research Project compound.

It was easily as large as all of Dunwich Town.

And coming from it was a horrible, wet sound. A sucking, slithering, *hungry* sound. And from the ground beneath Dunwich, even as far away as the Aylesbury Pike, could be felt a terrible, trembling, rumbling.

It could only have been a matter of minutes, perhaps even seconds, until the great creature struck the earth. All of the equipment on Sentinel Hill must have shorted in that moment, and for all that Cordelia Whateley was ever able to determine, it was the immense electrical field created by that equipment that caused all the other problems with electrical devices in Dunwich.

There was flash brighter than the noonday sun, and a coruscation of pulsing colors, and a strange display of chromatics that Cordelia Whateley could only describe, in the days and years that followed, as *the very sky and earth screaming in terror and in pain.*

Then all was silence and all was darkness, and Cordelia Whateley knew nothing until she opened her eyes and looked into the face of a brawny individual wearing the garb of a Massachusetts State Trooper. He was shining a flashlight into her eyes, and when she blinked and moaned he said, "Are you all right, ma'am?"

She lifted a hand to her face and said, "Yes. Yes. I just — I managed to escape from Dunwich Town."

The trooper frowned. "There's been a terrible disaster there, ma'am. Looks as if some kind of giant meteor crashed on Dunwich. Wiped out the town, the hull entire town." He shook his head. "Every man, woman and child. And there's some kind of horrid goop all over the place, and a stench like to make you throw up. Pardon me, ma'am. Sorry about that."

Cordelia Whateley struggled to stand up.

The trooper assisted her gently. "Can we take you somewhere, ma'am? Is there someone we should notify?"

"No." She shook her head. "I just want to leave. I just want to get back to Montreal and forget this — this horror."

The trooper's face was visible in the reflected illumination cast by his flashlight. "Should a lady your age be driving a car?" he asked. "Do you still have a driver's license, ma'am? I mean, I know the laws are different there in Quebec. Your car has Quebec tags, ma'am. Are you from Quebec?"

She said, "Yes. Thank you. I'm perfectly all right. I just want to get home."

The trooper looked dubious, but finally he said, "All right, ma'am. If you're sure you'll be all right."

"I'm perfectly all right," she repeated, annoyed. The trooper released her and she climbed into her car. Her purse lay on the seat beside her and she found the cassette player and rewound the tape and hit *play*. From the player's speaker there emerged only a hissing and crackling, and the occasional hint of an indecipherable whisper.

Cordelia shut the player off. She tossed it into the back seat of her automobile. She switched on the engine. This time it started without hesitation. She reached up to adjust the rear-view mirror, but on an impulse turned it first toward herself. By the dome-light of the sedan she studied her image. Her hair was white and her visage was the withered, wrinkled, desiccated face of a woman three times her age.

THE SECRET OF THE SAHARA

Although the Great Hall of the Republic could of course have been commandeered for the meeting, His Excellency the Governor General of the Province of Tunisie Francaise had chosen to entertain his distinguished guests in a smaller, private dining room. Such was a proper decision, for these more intimate surroundings were designed to encourage an open discussion of issues and exchange of views than would the more formal, even ceremonial, atmosphere of the flag-draped and sculpted Hall.

Here in the Governor General's private dining room, a sparkling table had been set and the Personal Representative of the President of the French Republic had entertained his guests in lavish manner. The meal had consisted of a local endive and olive salad, baked Saharan langouste stuffed with salt-water crab, lamb shish kebab, chick peas and tabouli washed down with Algerian wine, followed by baklava, thick Turkish coffee, and a sweet Hungarian Tokay.

Empty dishes, silver, and other detritus has been cleared away by silent and well-trained servants. Out of respect for their sole female member, the Italian Dottore Speranza Verde, a native of Tuscany, the men of the party had refrained briefly from lighting cheroots. The red-haired and green-eyed Tuscan physician had startled them by requesting a cheroot from her neighbor, the English historian, Mr. Black, and drawing upon it with obvious pleasure.

Now as the Governor General, M. Sebastiane LeMonde, rose, the buzz of conversation which had followed the meal ceased and a hush descended upon the room.

"Madame," the Governor General bowed toward the female physician, "and Messieurs, in the name of the President of the Republic I welcome you to French Africa and to our beautiful city of Serkout."

A murmur of approval rippled through the assemblage, following which the Governor General resumed.

"I am authorized by the President of the Republic to offer special felicitations to Colonel Dwight David White."

The Governor General nodded toward a tall, distinguished gentleman clothed in the gray uniform of the Army of the Confederate States of America. This officer's skin was black; his hair, its tight curls cropped close to his skull, shared the coloration of his military garb. The uniform bore the gold frogging and glittering decorations earned in his distinguished career.

The Colonel nodded his acknowledgement of the Governor General's felicitation.

"Sir, this year marks the one hundredth anniversary of a date in the history of your nation, the Declaration of Emancipation issued by your President, Mr. Jefferson Davis. As a student of North American history since my first days at the *Ecole de Paris*, I have long felt that President Davis's action was not only a matter of high morality, but a political move of the wisest. By declaring the enslaved persons of his nation free and equal citizens of that Republic and offering them fair compensation for the suffering and deprivation of their lives, he won for the Confederacy a new and most highly motivated Army, which led to the vanquishment of the Union forces and recognition of a new and shining ornament among the family of Nations."

The Confederate rose to his feet and responded, briefly and modestly, to the Governor General's words before resuming his seat.

M. LeMonde spoke once more. "You have assembled here, Madame and Messieurs, in regard to a situation unprecedented in human history. As you are aware, the greatest engineering feat of the past century, greater even than the Grand Canals de Lesseps which connect the Red Sea with the Mediterranean and the Atlantic Ocean with the Pacific at the Isthmus of Panama, was the creation of the Sahara Sea by the engineers of the Republic of France under the leadership of the great M. Roudaire, of happy memory."

A murmur of agreement was heard, accompanied by the nodding of distinguished heads.

"The world has known and applauded this great feat of engineering," LeMonde continued, "but at this moment we face a new puzzle of which only a handful of individuals are aware. The details will be revealed to you shortly. By your own consent, all contact with the general public and the outside world has been interdicted, and will remain so until you return from the mission which you have agreed to assay."

A grumble made its way around the table. The bearded, heavy-set archaeologist, Herr Siegfried Schwartz, ground his Cuban maduro cigar into an ashtray. "From Berlin I receive my instructions, Monsieur LeMonde."

The Frenchman expressed his concern. "All was agreed to beforehand, Mein Herr, was it not? I hope we are not to dissolve into disagreement at this point."

"Yes, I believe that was the agreement. Otherwise I should have to consult Whitehall at every turn. It just wouldn't do, sir." The blond moustache of the historian, Sir Shepley Sidwell-Blue, twitched as if with a life of its own.

"Very well," Herr Schwartz growled, "continue, Monsieur."

"At this point, if I may be excused," the Governor General stated, "I will turn the proceedings over to the Chairman of your Committee, Monsieur Jemond Jules Rouge." The Governor General bowed and took his leave. He was replaced at the podium by his goateed countryman.

Monsieur Rouge looked around the room, his eyes flashing. "Madame and Monsieurs, you represent not merely the great nations of the civilized world but the flower of your chosen professions. Throughout this day and evening we have socialized and exchanged credentials. In this room are assembled the world's most famed archaeologist, the author of many volumes which I may say cumulatively comprise nothing less than the history of civilization, the military officer whose brilliant campaigns have extended his nation's borders from the Mason-Dixon Line to the de Lesseps Inter-Oceanic Canal, and, may I offer my compliments to the lovely Dottore Verde, our most accomplished — pardon my crude pronunciation *s'il vous plait* — hydrologist."

Each participant in the conference — and the meal — nodded acknowledgment as his or her name was spoken.

The Italian hydrologist, Dottore Verde, had prepared for this moment. She rose to her feet and strode to the rostrum, relieving the Frenchman who resumed his place at the now cleared dinner table.

"Signori, when our colleagues French opened the northerly dunes of the Sahara desert and let in the waters of the Mediterranean to create the Sahara Sea, they created a new avenue for the ships of commerce and a new home for the fish of nourishment. We agree — yes? — that the people of the Africa North are blessed by this new sea. But also they created, perhaps unthinkingly, the so-they-say Fleuve Triste, the river which flows between Isola di Crainte and Isola di Doute. This fleuve, this so-they-say fiume, is not really a river, but a tidal phenomenon that flows first to the north, then to the south, again to the north, again to the south."

A sulfur match flared as Herr Schwartz lighted another maduro. He sucked loudly at the cigar, then exhaled a cloud of heavy, odorous smoke.

"I should think, perhaps, that Signor Schwartz of all, would take an interest in this phenomenon," the red-haired Tuscan continued. "For the action of scouring of the rushing water, back and forth, back and forth, has begun to carry away the sand accumulated between these two islands over a many thousands of years span. The French, by creating this new sea, have changed the — what we call the idrodinamica — the hydrodynamics — of the entire Mediterranean region as well."

"So?" Herr Schwartz growled, "to what result, Doktor?"

"Herr Schwartz," the Tuscan smiled, "you of all persons are familiar with the great and ancient civilizations to the east of our present location."

"Ah, of course. The Egyptians, the Mesopotamians, the Hebrews, the Hittites. But here in the Sahara — nothing but sand and palm trees, my dear Doktor. My time I could spend far better in my museum in Berlin. A channel perhaps deeper is made, larger ships it will permit to travel to this city of Serkit. Of interest to me this is not. Only because my government instructed, am I here."

"I see." Dottore Verde gave no indication that she was hurt by the German archaeologist's words. "But your knowledge of the archaeology may yet prove useful. You see, good sir, all is not sand beneath the Sahara seabed."

"Of course not," Schwartz frowned. "Bedrock we will find. Sooner or later, it this inevitable is."

"Not only bedrock, good sir. When the Sahara was a desert, the dunes they rose and fell with the action of mighty winds. But beneath the dunes, the ancient rocks had their own," she smiled, displaying white, even teeth, "their own topografia, you understand? The islands between which we cruise, Crainte and Doute, are of the ancient bedrock. But — "

"This lesson in geography, Dear Madame — any point at all, has it?"

The Tuscan hydrologist's monologue had turned into a dialogue with the archaeologist, then a debate, very nearly a quarrel.

"What we have found," Dottore Verde went on calmly, "is nothing less than dressed rock of a workmanship most assuredly artificial."

The historian let out a gasp. "Surely, Doctor, surely you do not realize the implications of what you say!"

Dottore Verde shook her head. A strand of her russet hair, until this moment held in place by an elaborate array of clips and long pins, broke loose from its moorings. With an annoyed gesture she swept it away from her face. She leaned forward, pressing the knuckles of a slim hand against white linen.

"I realize quite well the implications of what I say. We are about to discover the greatest mystery since the discovery of the ancient world. We are about to discover it, yes, but will we solve this mystery? That may be the work of many years and require the efforts of many scholars, but we will be the first to behold these great objects. My friends — "

She looked around.

"Miei amici, miene Freunde, mes amis, did the great Egyptians move to the west, did they leave traces of their art in the Sahara land once fertile, only to retreat before the advancing sands? Or did another race, perhaps even a greater race, once call this region their home? Could they have taught their arts and science to the Egyptians, only to disappear, themselves, beneath those sands? This mystery will be solved, and we are the first so honored to begin its unravelment."

*

An hour later Colonel Black and Dottore Verde sat in the lounge of the hotel where the members of the party had been inconspicuously housed. Every other customer had departed the room. A pair of Arab musicians played softly upon aoud and tabla, the voice of one rising in tones as soft and as mournful as the long, sad history of his people.

A bottle and two small glasses stood upon the table between the man and woman. A candle flickered beside the bottle, casting shadows on the faces of the two. Only an ornately tooled portfolio stood against one leg of the Tuscan hydrologist's chair to remind a viewer — had there been one — of the session but earlier completed with their colleagues from France, Germany, and England.

Colonel White reached to fill both glasses, not for the first time. The two raised their glasses, let them touch rim to rim, then sipped at the delicious beverage. "I didn't like that German," Colonel White whispered. "If he doesn't believe in this mission he shouldn't be here."

Dottore Verde shook her head. "Skepticism is healthy, Colonel. Perhaps it is different for a military man like yourself, but a scientist must treat each claim as a mere possibility, a suggestion perhaps, until it is supported by solid proof."

The Confederate looked into his companion's eyes, his usually serious countenance brightened by what might have been the merest suggestion of a smile. He did not reply, not yet, but instead waited for the Tuscan to resume.

"If we believed every report," Dottore Verde said at last, "we would live in a world of chimerae and of hobgoblins, every woods full of werewolves and ogres, every castle populated by a bevy of ghosts, every tomb the abode of a vampire or a ghoul, the sea filled with mermen and naiads, and the sky at night filled with visitors from the circling planets and the twinkling stars."

Now White did smile. "You don't believe in any of those things?"

"No." Dottore shook her head. The pins and clips had been removed now, and her russet locks fell in graceful waves about her oval face. "I do not say that none of those exist, the world is full of wonders and of mysteries. That is why we must investigate what lies beneath the Fleuve Triste. But until there is evidence, dear friend — I may call you that, I hope? For of all the members of our party, you seem the one to whom I am most attuned ..."

"I am honored, Dottore."

"Until there is evidence, we must reserve judgment. As for me, should I meet a merman or naiad, I should be delighted. But, alas, I do not expect ever to have that pleasure."

She smiled wistfully and lifted her glass. She peered through the smoky liquid it contained, or appeared to Colonel White to be doing so. She tilted her glass to her lips, then lowered it to the table and reached for her portfolio.

"Do you know the work of Herr Schwartz's countryman, Herr Doktor Professor Roentgen, Colonel White?"

"Indeed. We use his wonderful invention in military medicine. Thanks to the good professor I am here tonight, Dottore."

"And how is that?"

The Confederate held a hand to his side. "I don't like to talk about it much."

"As you will, then."

"Very well. It was at the First Battle of Belize. I took a piece of shrapnel between my third and fourth rib. A bomb had exploded and sent our position sky-high. I was just a lieutenant then." He smiled at the recollection.

"They say that I kept fighting, that I led my platoon through the rest of the battle before I collapsed. They say that I killed an entire squad of enemy troops with a bayonet held in one hand while I held myself together with the other. I wouldn't know about that, I don't remember it."

"Yet you received a medal for it, did you not?"

"The Order of Stonewall Jackson, yes."

"Well, then." There was a look of concern on the Tuscan's face. She reached for White's hand and steadied its trembling.

"You have not recovered in fullness, have you, Colonel?"

The Afro-Confederate shook his head. "I'm sorry, Doctor."

She held his hand in both of hers until the trembling subsided. "Please," she smiled at him, "I would appreciate if you might call me Speranza."

He nodded silently, tightening his grip on the hand he held in his own.

"And I may call you Dwight?"

This brought a small smile to the Confederate's features. He relaxed his grip on the Tuscan's hand, and she on his. "I prefer David. My parents must not have been thinking when they named me Dwight White." He managed a hint of a laugh. "It didn't take me long to realize that it was better to use my middle name."

"Sensible indeed." Speranza Verde held her glass between them and the Confederate poured. A waiter appeared, placed a small brass platter of sweetmeats on the table and withdrew without speaking.

"You mentioned Professor Roentgen," the Confederate said.

"Yes. And you said his work had saved you, did you not?"

"At Belize, yes." A faraway look came into White's eyes. He lifted his glass and drained its contents. "When I regained consciousness in the field hospital the doctors told me that I'd actually had a piece of shrapnel in my heart. They couldn't see what they were doing so they used a Roentgen apparatus to guide their instruments when they took it out. If it hadn't been for that, I wouldn't have lived a day."

Speranza Verde nodded. She laid her portfolio on the table between them and took from it a heavy envelope. From this she extracted several heavy celluloid sheets. Lying flat upon the envelope from which they had been removed, the celluloid sheets appeared solidly black. The woman lifted the top sheet from the stack and handed it to Colonel White.

He held it between himself and the flickering candle that stood on the table. After studying it for the better part of a minute he whistled softly and then extended it toward Speranza Verde. She took the sheet from him and handed him another. The procedure was repeated until White had examined all the sheets.

He said, "Do you want to tell me what I've just looked at?"

Before responding she replaced the sheets in their envelope and the envelope in the portfolio. She placed this in her lap. "These are imagistic plates. They were made by combining the technology of Wilhelm Conrad Roentgen with that of my countryman Louis Jacques Mande Daguerre. The Roentgen mechanism can look through solid material. The Daguerre camera records that which the Roentgen machinery sees. What you have seen, David, is that which lies beneath the dressed rocks of the Marée de Fureur, the tidal bed that lies between the Isole de Crainte and Doute."

"Impossible."

"Not impossible."

"But Dottore — "

"*Per piacere* , Speranza."

"Speranza."

She smiled.

"I saw living things. At least, I think they were living things. But things not like any I have ever seen before. Were they alive?"

"No." The russet waves moved as if with a will of their own as she shook her head. "They have not moved. They show no signs of life. But I believe they were once alive, David."

"Creatures like that — mixtures of human and beast. They look like the product of the imagination of a madman."

She shrugged.

"I saw things in the jungle of Belize that I would never have imagined at home in Creston, South Carolina. I spent half my childhood in the water of Lake Marion along with other children. We came to know every creature in that little aquatic world, from the smallest water-bugs to tortoises with the wisdom of eternity in their eyes to eels that could eat a dog in two bites if that dog was foolish enough to swim too close. But in Belize I saw spiders that eat careless birds and plants that eat baby pigs. But still, the eels were eels, the spiders were spiders."

"I did not make these up." Speranza tapped a graceful fingernail on the portfolio containing the Roentgen-Daguerre plates. "The machine has no imagination, even if a madman might."

Colonel White pondered in silence, then shook his head. "Those things," he tapped a powerful finger against the Tuscan's portfolio, "those great star-headed, conical things, and that other, that incredible beast with tentacles like ropes, with legs like a giant beetle and with the mockery of a human face on its carapace — do they really exist?"

A rectangle of light broke the mood. Speranza Verde had reached toward the portfolio, perhaps to open it and remove the envelope of celluloid image plates once again, perhaps to touch Dwight David White's hand with her own, but instead she grabbed the portfolio and placed it protectively on her lap. The Tuscan hydrologist and the Confederate soldier turned to see a trio of silhouettes in the illuminated doorway of the lounge.

As Dottore Verde and Colonel White watched, the three newcomers advanced toward them. The latter trio halted beside the table from which Colonel White rose, his military bearing giving him the appearance of a man taller than his actual stature.

"Herr Schwartz, Monsieur Rouge." The Colonel raised his hand in suggestion of a military salute. The German archaeologist clicked his heels and bowed; the Frenchman bent over the white linen covered table, took the reluctantly offered hand of Speranza Verde in his own and brushed his lips over it.

"We have a pleasant chat been enjoying, Monsieur Rouge and I," Schwartz stated. "We had thought to share a — what I believe you call in your Confederacy a night hat, Colonel White? — before retiring for a few hours' sleep."

"A nightcap, Herr Schwartz. Won't you join us?"

Monsieur Rouge bowed once again. "May I present Captain Alexandre, of the Rosny."

The third newcomer advanced to the table. She was as tall as a man, like Colonel White she was attired in a uniform, its midnight blue color contrasting with the Colonel's Confederate gray. Her features were strong but not masculine. Her hair was so dark that it appeared almost to blend with the blue of her jacket, flashes of candlelight seeming to be caught and thrown back from her coiffure. The door through which the trio had entered was closed now, the sole illumination coming from the candle on the table. The Arab musicians had packed their instruments and retired.

Brass buttons on the woman's tunic gave back the flickering light of the candle. The cuffs of the tunic were wrapped in wreaths of gold braid and on her chest the orders and decorations gave testimony of a distinguished naval career. A dark, pleated skirt fell below her knees.

Herr Schwartz and Monsieur Rouge drew chairs from a nearby, unoccupied table. Rouge held one for Captain Alexandre before seating himself. A waiter brought a bottle of schnapps and placed it before Herr Schwartz and one of cognac which the French explorer and the naval officer would share; glasses were provided for all.

Shortly the quintet were engaged in conversation. Colonel White waited for Speranza Verde to place her portfolio on the table again and share its contents with Schwartz and Rouge, but she gave no indication of doing so. In fact, at one point Jemond Jules Rouge asked if there was something she wished to share, but Speranza Verde brushed aside the obvious suggestion.

"Just a few minor items, Monsieur, nothing of importance."

"We are all together," Colonel White said, "except for our English colleague. Does anyone know where Sir Shepley Sidwell-Blue has disappeared to?"

"I am sure he is preparing for our expedition."

Captain Alexandre drew an ornately engraved watch from a uniform pocket. Holding it close to the candle she announced, "We must be aboard Rosny in two hours, so as to depart in three."

"So soon?" Speranza Verde exclaimed.

"It is the tides," Captain Alexandre explained. "The Mareé de Fureur is a tidal body the most unusual. It will offer sufficient draft for the Rosny today, and she can make faster headway using the electro-atomic power of her Curie engines than creeping along on the Wells track drive. Surely, Mademoiselle Verde, you are familiar with the behavior of the marée."

"Of course, Captain."

"Have you studied the tide tables for this month, Mademoiselle Docteur?"

"I have. Of course we have only a limited record of tides. The creation of the Sahara sea in 1930 had unexpected results, creating tides in the Mediterranean where none had previously existed, and providing for my profession wondrous new food for thought. The northerly flow will begin at four o'clock in the morning."

"Indeed." Captain Alexandre raised her glass, tested the nose of the cognac, sampled its flavor only with the tip of her tongue, then lowered her glass smiling. "*Bon.*" Her gaze flicked from face to face of her companions. "I trust you have all stowed your scientific equipment and your personal gear — Mademoiselle, Monsieurs?"

Speranza Verde said, "I prefer the title of Dottore alone."

"Very well. As you wish, Dottore Verde. My point, however, is that we must sail with the tide or we lose the opportunity. The French Republic has a great fleet but no nation's resources are without limit. We do not wish to waste this time."

"And Sir Sidwell-Blue?" the German asked.

"He will board *Rosny* on schedule or he will find only a sealed bulkhead or a vacant quay. We sail with the tide."

The party dispersed, some to gather such brief moments of slumber as they could, others to remain awake pending the time to board the submersible.

Rosny was an example of the newest and smallest *Nautilus IV* class of submersibles. Barely sixty meters in length, the submersible carried a small crew. Propelled by her Curie engines, she could outspeed and outmaneuver any other known submersible craft on the planet. She was also capable of crawling over dry or muddy terrain on extended tracks based on the designs of the Englishman Wells.

Her interior fittings, in the tradition of her kind stretching back to the original *Nautilus* , were of mahogany and polished brass. Her floors were carpeted. Her galley was filled with fresh viands and fine vintages produced by the enological artists of Metropolitan France and her North African provinces.

Only in the department of weaponry might *Rosny* be deemed deficient. Outfitted as the submersible was for purposes of reconnaissance and exploration, she carried neither cannon nor torpedo nor submarine bomb. Her crew had been trained in riflery and such arms were stowed in the submersible's armory; her officers, also, were furnished with sidearms.

Colonel Dwight David White of the Army of the Confederate States of America stood at the foot of *Rosny's* gangplank. He held a single item of luggage, containing changes of clothing, necessary toiletries, and certain equipment with which he had been furnished by the technicians and planners of his nation's embassy and military legation in Serkout.

The Colonel was of course thoroughly familiar with the courtesies and ceremonies of both the military and diplomatic communities of the world. When he boarded the submersible he saluted the colors of the French Republic, offered his sidearm, a Harrington and Richardson .32 automatic, to Captain Alexandre and received permission to retain possession of the weapon.

The quay, of course, had been illuminated with spotlights to facilitate boarding *Rosny* in the hours of the night. A crescent moon had been visible from Colonel White's hotel room; from the quay its pale radiance was utterly obliterated by the brilliance of artificial illumination.

Once on board, Colonel White declined the assistance of a crew member in carrying his single item of luggage to his tiny but richly furnished cabin. Here he distributed his personal items, retaining only his firearm and technical gear in a smaller case which he removed from his principle luggage and locked to his wrist with a specially designed handcuff.

Thus prepared he brushed his hair, straightened his uniform, and made to join his fellow inquirers.

As had been prearranged, the investigative team assembled in the Captain's cabin as they arrived and settled into their respective quarters. The cabin was furnished with a polished conference table and plush chairs. An ornate instrument panel comprising a great clock-face, compass, barometer, and navigational tools filled most of one wall. An electrical lighting system furnished illumination and the soft susurrus of fresh air, processed and piped throughout *Rosny* by the most up-to-date means, gave evidence that the submersible was a self-sufficient and self-contained world of its own.

The cabin was located above the main body of the submersible and was fitted with large glass panels on both starboard and larboard sides. Upon arriving in the cabin, Colonel White observed the activity of sailors and dockmen on the quay. Not a word was spoken before *Rosny* began to move, so smoothly and gradually as to create the illusion that the submersible remained stationary while the quay with its brilliant lights and scurrying workers was retreating.

But within fleeting moments, to *Rosny's* forward motion was added a horizontal movement. The black sky with its crescent moon and glittering Saharan stars appeared overhead only briefly, then *Rosny* opened her buoyancy tanks to the Saharan brine.

Soon the world outside *Rosny's* heavy glass panels became one of utter blackness. Eventually brightly luminescent denizens of the Saharan deep would reveal themselves, Colonel White and his companions knew, but for the moment they might as well have been in the depths of interplanetary space, for all the commerce they held with the sea that surrounded them.

They sat around the polished wooden table, Jemond Jules Rouge at its head, Colonel Dwight David White, Dottore Speranza Verde, Herr Siegfried Schwartz and Sir Shepley Sidwell-Blue. The submersible's Captain, Melisande Alexandre, had taken her place inconspicuously away from the table, clearly indicating a desire to observe but not to dominate the proceedings to follow.

Yes, Sir Shepley Sidwell-Blue had arrived at the quay in time, barely in time, to make the sailing of *Rosny*. He was disheveled, he was followed to the boarding ramp by a driver and footman carrying valises from which loose shirt-ends and stocking garters hung, his shirt was rumpled and his blond hair fell across his forehead, but he did not miss the sailing.

After messmen had served coffee and biscuits, M. Rouge made welcoming remarks to the assembled group. "We are proceeding beneath the surface, my friends. The tide is with us, flowing in a northerly direction. We should reach our destination within a half-day's cruise. Until then, I hope that we may discuss our plan of investigation."

Gazing around the table, he continued. "Each of you has been selected as the outstanding representative of your chosen profession. Dottore Verde was of course our first chosen expert. Her study of the tidal flow through the Marée de Fureur has been vital, for the hydrological patterns and alterations of the sea bed encountered in this new body of water is a challenge unique."

He bowed to Speranza Verde.

"Herr Schwartz and Sir Shepley are representatives of converging disciplines. Our preliminary findings indicate that the relics we are about to examine are of an Egyptian or pre-Egyptian origin. Their significance and value to the modern world, beyond that of the purely scholarly, are, one surmises, incalculable."

The German nodded acknowledgement of Rouge's words. Schwartz had lit a black cigar and gestured with it. The Englishman, clad in soft tweeds that complimented his light hair and moustache, fumbled in his pockets for a pipe and tobacco. Finding them, he packed the pipe and held a match to its bowl. The smoke that rose was drawn away by the submersible's ventilation system. Sidwell-Blue muttered his acknowledgement.

"And Colonel White," the Frenchman concluded, "is our military man. A grand concession by France to nominate a representative of the Confederacy to this position, but of course the friendship of our two great Republics is of historic nature, known to all around the world."

Before David White could reply, the room was startled by the clatter of Sir Shepley Sidwell-Blue's pipe on the polished mahogany table. "I say," the Englishman exclaimed, "I fear we're under attack. Just look at that!"

He pointed to the oblong window on the starboard side of the cabin.

A vast creature was charging at *Rosny*. Its eyes were huge, its open mouth contained rows of gigantic, murderous teeth. Its fins were clawed like those of certain tropical frogs the David White had encountered in his service in the jungles of Belize, and it used them in a manner suggestive of an amphibian crawling toward its hopeless prey.

Strangest of all, the creature appeared to be carrying a lighted lantern in its single hand. Upon more considered observation the seeming lantern proved to be a naturally luminescent organ mounted on a flexible stalk that rose from the creature's forehead.

David White's hand moved instinctively to his sidearm. But he realized almost at once that the Harrington and Richardson would do little to help the voyagers if their aquatic attacker succeeded in bursting through *Rosny's* glass plate. To his astonishment, the creature swam to within seeming inches of the glass, then hovered, its clawlike fins moving slowly to and fro. At the submersible's rate of speed the creature was obviously a mighty swimmer to maintain pace at all, no less with such seeming ease.

Even as the voyagers, recovering from their initial startlement, left their seats to cluster at the glass, the creature held pace, returning their curious stares with an expression of its own that seemed to duplicate their surprise.

The laughter of Monsieur Rouge drew their attention back from the sea. "A common sight nowadays, my friends. Since the creation of the Sahara Sea, creatures have invaded this new body of water, making their way from the Mediterranean and even in some cases from the cold waters of the Atlantic. The Sahara Sea offers the appeal of a warm and mostly gentle body, and in less than a century that the Sahara Sea has existed, numerous species have come to visit and stayed to raise their progeny."

"By Jove," the Englishman inquired, "are there no native species in this lovely little pond?"

At this moment the ferocious-appearing lantern bearer, its curiosity as to *Rosny* and her occupants satisfied, flashed away from the submersible and disappeared into the darkness.

"Perhaps, if you will return to your places, Mademoiselle et Messieurs, Dottore Verde will enlighten us as to the plan of action once we reach our destination.

Speranza Verde rose to her feet.

"With permission of Captain Alexandre, I have plotted our course to bring us to our destination as the tidal flow ceases. Of course it will in due time reverse its direction and flow back from the Bay of Sidra toward the City of Sercout from which we departed. Such tidal reversals are of course entirely normal."

She paused in her presentation to draw from a cylindrical case which had previously been placed in the cabin a nautical chart of the Sahara Sea, centering up the Iles de Crainte and Doute. This she spread on the table so that all the travelers might see it.

"The lunar and solar attractions that control earthly tides are at this time in unique conjunction. The result will be a period of several hours during which the channel between the two isole becomes a dry bed. This phenomenon is not unknown, of course."

She paused to smile, and David White was struck by the brightness and gentleness of her expression.

"Students of the Bible," Speranza Verde went on, "will recall the parting of the Red Sea upon the command of Moses. It is my belief that this event was in fact a tidal anomaly similar to that which is about to occur. When we reach our destination, Captain Alexandre informs me, *Rosny* will rest upon her Wells tracks and use them for any needed short-distance travel. You may rest assured that we will be safe from the waters during this period, but we must all complete out work before the Marée rushes back upon us, however. Our period of safety, according to my calculations, will be approximately four hours, thirty-two minutes, and sixteen seconds."

"I say," Sidwell-Blue put in. He had long since recovered his pipe and was puffing furiously away at it, challenging the ability of the air-circulator to keep up with his production of bluish smoke. "I say, are you *sure* this won't be dangerous? Perhaps we should try this another time?"

From her position in a corner of the cabin, Captain Alexandre put in, "Quite sure, Sir Shepley. There is nothing to fear."

"And as for another time," Speranza Verde put in, "do you know how long it is since Moses parted the Red Sea? That is how often this peculiar phenomenon occurs. If we do not take advantage of our opportunity, we will all be several thousand years old before another such presents itself."

"Well," Sidwell-Blue said, "well, if you're really certain, Captain. And, ah, Doctor. But, it strikes me that this is a damned dangerous undertaking. You know, I've always worked in the museum. This is all quite new to me, this racing about like a pack of Alan Quatermains and Captain Nemos."

Out of the corner of his eye Colonel White saw what appeared to be a gray-cloaked and death-white-masked figure streak across the room and launch itself through the air. It bounced off the paunch of the unsuspecting Herr Schwartz, eliciting a startled grunt and a violent exclamation, then landed with a skid in the center of the nautical chart that had been spread on the conference table.

"The apologies of *Rosny*, Mein Herr," Captain Alexandre laughed. "Madame et messieurs, may I present My Lady Bast, our ship's mascot and mouser par excellence."

The large cat studied each of the conferees in turn, directing a piercing glance from golden eyes that punctuated a snowy white face while she twitched her powder-gray tail thoughtfully. She made her opinion obvious, redirecting her attention from the conferees to the task of washing her paws.

"You should not barnyard animals on a ship carry," Herr Schwartz growled, "unless they are cargo to market being transported."

Captain Alexandre ignored the German's complaint. She stroked the luxurious fur; My Lady Bast twitched her ears in response. Captain Alexandre compared the time according to her watch, with that indicated by the ship's clock. She nodded to the hydrologist, Speranza Verde, then to the others. "I think it is time to begin your explorations. I will remain aboard *Rosny*. You understand the constraints of time under which you operate."

At Captain Alexandre's command the submersible rose to the surface of the Fleuve Triste. Colonel White found himself standing between Dottore Verde and Monsieur Rouge. A polished metal railing surrounded *Rosny's* deck. Sea water dripped from it and ran from the submersible's deck into the fleuve.

The sky above was still black. The tropic stars blazed like the flames that astronomers stated that they were.

Each of the explorers carried an electro-atomic powered portable lantern. Further, Colonel White noted to his amusement that the costume of each showed a mysterious bulge which he took to reveal the presence of a clandestinely carried firearm. Even Dottore Verde was so armed. Her weapon, he inferred, was most likely a small but efficient Gilsenti automatic pistol.

Now the sun's first rays illumined the western sky, and within moments the edge of the solar disk appeared over the waters of the Sahara Sea. Bright points of light danced across the brine.

At this moment a buzzing sound was heard, and Colonel White along with his companions turned his eyes skyward. The daily flight from Rome to Serkut appeared, the sun's early rays reflecting off its polished metal exterior. The Bleriot trimotor's propellers were powered by Curie electro-atomic engines similar to those that furnished *Rosny's* propulsion. The aeroplane's passengers, business travelers, tourists, diplomats, might well be gazing downward at *Rosny* even as *Rosny's* explorers were gazing upward at the Bleriot.

Now there came a great rushing, roaring sound; the submersible rocked, bounced once, and settled onto the rocky sand at the bottom of the Fleuve Triste. The Curie engine hummed and the submersible's Wells tracks found their footing on the sand and steadied the submersible.

"Alors," Captain Alexandre announced with a smile, "madame et monsieurs, we are here. You have my permission to depart my ship. I wish you well, and shall expect your safe return in four hours, thirty-two minutes, sixteen seconds."

She exchanged handshakes with Jemond Jules Rouge and Shepley Sidwell-Blue. Herr Schwartz instead offered a bow and click of his heels. With Speranza Verde she exchanged a brief embrace, and with Colonel Dwight David White a crisp military salute.

The explorers clambered down the ship's ladder. Standing on the still moist sand of the Fleuve Triste they found it drying rapidly. The tropical sun seemed to have sprung into a brilliant and cloudless sky. Here and there specks of crystal in the Sahara sand reflected as points of brilliance.

Speranza Verde had brought with her the Roentgen-Daguerre plates that she had shown David White the night before, and Herr Schwartz carried a smaller version of the nautical chart that had been left on the conference table aboard *Rosny*.

A gray and white streak whizzed past the exploration party, raced up a sandy hillock and disappeared.

"That was My Lady Bast!" Sir Shepley Sidwell-Blue exclaimed. "The creature will be lost. The water will rush back in four hours and she will be lost."

"Too bad for her," Herr Schwartz growled. "But a good thing she did, the way showing us to the finds." He held the map before him and pointed in the direction My Lady Bast had taken. "March!" he commanded.

My Lady Bast had left behind a track of feline footprints in the drying sand. The explorers followed the cat's trail. The sun's rays had already dispersed the chill of night air, and this small stretch of seabed was assuming the torrid glare it had known before the creation of the world's newest sea.

Upon reaching the crest of a hillock the explorers were able to look back and see the submersible *Rosny* resting upon her Wells treads. Sailors moved on her decks polishing metalwork and cleaning hardwood, looking for all the world like miniatures performing in a puppet theater. And in the other direction appeared a vision denied to human eyes by the dark waters of the Sahara Sea for three decades, and before that by the white sands of the erstwhile Sahara Desert for ten times as many millennia.

These were the rocks, dressed and polished, rising but a short distance from their position that hid the secret of the Sahara.

Herr Siegfried Schwartz and Sir Shipley Sidwell-Blue raced ahead and dropped to their knees. Bending to examine the carven rocks on which they knelt, the ill-matched pair resembled nothing more than two worshippers come to make obeisance at an ancient shrine.

The uppermost rocks of the formation reflected the sun's rays with a white brilliance; those lower in the ancient structure were still protected from direct illumination by the intervening crest. Schwartz and Sidwell-Blue were running their hands over the carven rocks, studying the figures placed there untold ages before by hands long since turned to dust.

As the sun's illumination spread and the shadows crept away solar brightness struck a glittering point so cleverly concealed within the intricacies of a carving as to be for all practical purposes invisible. As it did so the rock in which it had rested for thousands of years in utter darkness fell away from the kneeling explorers. There was exposed before them a dark opening, its walls as smooth and as carefully crafted as those of the Great Pyramid of Cheops.

There was a flash of gray as My Lady Bast, returning from some place of concealment, streaked past the explorers and disappeared into the blackness.

Herr Schwartz switched on his electro-atomic lantern and sent its rays into the blackness, flashing them this way and that. Still on his knees, the German started down the passageway. As he did so, Colonel White took note, he reached inside his jacket and drew a weapon which the White immediately identified as a Bergmann Model Five automatic pistol.

As Schwartz disappeared into the darkness he was followed by Jumond Jules Rouge and Speranza Verde, each brandishing a lantern and a firearm; Rouge's weapon was a Lebel revolver and Verde the Gilsenti that White had expected.

Sir Shepley Sidwell-Blue alone stepped aside as Colonel White moved toward the opening. "I think it would be best if one of us stood guard out here, Colonel. Just in case, well, in case of need."

David White nodded and followed Speranza Verde into the darkness.

The tunnel slanted downward into bedrock. To David White's surprise the air tasted fresh. He could see only a short distance ahead, thanks to the procession of bodies, but at length he heard a grunt and a guttural exclamation, followed by a series of increasingly excited vocalizations as first Schwartz, then Rouge, than Speranza Verde emerged from the slanting passage.

White paused momentarily, pointing his lantern this way and that, then dropped the few feet from the mouth of the passageway into the chamber. Two men and a woman had separated in the chamber; flashing beams from their lanterns crisscrossed in a virtual museum of unknowable antiquity. Statues cast great monolithic shadows in the flashing lantern-beams. Some were tiny and were exhibited on plinths as high as his own waist; others were of human size. At the far end of the chamber a figure rose to herculean heights, its details concealed by distance and darkness.

The walls were covered with paintings that appeared as fresh as though they had been created this very day. The scenes portrayed were those of nature, of forests and rivers, of hippopotami and crocodiles and okapi, the beasts that must have roamed the once-fertile plains of the Sahara before it had dried to form the desert now covered by the waters of the sea.

Colonel White paced slowly past paintings executed with impressive craftsmanship and skill. Yet there was something disquieting and unpleasant about the images.

The paintings, he inferred, represented a chronology, for after a time there appeared among the beasts of the forest primitive human figures, and even more disquietingly, other figures that were those of neither humans nor beasts, but of something — other. He thought briefly of the fierce-looking lantern fish that had studied the explorers through the cabin glass of *Rosny* even as they had studied it.

The lantern-fish, of course, was fitted by nature with fins for propulsion and with a form adapted to life beneath the surface of the sea. But the creatures in the paintings appeared as if they were distant evolutionary relatives of the lantern-fish, great, pop-eyed, piscine beings. White remembered a lecture in a long-ago classroom, where he had heard a savant expound upon the theory that whales, dolphins, sea lions and seals had all evolved from marine creatures onto the land, and had then returned at some time to their ancestral home to become once again creatures of the deep.

Could the unpleasant beings pictured on the carven walls have followed a parallel but opposite evolutionary path, emerging from the sea to live on the surface of the earth even as mammals were returning from the land to live beneath the sea?

More panels of ancient art revealed an ongoing march of progress, if progress it might be called, as both humans and piscines advanced. Cities appeared, and great sky-going machines. The two civilizations developed side by side but there was little commerce and no friendship between them, until in a series of paintings portraying a terrible war the human civilization was destroyed and that of the fish-men emerged triumphant.

There was a yowl from the end of the gallery and White whirled to see My Lady Bast the cat rising on her hind legs, her coat standing on end to give her the appearance of a beast three times her actual size. Her paws were raised and her saber-like claws were extended. Her needle-sharp teeth seemed to have grown into the fangs of a feline many times her size but no less outraged than was My Lady Bast.

She stood poised before the great statue that ended the gallery, and as Colonel White and his companions stood in stupefaction she dropped to all fours, ran forward, launched herself into the air and caught at the convolutions of the lowermost part of the statue.

The brilliant beams of four Curie lanterns followed the cat as she clawed and fought her way upward on the statue. The thing was monstrous, a variant of the horrible image the Speranza Curie had shown Colonel White the night before.

The thing was fitted with tentacle-like stalks, uncounted numbers of them, some terminating in sucker-like mouths, others in shining eyes. It had a head, or what must serve as a head, shaped like a five-pointed star, each extremity of this bearing a great, dark eye.

Most horrifying of all, David White stood paralyzed with shock and fear. And know well, even the noblest of men know fear; it is the overcoming of this experience that comprises true courage. That which had paralyzed White was the sight of the five points of the statue's face writhing and turning, turning horribly, until the eyes focused upon My Lady Bast the cat.

From all directions, tentacles tipped with horrid mouths and rows of teeth resembling those of giant, extinct sharks, wove toward My Lady Bast. From the cat there came a blood-freezing scream of raging ferocity as the pleasantly disposed ship's mascot was transformed into a whirlwind of fury and violence.

My Lady Bast flew from the grasping, mouth-tipped tentacles, the points of her claws leaving a trail of punctures from which there spurted a steaming green ichor. Blobs of the foul liquid splashed on the great paving stones with which the room was floored. Each point of contact was transformed into a miniature cauldron that seethed and bubbled and from which a noxious greenish vapor arose.

The cat by now had reached the star-shaped head of the monstrous living statue. Using the claws of two paws while she clung to the monstrous visage with the others, she shredded one baleful eye, then moved to the next and the next. The monstrous living statue yielded to a series of spasms.

David White, watching the incredible battle of a feline analog of his Biblical namesake against this titanic alien Goliath, realized to his astonishment that the star-headed monster was actually terrified. He was aware that Siegfried Schwartz had drawn his Bergmann automatic and was firing at the monstrosity. Other members of the exploring party, Rouge, Sidwell-Blue, Speranza Verde, had drawn their own weapons and were pointing them upward.

Bounding forward to place himself between his comrades and the monster, David White waved his arms and cried out, "Careful! Careful! Don't hit the cat!"

Even as the sound of two revolvers and an automatic pistol echoed off the walls and ceiling of the chamber, the great monstrosity, blinded now and bleeding green ichor from its wounds, gave forth a mighty roar that echoed and re-echoed through the hall. It gave a mighty spasm and My Lady Bast, the gray and white warrior, her grasp on the star-shaped head broken by the jolt, was flung from the monster. As if fully accustomed to flight she soared through the darkened reaches of the tomb, falling at last into the welcoming arms of Colonel David White.

But this was no gentle pussy. My Lady Bast had been transformed into a warrior-goddess and she was not so quick to resume her domestic mien. Raking claws shredded White's military tunic and suddenly terrifying fangs snapped within millimeters of his eye, removing a gobbet of flesh just at his cheekbone. Then My Lady Bast flexed powerful legs, launched herself from his torso and disappeared into the darkness of the tomb.

Rouge, Schwartz and Verde had advanced cautiously toward the monster. In its great spasm it had flung itself from its plinth and lay thrashing on the stone floor. Its mouths seemed to possess the power of speech independent of one another, and they uttered sounds that resembled human speech as a horrid parody of the human form might resemble a beautiful woman.

Siegfried Schwartz, surely crude and perhaps cruel as well, was by no means lacking in courage. He had advanced to within an arm's reach of the monster and was speaking to it in a language which David White did not understand, but which he inferred to be that of ancient Egypt. Astonishingly, the monster seemed to hear and understand the German archaeologist, and to reply in a strange and terrible variant of the same language.

Without warning the monster managed to raise itself halfway to a vertical position. It turned its eye-tipped tentacles toward the roof of the chamber.

There, its rays focused through a lens of tinted mica, the sun casting a single, bright beam into the chamber. The beam had obviously been aimed, how many millennia before there was no way of calculating. In its light one of the painted panels on the tomblike wall seemed almost to come to life.

A row of half-human figures knelt in postures of worship. There was a man with the head of a falcon, a woman with the features of a lioness, a hawk-man, a woman in the grotesque form of a hippopotamus, a being with a human body and the head of a crocodile. David White did not know their names, but he recognized them as Egyptian deities. And they were kneeling in submission.

Before them stood a party of star-headed, tentacled monsters like the one whose statue had seemingly come to life only to be slain by the ferocity of a ship's gray and white mascot. And behind the alien beings could be seen a sleek machine, obviously a vehicle that had brought it occupants from some home unimaginable to mere humanity.

From the shadowed passageway through which the explorers had entered the tomb there came an echoing voice. "It's time," came the voice of Sir Shepley Sidwell-Blue. "We'd best get back to *Rosny* . Our time is running out."

The explorers turned toward the passageway. Jemond Jules Rouge leading the way, followed by Speranza Verde and Siegfried Schwartz, preceded Colonel Dwight David White into the passage. White realized that they had all been so busy in dealing with the wonders and terrors of the tomb that they had forgotten the time. It was a good thing that the Englishman had stayed outside the tomb, keeping track of the passing hours.

Once outside the tomb the party formed up and moved off in the direction of the temporarily dry bed of the Fleuve Triste.

They had gone only a score of paces when Sidwell-Blue cried out, "Halt!" The decisive and authoritarian utterance from the hitherto timid and uncertain Englishman startled the others into obedience. To their disbelieving eyes Sidwell-Blue ran back toward the dark opening in the rock. He disappeared into the shadowed passageway. Minutes passed. David White studied his own pocket watch, performed a rapid mental calculation and said, "If we don't move quickly we'll be trapped by the returning Marée."

"But we cannot leave poor Sir Shepley in that tomb!" Speranza Verde cried. She started back toward the rock sepulchre, followed by the others, but before she could reach the opening Sir Shepley Sidwell-Blue emerged into the Saharan sunlight, My Lady Bast nestled comfortably in his arms.

As they approached the submersible *Rosny* a mighty aqueous roar was heard and two walls of water became visible, speeding toward them from both directions. The explorers ran at top speed to the submersible and scrambled up *Rosny's* boarding ladder. Captain Alexandre herself had awaited them, and followed them into the submersible, counting off as they descended:

"Rouge."

"Schwartz."

"Blue."

"Verde."

"White."

"My Lady Bast."

Even as the first spray of the onrushing waters spattered her midnight-tinted uniform sleeve, the Captain slammed the hatch shut and turned its dogs to seal the submersible against the waters of the Saharan Sea.

Soon all had refreshed themselves and reassembled in the Captain's conference room. Hot coffee spiked with strong brandy was served, along with nourishing sandwiches. Outside *Rosny's* oblong panels of glass, marine creatures swam up to this strange invader of their realm and studied its occupants with as much curiosity as the men and women of *Rosny* exhibited toward them.

In a corner of the room, My Lady Bast, her coat now restored to its proper state, enjoyed a treat of fresh fish and rich cream.

At the table, the explorers gave their complementary reports on their experiences in the ancient tomb. Speranza Verde took special note of Shipley-Blue's unexpected heroism. "Beneath this *senza pretese*, how you say, unassuming exterior, eh, there beats the heart of a lion. I salute you, Sir Shepley."

The Englishman turned away shyly. "One couldn't abandon that splendid cat, you know." Even in the artificial light of Rosny's cabin, his furious blush was obvious.

At the end, it was Colonel White who asked Herr Siegfried Schwartz, "What was it that the monster said before it died?"

The German stroked his beard as if in deep thought. "To understand what said the creature, Mein Herr White, it was for me not easy. Its language that of ancient Egypt was almost, but certain differences there were."

He paused and drained his cup. When it was refilled he instructed the crewmember to omit the coffee.

"I think it said, 'My parents for me will come. Someday my father and mother for me will come.' You see, Herr Colonel, to us a great monster it was, but in truth that sleeping creature that we awakened, that we killed, of its own kind was a baby."

THE TURRET

I was not really surprised when my employer, Alexander Myshkin, called me into his office and offered me the assignment to troubleshoot our Zeta/Zed System at the Klaus Fuchs Memorial Institute in Old Severnford. The Zeta/Zed System was Myshkin Associates' prize product, the most advanced hardware-software lashup in the world, Myshkin liked to boast, and the Fuchs Institute was to have been our showpiece installation.

Unfortunately, while the Zeta/Zed performed perfectly in the Myshkin lab in Silicon Valley, California, once it was transported to the Severn Valley in England, glitches appeared in its functioning and bugs in its programs. The customer was first distressed, then frustrated, and finally angry. Myshkin had the Fuchs Institute modem its data to California, where it ran perfectly on the in-house Zeta/Zed and was then modemed back to England. This was the only way Myshkin could placate the customer, even temporarily, but we knew that if the system in Old Severnford could not be brought online and into production, the Institute could order our equipment removed. They could replace it with a system from one of our competitors, and further could even sue Myshkin Associates for the lost time and expense they had put into our failed product.

"Park," Alexander Myshkin said to me as soon as I entered his office in response to his summons, "Park, the future of this company is in your hands. If we lose the Fuchs Institute, we could be out of business in six months. We're hanging onto that account by our fingernails. You've got to get that system running for the customer."

I asked Myshkin why our marketing and technical support teams in the UK had not solved the problem. "We have good people over there," I told my employer. "I know some of them, and I've seen their work."

Myshkin said, "You're right, Park." (My name is Parker Lorentzen; Lorentzen for obvious reasons, Parker in honor of a maternal ancestor who actually hailed from the Severn Valley. I had never seen the region, and was inclined to accept the assignment for that reason alone.)

"You're right," my employer repeated, "but they haven't been able to solve it. Somehow I don't think they *like* visiting this account. They don't like staying anywhere in the Severn Valley and they absolutely refuse to put up in Old Severnford itself. I've never been there myself, but I've seen the pictures, as I'm sure you have."

I admitted that I had.

"The countryside is beautiful. Rolling hills, ancient ruins, the Severn River itself and those smaller streams, the Ton and the Cam. I'll admit, a certain, well, call it sense of *gloom* seems to hang over the area, but we're modern people, enlightened technologists, not a pack of credulous rustics."

"True enough, chief. All right, no need to twist my arm." I gazed past him. Beyond the window the northern California hills rolled away lush with greenery. I found myself unconsciously touching the little blue birthmark near my jawline. It was smaller than a dime, and oddly shaped. Some claimed that it resembled an infinity sign; others, an hour-glass; still others, an ankh, the Egyptian symbol of immortality. My physician had assured me that it was not pre-cancerous or in any other way dangerous. Nor was it particularly unsightly; women sometimes found it fascinating.

My mother had had a similar formation on her jaw. She called it a beauty-mark and said that it was common among the Parkers.

"Thanks, Park," Alexander Myshkin resumed. "You're my top troubleshooter, you know. If you can't fix a problem, it can't be fixed."

Within twenty-four hours I had jetted across the country, transferred from my first-class seat in a Boeing jumbo to the cramped quarters of the Anglo-French Concorde, and left the Western Hemisphere behind for my first visit to England, the homeland of half my ancestors.

I stayed only one night in London, not sampling that city's fabled theatres or museums, but simply resting up, trying to rid myself of the jet lag inherent in a body still running on California time even though it had been relocated some eight or nine time zones. I boarded a wheezing, groaning train that carried me from fabled Victoria Station through Exham and the very peculiar-looking town of Goatswood and thence to its terminus at Brichester.

My luggage consisted of a single valise. In this I had placed my warmest clothing, a tweed suit and Irish hat that I had purchased years before in an English shop in San Francisco and reserved for trips from California to areas of less salubrious climate. I carried an umbrella and, slung from my shoulder, a canvas case containing a notebook computer.

In Brichester I spent my second night in England. The inn where I lodged was old and run down. It contained a pub on its ground floor, and I looked forward to an evening of good-fellowship, a tankard of beer (perhaps more than one!) and a platter of hearty English beef before bed.

Alas, I was disappointed on every count. The beef was tough, stringy and overdone. The beer was watery and flat. But most disheartening of all, the local residents, for all that they appeared just the colorful and eccentric folk that I had hoped to encounter, proved a taciturn and unforthcoming lot. They responded to my opening conversational ploys with monosyllabic grunts and rejected my further attempts at camaraderie by pointedly turning their backs and engaging in low, muttered dialogs, casting unfriendly glances from time to time at the obviously unwelcome interloper in their midst — myself.

After chewing futilely at the beef until my jaws ached, and giving up on the poor beer that the innkeeper served, I finally retired early, not so much from fatigue, for my body was beginning to recover from its jet lag, but simply because I could find no comfort in the surroundings of this disappointing pub and its hostile clientele.

In the morning I was awakened by a pale wash of sunlight that seemed barely able to penetrate the gray and louring sky that I soon learned was typical of most days in the Severn Valley. I found myself wondering why the residents of these towns remained there — why, in fact, their ancestors had ever settled in this gloomy and unpleasant region.

At first I thought it fortunate that I had brought my cellular telephone with me — my room at the inn, of course, had no such modern convenience — but of course I got nowhere with the local telephone system when I tried to place a call. Eventually I located a call box, however, and spent most of the day conducting business. I spoke several times with Alexander Myshkin, and let me not rehearse the agonies of placing a call from a decrepit call box in the Severn Valley town of Brichester to Myshkin Associates in Silicon Valley, California. I finally reached my employer after being cut off several times by malign operators somewhere in the British telephone system, and at least once by Myshkin's own secretary, who apologized effusively once the connection was re-established, only to cut me off again.

Myshkin brought me up to date on further tests which were being run continuously on the Zeta/Zed System in our California laboratory. The system, of course, performed flawlessly, leaving me no less baffled than beforehand by the reported problems at the Fuchs Institute installation.

I succeeded in reaching the Institute as well, for all that I was distressed at how difficult it was to do so. Silicon Valley was some 6,000 miles from the Severn Valley. That was at least some mitigation for the difficulties in communication. But my call from Brichester to Old Severnford, a matter of a mere few miles, was interrupted several times by unexplained disconnections. Even when I was in communication with my opposite number at the Fuchs Institute, one Karolina Parker — I found myself wondering if we might be related through my mother's side of the family — conversation was not easy. There was a curious *buzzing* and an occasional unpleasant *scraping* sound on the wire. I asked Karolina if she was not disturbed by these noises, but she denied hearing them. She suggested that they were all at my end of the hook-up — or perhaps in my mind. The latter implication did not sit well with me, but I made no point of it at the time.

Eventually I took a late and unpleasant dinner in Brichester, in a restaurant some distance from my inn. There was not a single other customer in the establishment, and yet it took the waiter a long time to approach me. His manner was surly and I got the feeling that the management would have been happier to forego my trade than to have it. The surroundings were stuffy and utterly devoid of decoration or distraction. As had been the case with my dinner the previous evening, the food was bland in flavor, unpleasant in texture, and served at a uniform degree of lukewarmness, whether the dish was a supposedly chilled madrilène or an allegedly freshly broiled mutton chop.

Abandoning the sorry repast after a half-hearted attempt to consume it, I paid my bill and, leaving the restaurant with a silent vow never to return, hefted my single valise and began the trek to Old Severnford. With difficulty I was able to hire a car and driver who insisted on being paid in advance for his services. I was not pleased with the arrangement, but, feeling that I had no choice, I consented.

The car was of uncertain ancestry and vintage; its suspension was badly sprung and I suspected that its heater was connected directly to its exhaust pipe — the chill of the day was dispelled, all right, but was replaced in the car by a choking unpleasantness far worse.

The afternoon had turned a dark gray, and it was impossible to tell just when the sun dropped beneath the rolling, sinister hills beyond the Severn River to the west, save for the moment when my driver switched on the car's headlamps. They cast a feeble, amber patch of light on the narrow and ill-repaired roadway ahead of us.

The driver stayed muffled deep in his sweaters and overcoat, a visored cap with furry earflaps covering most of his face. He wore a pair of mirrored eyeglasses — a peculiarly modern touch in this archaic valley — and between his upturned collar and the visor and earflaps of his headgear, all that I could see of his face was the mirrored lenses and a huge, walrus moustache, grayed with age and yellowed with I knew not what.

We reached the Severn River without incident, save for a few bicycling schoolchildren — these, among the *very* few children I ever saw in the Severn region — who halted their bikes and pointed as we passed them in the roadway. I thought at first that they were waving a friendly greeting, and waved back at them, pleased at this sign, however slight, of cheer and goodwill.

Once more I was mistaken. Quickly I realized that their gestures were not friendly waves, but some sort of mystical sign, whether intended to ward off evil or to bring harm upon me. One boy, who seemed almost unnaturally large and muscular for his age, but whose face appeared unformed and vaguely animal-like, hurled a large rock after my car. The rock struck the rear of the car, and for a moment I thought the driver was going to stop and berate the children, but instead he pressed down on the accelerator and sped us away from there, muttering something beneath his breath that I was unable to make out.

The driver brought the car to a halt in a decrepit dockside district of Severnford. Full night had fallen by now, and the quays and piers before us seemed utterly deserted. I asked the driver if he would wait for a ferry to carry us to Old Severnford, and if he would then drive me to the Klaus Fuchs Memorial Institute.

He turned around then, glaring at me over the rear of his seat. I had switched on the car's tiny dome-light, and it reflected off his mirrored glasses. "Last ferry's run, mister," he husked. "And me'uns don't fancy spending no night by these docks. You get out. Get out now, and you're on your own."

I started to protest, but the driver leaped from the car with surprising agility for so bulky and aged an individual. He yanked open the door beside which I sat, caught my lapels in two thickly-gloved hands, and lifted me bodily from the car, depositing me in no dignified condition on the cracked and weedy sidewalk. He hurled my valise after me, jumped back into his vehicle and sped away, leaving me angered, puzzled, and utterly uncertain as to how to resolve my predicament.

I recovered my valise and tested my notebook computer to reassure myself that it was undamaged. I then pondered my next move. If the Severn ferry had indeed ceased its runs for the night, I could not possibly reach Old Severnford before morning. I did not know my way around the town of Severnford itself, and with a shudder of apprehension I set out to explore.

At first I walked beside the river. A moon had risen, apparently full, yet so cloaked by heavy clouds as to appear only a vague, pale disk in the sky, while furnishing the most minimal of watery illumination to the earth. But as my eyes grew accustomed to the darkness, I realized that there was another source of illumination, faint and inauspicious.

A glow seemed to come from beneath the surface of the Severn River. Seemed? No, it was there, it was all too real. I tried to make out its source, but vague shapes seemed to move, deep in the river for the most part, but darting toward the surface now and again, and then slithering away once more into the depths. And a mist arose from the sluggishly flowing water, and gave off a glow of its own, or perhaps it was that it reflected the glow of the river and the vague, luminous shapes therein. Or yet again, were there shapes *within the mist* as well, floating and darting like fairies in a garden in a child's book?

The sight should have been charming, almost pretty, but for some reason it sent a shudder down my spine. With an effort I turned away and made my way up an ancient street, leading at a slight uphill slant from the river and the docks and into the heart of town.

Perhaps I had merely strayed into the wrong part of Severnford, or perhaps there was something about the town itself that set off silent shrieks of alarm within me. I could find no establishment open, no person to ask for assistance. Instead I paced darkened streets, chilled and dampened by the night. Once I thought I heard voices, rough and furtive in tone, murmuring in a language I could neither comprehend nor identify. Twice I heard scuffling footsteps, but upon whirling clumsily with my valise and computer weighing me down, I saw nothing. Thrice I thought I heard odd twitterings, but could find no source or explanation for them.

How many miles I trudged that night, finding my way from alley to courtyard to square, I can only guess. I can only say that the first pallid gray shafts of morning light were as welcome to me as any sight I had ever beheld. I was able, by heading steadily downward, to find my way back to the docks.

In the morning light the mist was lifting off the Severn, the hills on its far shore looked almost welcoming, and the disquieting shapes and lights beneath the river's surface were no longer to be seen.

I located the quay where the Severn ferry made its stops and waited for the morning's first run. I was rewarded soon by sight of an ancient barge, something more suitable to a motion picture about Nineteenth Century life than to a modern enterprise. Nonetheless cheered, I climbed aboard, paid my fair, and waited with a small party of taciturn passengers until the ferryman saw fit to weigh anchor and transport us across the slowly flowing water.

I tried my cellular telephone from on board the ferry, and by some miracle of electronics managed to get through to the Fuchs Institute. I spoke with Karolina Parker, who expressed concern as to my welfare and my whereabouts. As briefly as possible, I explained my situation and she said that she would personally greet me at the pier in Old Severnford.

She proved as good as her word. I found her a delightful young woman, perhaps a few years younger than I, but showing so marked a family resemblance as to remove all doubt as to our being related. I explained to her about my Parker ancestors, and she astonished me by planting a most un-cousinly kiss on my mouth, even as we sat in her modern and comfortable automobile.

I was still puzzling over this remarkable behavior when we arrived at the Klaus Fuchs Memorial Institute. Karoline Parker introduced me to the director of the institute, whose friendly greeting was tempered by his assertion that I was expected to resolve the troubles of the Zeta/Zed system *post haste*, if Myshkin Associates was to retain the Fuchs Institute as an account.

Without stopping to arrange lodging in the town of Old Severnford itself, I set to work on the Institute's Zeta/Zed machines. The system was taken offline, which did not please the director, and I ran a series of diagnostic programs in turn on the mainframe processor, the satellite work stations, and the peripheral units that ran under system control.

As long as I used only sample data for testing, Zeta/Zed performed to perfection. It might be thought that I would be pleased with this result, but in fact the opposite was the case. If the system had malfunctioned, I possessed the tools (or believed that I did) to narrow down the area of malfunction until a specific site in the hardware or software remained. This could then be examined for its flaw and repaired or replaced.

When nothing went wrong, I could correct nothing.

"Very well," my hostess, Karolina Parker, suggested, "let's go back online while you observe, Mr. Lorentzen." I was as surprised by the coldness of her address as I had been by the warmth of her greeting in the car, but I could think of no response better than a simple, "All right."

Zeta/Zed was placed back on line. Almost at once error messages began flashing on the main monitor screen, but the system did not shut down. I permitted it to run until a batch of data had been processed, then attempted to print out the results.

The high-speed laser printer hummed, then began spitting out sheet after sheet of paper. I tried to read the top sheet, but it seemed to contain sheer gibberish. The printout comprised an almost random pattern of numbers, letters, and symbols which I knew were not part of any font supplied by Myshkin software. I asked Karolina Parker about this, but she insisted that no one had tampered with the software and no virus could have been introduced into the system as it was swept by anti-virus software regularly.

What could be the answer?

I asked Karolina Parker the source of the Institute's power supply, and was told that the Institute generated its own power, the Severn River turning a generator housed in a separate building. In this manner the Institute was independent of the vagaries of the local power system, antiquated and unreliable as it was known to be.

Furnished with a sparse cubicle from which to conduct my affairs, I soon sat alone with the enigmatic printouts. I had been furnished with a meal of sorts from the Institute's commissary, and I sat eating a stale sandwich, pausing to wash it down with occasional swigs of cold, bitter coffee, trying to make head or tail of these pages.

After a while I found a passage that seemed less chaotic than what had gone before. The printing was in Roman letters, not mathematical formulas, and by concentrating on the "words" (which were in fact not any words I recognized), moving my lips like a child just learning to read, and letting the sounds that were suggested pass my lips, I realized that this was the same language I had heard the previous night as I wandered the streets of Severnford.

By quitting time I was tired, nervous, and eager to find a warm meal and a soft mattress, if such amenities even existed in this accursed Severn Valley.

To my astonishment, Karolina Parker offered me a ride home in her automobile, and even offered me room and lodging in her house. I insisted that such hospitality, while appreciated, was excessive, but she replied that everything should be done to make my visit pleasant. We were, after all, family!

Karolina Parker's home was a pleasant house set in the center of a modest but beautifully tended park-like estate. The house itself was of late Tudor style, with half-timbered beams and diamond-pane windows. There was a great fireplace in the living room, and through the front windows I could see the peculiar topiary shrubs that stood outside like unfamiliar beasts grazing an alien landscape.

My hostess explained to me that she lived alone, and showed me to a comfortable bedroom which she said would be mine during my stay in Old Severnford. She suggested that I refresh myself while she prepared dinner for us both.

An hour later I was summoned to dine in a charming informal room. Karolina apologized for her impromptu mode of entertaining, but I found both her manner and the meal which she served me the high points of my, until now, dismal journey. She had decked herself out in a pair of tight-fitting blue jeans and a tee shirt with a portrait of Klaus Fuchs himself blazoned on it. Over this amazing outfit she wore a frilly apron.

She served me a delicious *ratatouille* accompanied by an excellent white wine (imported from northern California, I noted with some pride) and a crisp green salad. How this attractive young woman could work all day at the Institute and still entertain in such delightful fashion afterwards, was quite beyond my power of comprehension.

After the meal we repaired to the living room and shared coffee (hot, fresh and strong!) and brandy before a roaring fire. Oddly portentous selections of Carl Philipp Emanuel Bach and Georg Philipp Telemann came from the speakers of a superb sound system. Karolina and I spoke of computers, of her work at the Fuchs Institute and mine at Myshkin Associates. We tried to trace our common ancestry but ran into a blank wall somewhere around the year 1665. At no time did we speak of our personal lives. I did not know whether she had ever been married, for instance, or seriously involved with a man, nor did she query me with regard to such sensitive (and for me, painful) matters.

The sound system must have been preprogrammed, for after a while I found myself drawn into a complex composition by Charles Ives, and then into one of the stranger sound pieces of Edgar Varese. Our conversation had turned to the history of the Severn Valley, its peculiar isolation from the rest of England, and the odd whispered hints that were sometimes heard regarding the dark countryside and its inhabitants.

I fear that my stressful journey and my lack of sleep the previous night caught up with me, for I caught myself yawning at one point, and Karolina Parker, gracious hostess that she was, suggested that I retire.

"I'll stay downstairs to clean up a little," she volunteered. "You can find your room again, of course?"

I thought to offer a familial hug before retiring, but instead I found Karolina returning my gesture with a fierce embrace and another of her incredible kisses. I broke away in confusion and made my way to my room without speaking another word. I locked the door and placed a chair beneath the doorknob before disrobing, then climbed gratefully into bed and fell asleep almost at once.

I do not know how much later it was that I was awakened by — by what, I asked myself. Was it a careful rattling of the doorknob of my room? Was it a voice calling to me? And in words of what language —

the familiar tongue which Americans and Britons have shared for centuries, or that other, stranger language that I had heard in the streets of Severnford and had myself spoken, almost involuntarily, as I struggled to decipher the peculiar printouts of the Zeta/Zed system at the Fuchs Institute?

Whatever it was — whoever it was — quickly departed from my ken, and I sought to return to sleep, but, alas, I was now too thoroughly wakened to do so easily. I did not wish to leave my room; I cannot tell you why, I simply felt that there were things, or might be things, in that pleasant, comfortable house that I would rather not encounter.

So instead I seated myself in a comfortable chair near the window of my room and gazed over the Severn landscape. I could see but little of the village of Old Severnford, for this was a community where the residents retired early and stayed in their homes, the doors securely locked and the lights turned low, perhaps for fear that they attract visitors not welcome.

Raising my eyes to the hills above, I saw their rounded forms as those of ancient, sleeping beings, silhouetted in absolute blackness against the midnight blue sky. The clouds that had obscured the moon and stars earlier had dissipated and the heavens were punctuated by a magnificent scattering of stars and galaxies such as the city lights that blazed all night in the Silicon Valley could never reveal.

I permitted my gaze to drift lower, to the Severn Hills, when I was startled to perceive what appeared to be an artificial construct. This structure was in the form of a tower surmounted by a peculiarly made battlement or turret. I had thought the Severn Hills uninhabited save for a few examples of sparse and ill-nourished wildlife, hunted on occasion by locals seeking to add to their meager larders.

Even more surprising, the turret appeared to be illuminated from within. I strained my eyes to see clearly that which was before me. Yes, there were lights blazing from within the turret — if blazing is a word which may be applied to these dim, flickering, tantalizing lights. If I permitted my fancy to roam, the lights would almost form themselves into a face. Two great, hollow eyes staring blindly into the darkness, a central light like a nasal orifice, and beneath that a wide, narrow mouth grinning wickedly with teeth — surely they must be vertical dividers or braces — eager to invite… or to devour.

I stared at the turret for a long time. How long, I do not know, but eventually the night sky began to lighten, the moon and stars to fade. Were the lights in the turret extinguished, or was it the brightness of morning that made them fade?

A chill wracked my body, and I realized that I had sat for hours before the open window, clad only in thin pajamas. I climbed hastily back into bed and managed to catch a few winks before the voice of Karolina penetrated the door, summoning me to a lavish breakfast of bacon and eggs, freshly squeezed orange juice and a rich, hot mocha concoction that offered both the satisfying flavor of chocolate and the stimulation of freshly-brewed coffee.

In Karolina's car, on the way to the Klaus Fuchs Memorial Institute, I sought to gain information about my peculiar experience of the night before. I realized that my suspicion of my dear, multiply-distant cousin (for as such I had chosen to identify her, for my own satisfaction) had been the unjustified product of my own fatigue and depression, and the strangeness and newness of my surroundings.

Almost as if the turret had been the figment of a dream, I grappled mentally in hopes of regaining my impression of it. To a large degree it eluded me, but I was able at length to blurt some question about a turreted tower in the hills.

Karolina's answer was vague and evasive. She admitted that there were some very old structures in the region, dangerous and long-abandoned. In response to my mention of the flickering lights and the face-like arrangement in the turret, Karolina became peculiarly agitated, insisting that this was utterly impossible.

I averred that I would like to visit the tower and see for myself if it were inhabited, even if only by squatters.

To this, Karolina replied that there had been an earthquake in the Severn Valley some years before. A fissure had opened in the earth, and the row of hills in which the tower was located was now totally unreachable from Old Severnford. I would have to abandon my plan and give up my hopes of learning about the turret and its lights.

I spent the day at the Fuchs Institute working diligently on the Zeta/Zed system. Since my attempts of the day before had led me only to frustration, on this day I determined to tackle the problem on a smaller, more intensive basis. I powered down the entire system, disconnected all of its components from one another, and began running the most exhaustive diagnostic programs on the circuitry of the central processor.

During a luncheon break I thought to ask another employee of the Institute — *not* Karolina Parker — about my experience of the previous night. But strangely, I was unable to recall just *what* I had experienced, that I wished to inquire about.

This was by far the most peculiar phenomenon I had ever encountered. I *knew* that something odd had happened to me, I *knew* that I wanted to seek an explanation for it, but I was absolutely and maddeningly unable to remember just *what* it was that I wanted to ask about.

Humiliated, I terminated the conversation and returned to my assigned cubicle to study manuals and circuit diagrams associated with Zeta/Zed.

That night Karolina furnished another delicious repast, and we shared another delightful evening of conversation, coffee-and-brandy, and music. Karolina had attired herself in a shimmering hostess gown tonight, and I could barely draw my eyes from her own flowing, raven hair, her deep blue orbs, her pale English skin and her red, generous lips.

When the time came for us to part to our rooms and retire for the night, I no longer recoiled from my cousin's ardent kiss, but luxuriated in it. As I held her, our faces close together, I saw that she, too, carried the familiar Parker mark on her chin. I placed my lips against the mark, and she sighed as if I had touched her deeply and erotically. Images and fantasies raced through my mind, but I banished them and bade her good-night, and climbed the flagstone staircase to my quarters.

I wondered whether I really wanted to lock my door tonight, whether I really wanted to place a chair against it, but I finally did so, and climbed into bed, but this time I was not able to sleep, so I attired myself more warmly than I had the previous night, and placed myself in the comfortable chair before the window.

In the darkness of the Severn Valley my eyes soon adjusted themselves, and the utterly murky vista that greeted me at first once more resolved itself into rows of hills, clearly old hills smoothed and rounded by the passage of millennia, silhouetted against the star-dotted heavens. And as I simultaneously relaxed my body and my concentration, yet focused my eyes on the area where I had seen the turret rising the night before, once again I beheld its shape, and once again I perceived what appeared to be faint, flickering lights in its windows, making the suggestion of a face that seemed to speak to me in the peculiar tongue of the night-prowlers of Severnford and of the enigmatic computer printout.

I did not fall asleep. I wish to make this very clear. What next transpired may have been a vision, a case of astral travel, a supernatural or at least supernormal experience of the most unusual and remarkable sort, but it was absolutely *not a dream.*

Some force drew me from my chair in my room in my distant cousin Karolina Parker's home. That which was drawn was my soul.

Now you may think this is a very peculiar statement for me to make. I, Parker Lorentzen, am a thoroughly modern man. I hold degrees in mathematics, linguistics, philosophy, psychology, and computer science. I could, if I chose to do so, insist upon being addressed as Dr. Lorentzen, but I prefer not to flaunt my education before others.

I opt philosophically for the kind of scientific materialism that seeks explanations for all phenomena in the world of physical reality. I know that there are great mysteries in the universe, but I think of them as the *unknown* rather than the *unknowable.* Research, careful observation and precise measurement, computation and rigorous logic will eventually deliver to inquisitive intelligence, the final secrets of the universe.

Such is my philosophy. Or such it *was* until I visited the turret which my cousin Karolina claimed was unreachable.

At first I was frightened. I thought that I was being summoned to hurl myself from an upper-story window, from whence I would fall to the garden below and injure myself. I looked down and the weird topiary beasts seemed to be gesturing, urging me to fly from the house. I knew that this was impossible — in my physical being — but by relaxing ever more fully into my chair, while concentrating my vision, my mind, my whole psychic being on the distant turret in the Severn Hills, I felt my soul gradually separating from my body.

Why do I use the word, "soul," you may ask. Did I not mean my mind, my consciousness? Was I not having an out-of-body experience, a controversial but nevertheless real and not necessarily supernatural phenomenon?

But no, it was more than my mind, more than my consciousness that was leaving my body. It was my whole *self,* which I choose to refer to as my soul. For all my scientific skepticism, I have been forced to the conclusion that there is some part of us that is neither material nor mortal. Just what it is, just how it came into being, I do not pretend to know. I have heard every argument, faced every scoffing comment — have made them myself, or did so when I was a younger man — but I cannot now deny the reality of this thing that I call the soul.

For a moment I was able to look back at my own body, comfortably ensconced in the chair. Then I was off, drifting at first languorously through the open window, hovering briefly above the topiary figures in my cousin's garden, then rising as if on wings of my own, high above the town of Old Severnford, and then speeding into the black night, soaring toward the hills to the west of town.

I did see the fissure that Karolina had described, a horrid rent that seemed to penetrate deep into the earth. Its walls were strewn with boulders, and brushy vegetation had made its way down the sides of the fissure, attracted, perhaps, by the heat that seemed to radiate from its depths, or from the water that I surmised would gather in its depths.

As I approached the turret I had seen from my window, I could again perceive the flickering lights within, and the face-like formation of the illumination. From the distance of my cousin's house, and against the blackness of the Severn Hills, the tower had been of uncertain shape. Seen from a lesser distance, it assumed a clear shape and a surprisingly modern architectural aspect. It seemed to rise almost organically from its surroundings, a concept which I had come across more than once while browsing architectural journals.

Entering the largest and most brightly illuminated window, I found myself in a large room. It was unlike any I had ever seen before. As familiar as I am with every sort of modern device and scientific equipment, still I could not comprehend, or even describe, the titanic machinery that I beheld.

Figures utterly dwarfed by the machines tended them, tapping at control panels, reading indicators, adjusting conduits. Lights flashed on the machinery, and occasionally parts moved. Just as the building itself had exhibited an almost organic quality of architecture, so the machines within it seemed, in addition to their other characteristics, to be, in some subtle and incomprehensible way, *alive*.

Strangest of all was a gigantic, rectangular plane that filled an entire section of the monstrous room. Its surface was of a matte gray finish and had a peculiar look to it as if it were somehow *tacky*, as sticky as if a thin coating of honey had been spread on it, and let to stand in the sunlight until it was mostly but not entirely dry.

I approached the gray rectangle by that peculiar sort of disembodied flight that I had used since leaving my body in my cousin's house in Old Severnford, and hovered effortlessly above the gray plane. From my first vantage point at the window of the turret room, the plane had looked large, but was still contained within the single, large chamber. If I had been forced to make an estimate of its dimensions, I would have described it as three to four yards in width, and as much as forty yards in length.

But as I hovered above it, I realized that it was incredibly larger than I had first estimated. That, or perhaps it was merely my change of perspective that gave it the appearance of great size.

Have you ever played with one of those optical illusions, in which you are asked to look at two curved rectangles, or sections of arc cut from the perimeter of a circle or torus? One may appear far larger than the other, yet the instructions that come with such games always urge you to measure the rectangles and see that they are exactly the same size.

Maybe something like that is what happened to me. I cannot testify with any degree of certainty.

But I can tell you that, as I hovered above the gray plane (perhaps I should refer to it, now, as a gray *plain*) it was gigantic. It was miles in width and hundreds of miles in length — or perhaps it was thousands or even millions of miles in each dimension. I felt myself being drawn down toward it, and feared that if I approached too close to it I would be caught in its gravity — or in the tackiness of its surface — and be unable to escape.

With a huge effort I managed to halt my descent, but already I was so close to the plain that I had lost sight of its termini. Grayness stretched to infinity in all directions. I could turn, and above me I saw only star-studded blackness. Was the turret room open to the Severn sky, I wondered.

Beneath me I thought I saw stirrings in the gray. At this range it was not a smooth and stationary surface, but seemed textured, as if it were of wet concrete, and tiny specks that at first seemed to be merely part of this texture, could be seen to move. They reminded me of insects caught in the sweet, tacky covering of a roll of old-fashioned fly-paper.

I descended farther, and realized that the moving specks were alive, and in some inexplicable way I realized just what they were: they were the souls of human beings, trapped in the hold of the gray plain, struggling futilely for their release.

How could such a thing be, I wondered. Whose souls were these? Were they the immortal parts of residents of the Severn Valley, the souls perhaps of local residents who had died, and been trapped here in this bizarre limbo, neither attaining heaven nor being consigned to hell? Had they been summoned by the shapes tending the titanic machines? And if such was the case, what mad motive had moved these weird scientists to set such a trap?

A sudden fear overcame me, lest I be drawn down into the gray plain and be trapped with the other souls, and I beat my ethereal wings with all my strength, struggling to rise above that horrid gray surface. For a time the struggle seemed hopeless, but I persevered to the limits of my strength and beyond, forcing myself as great athletes are said to do, to find and call upon unknown reservoirs of determination. And at last my efforts were rewarded, for I found myself rising with painful slowness above the gray plain.

In time the laboratory, if that is what it was, reappeared around me. The gray plain was reduced to a rectangular area in the great room. The shadowy figures continued to tend their titanic machines, either unknowing or uncaring of my presence.

I struggled to the window and darted back toward my cousin's house. Despite the great distance, I could see myself — that is my body — seated before the window in my bedroom. My eyes were hooded, my chin rested on my chest as if I had fallen asleep.

The turret fell behind me. I passed over the fissure in the Severn Hills, down their lower slopes and the darkling meadows that separated them from Old Severnford. I passed over the modernistic buildings of the Klaus Fuchs Memorial Institute, flashed over the topiary garden that surrounded by cousin's house, and entered my bedroom.

I was able to circle the room once, gazing down with a peculiar detachment at the body that had been my residence for so many years, then slipped back into it. I rose, yawned, and climbed into my bed.

In the morning I tried to discuss the matter with my cousin as we motored to the Institute, but I found myself able to speak only in vague and indefinite terms about that which had been so concrete and specific when I experienced it during the night. Once within the confines of the Institute, even more strangely, I found that my memory of the experience deserted me altogether. I knew only that I had seen and done *something* odd during the night. Twice I fell asleep over my work, which conduct would certainly not help the standing of Myshkin Associates with this, its most valued account.

Progress on the problems with the Zeta/Zed System were small or nil. I found myself wondering if the cause of the system's failures were not external to the system itself. The old computer slogan, GIGO — Garbage In, Garbage Out — suggested itself to me. But one does well to tread carefully before suggesting such an explanation to the customer. It can be offensive, and can alienate an important executive even if it is true.

I spoke with Alexander Myshkin by telephone. He was disheartened by my lack of progress on the Zeta/Zed System problem, but urged me to pursue my theory of external sources for the failure of the system. "You're a diplomat, Park, my boy. You can handle these Brits. Be honest with 'em, be tactful but be firm."

Following another frustrating day, Karolina Parker and I returned to her house. Once away from the Institute, I was able to recall something of my strange experience. Karolina suggested that we repair to a local restaurant for dinner rather than return directly home. Astonished to learn that an establishment existed in Old Severnford which Karolina considered worth visiting, I agreed with alacrity.

The restaurant was located in a converted country manor — in another context I would even have termed the venue a chateau. Waiters in formal garb attended our every whim. The pre-prandial cocktails which we shared were delicious. Our table was covered with snowy linen; the silver shone, the crystal sparkled, the china was translucently thin and delicate.

The meal itself was superb. A seafood bisque, a crisp salad dressed with a tangy sauce, tiny, tender chops done to perfection and served with delicious mint jelly, baby potatoes and tiny fresh peas. For dessert a tray of napoleons and petit-fours was passed, and we ended our repast with espresso and brandy.

Our surroundings had been as splendid as our meal. We dined in a hall with vaulting ceilings, ancient stone walls and a flagged floor. A fire blazed in a huge walk-in fireplace, and suits of armor, ancient weapons and battle flags set the establishment's motif.

A single disquieting note was sounded when, in the course of my table-talk with Karolina, I happened to mention the turret. Karolina gestured to me to drop the subject, but I realized that I had already been overheard. The table nearest ours was occupied by a dignified gentleman in dinner clothes, with snowy hair and a white moustache. His companion, a lady of similar years, was decked out in an elaborate gown and rich-appearing pearls.

The gentleman summoned the waiter, who hustled away and returned with the *maitre d'hotel* in tow. After a hurried conference with the elderly gentleman, the *maitre d'* approached our table and, bending so that his lips were close to my companion's ear, hastened to deliver a verbal message to her.

Karolina blanched, replied, then nodded reluctantly as the *maitre d'* took his leave.

I had not fully understood a word of their brief conversation, but I could have sworn that the language in which it was conducted was that strange tongue I had heard in the streets of Severnford, and read from the faulty computer printout at the Fuchs Institute.

In any case, Karolina immediately settled our bill — she would not permit me to spend any money — and hustled us to her automobile. She spoke not a word *en route* to her domicile, but spun the car rapidly up the driveway, jumped from her position behind the wheel and hastened inside the house, casting a frightened look over her shoulder at the topiary garden.

Once in the main room of her home, Karolina did an extraordinary thing. She stood close to me and reached one hand to my cheek. She moved her hand as if to caress me, but as she did so I felt a peculiar pricking at my birthmark. Karolina peered into my face while a frown passed over her own, then she stood on her toes to reach my cheek (for I am a tall man and she a woman of average stature) and pressed her lips briefly to the birthmark.

I placed my hands on her shoulders and watched as she drew back from me. She ran her tongue over her lips, and I noticed a tiny drop of brilliant scarlet which disappeared as her tongue ran over it.

What could this mean? But I had no time to inquire, for Karolina made a brusque and perfunctory excuse and started up the stairs, headed for her room, with a succinct suggestion that I proceed to my own.

Once attired for repose, I found myself drawn to the comfortable chair which stood before the open window of my chamber. My eyes adjusted rapidly to the dim illumination of the night sky, and almost at once I found my consciousness focused on the illusion (if it was an illusion) of a face, gazing back at me from its place high in the Severn Hills.

Almost effortlessly I felt my soul take leave of my body. For the second time I flew across the topiary garden, across the village of Old Severnford, across the modernistic buildings of the Fuchs Institute. The brush-choked earthquake fissure in the Severn foothills passed beneath me and the tower loomed directly ahead.

Strangely enough, it seemed to have changed. Not greatly, of course, and in the pallid light that fell from the English sky it would have been difficult to make out architectural features in any great detail. But the tower looked both *older* and *newer* at the same time.

Hovering motionlessly in my weird ethereal flight, I studied the tower and in particular the turret which surmounted it, and I realized that the architectural *style* had been altered from that of modern, Twentieth Century England, to the form and designs of an earlier age. As I entered the turret through its great illuminated window, I briefly noted the cyclopean machines and their scurrying attendants, but sped quickly to the gray rectangular plain I had observed the previous night.

I sank toward its surface, bringing myself to a halt just high enough above the plain to make out the struggling souls there imprisoned. They had increased in number from the night before. Further, I was able to distinguish their appearance.

Again, you may wonder at my description. If a human soul is the immortal and disembodied portion of a sentient being, it would hardly be distinguished by such minutia as clothing, whiskers, or jewelry. But in some way each soul manifested the *essence* of its owner, whether he or she be soldier or peasant, monarch or cleric, houri or drab.

And the souls which I had seen on my first visit were the souls of modern men and women, while those I beheld on this, my second visit to the turret, were clearly the souls of people of an earlier age. The men wore side-whiskers and weskits; the women, long dresses and high hair styles and broad hats. No, they did not wear hair or clothing — it was their essences, as of the England of a century ago, that *suggested* as much.

How they had come to the turret and how they had become entrapped on the great gray plain I could not fathom, but their agony and their despair were manifest. They seemed to reach out psychic arms beseeching me to aid them, but I was unable to do so; I was totally ignorant of any way to alter their condition.

My heart was rent by pity. I flew to the attendants of the cyclopean machines, intending to plead with them to help these poor trapped creatures, but I was unable to communicate with them in any way. I studied them, hoping to discern some way of reaching them, but without success.

At last, in a state of despair, I began to move toward the great open window. I turned for one last look back, and had the peculiar sense that the attendants of the machines were themselves not human. Instead, they resembled the vague, yellowish creatures I had seen swimming beneath the surface of the Severn River.

A shudder passed through my very soul, and I sped frantically back to Old Severnford, back to Karolina Parker's house, back to my physical form. I reentered my body, dragged myself wearily to my bed, and collapsed into sleep.

Again in the morning my recollections of the strange experience were vague and uncertain. By the time I reached my cubicle at the Institute I was unable either to summon up an image of the night's activities, or to speak of them to anyone. I did, at one point, catch a glimpse of myself, reflected in the monitor screen of the computer work-station beside my desk. I must have nicked myself shaving, I thought, as a drop of blood had dried just on the blue birthmark on my jawline. I wiped it away with a moistened cloth, and was surprised at the fierceness of the sting that I felt.

Struggling to resolve the problems of the Zeta/Zed System, I had arranged an appointment with the chief engineer of the Fuchs Institute, a burly individual named Nelson MacIvar. When our meeting commenced, I surprised MacIvar by inquiring first as to why the Institute had been situated in so out-of-the-way a place as Old Severnford, and on the outskirts of the town at that.

MacIvar was blessed with a thick head of bushy red hair, a tangled beard of the same color, save that it was going to gray, and a complexion to match. He tilted his head and, as my employer Alexander Myshkin was sometimes wont to do, answered my question with one of his own.

"Why do you ask that, Mr. Lorentzen? What bearing has it on this damned Zeta/Zed machine and its funny behavior?"

I explained my theory that some exterior factor might be causing the system's problems, and reasserted my original question.

"You think this is an out-of-the-way place, do you?" MacIvar pressed. "Well, indeed it is. And that's why we chose it. I've been here for two-and-thirty years, Mr. Lorentzen, I was one of those who chose this spot for the Institute, and I'll tell you now, if I had it to do over, I'd have chosen a far more out-of-the-way location. The middle of the Australian desert, mayhap, or better yet the farthest Antarctic glacier."

I was astounded. "Why?" I demanded again. "This location must make it hard enough to bring in supplies and equipment, not to mention the difficulties of recruiting qualified workers. The people of the Severn Valley — well, I don't mean to be offensive, Mr. MacIvar, but they don't seem to be of the highest quality."

MacIvar gave a loud, bitter laugh. "That's putting it mildly, now, Mr. Lorentzen. They're a degenerate stock, inbred and slowly sinking back toward savagery. As is all of mankind, if you ask me, and the sooner we get there, the better. This thing we call civilization has been an abomination in the eyes of God and a curse on the face of the earth."

So, I was confronted with a religious fanatic. I'd better change my tack, and fast. "The water that drives your generators," I said, "Miss Parker — " MacIvar raised a bushy eyebrow — "Dr. Parker then, tells me that you use the Severn River for that purpose."

"Aye, and she is exactly right."

"Do you make any further use of its waters?"

"Oh, plenty. We drink it. We cook with it. We bathe in it. The Severn is the lifeline of this community. And we use it to cool our equipment, you know. Your wonderful Zeta/Zed machines can run very hot, Mr. Lorentzen, and they need a lot of cooling."

I shook my head. "Have you tested the river for purity? Do you have a filtering and treatment system in place?"

"Yes, and yes again. Just because we're out here in the country, Mr. American Troubleshooter, don't take us for a bunch of hicks and hayseeds. We know what we are doing, sir."

I gestured placatingly. "I didn't mean to cast aspersions. I'm merely trying to make sure that we touch every base."

"Touch every base, is it? I suppose that's one of your American sports terms, eh?"

By now I felt myself reddening. "I mean, ah, to make sure that no stone goes unturned, no, ah, possibility unexamined."

MacIvar glared at me in silence. I asked him, "What happens to the water after it's been passed through the heat-exchange tanks?"

"It goes back into the river."

"Has this had any effect on the local ecology? On the wildlife of the valley, or the aquatic forms found in the river itself?" I thought of those graceful yet oddly disquieting yellowish shapes in the river, of the glow that emanated from their curving bodies and reflected off the mist above.

"None," said MacIvar, "none whatsoever. And that is an avenue of inquiry, Mr. Troubleshooter, that I would advise you not to waste your precious time on."

With this, MacIvar pushed himself upright and strode ponderously from the office. Something had disturbed him and I felt that his suggestion — if not an actual warning — to steer clear of investigating the Severn River, would have the opposite effect on my work.

At the end of the working day I feigned a migraine and asked Karolina Parker to drive me home and excuse me for the remainder of the evening. I took a small sandwich and a glass of cold milk to my room and there set them aside untouched. I changed into my sleeping garments and stationed myself at the window. At this time of year the English evening set in early, for which I thanked heaven. I located the flickering face and flew to it without hesitation.

The tower had changed its appearance again. From its Victorian fustian it had reverted to the square-cut stone configuration of a medieval battlement. Once within the great turret room I sped by the cyclopean machinery and its scurrying, yellowish attendants and headed quickly to the gray plain.

Hovering over the plain, I dropped slowly until I could make out the souls struggling and suffering there. More of them were apparent this night than had previously been the case, and from their garments and equipage I could infer their identity. They were members of Caesar's legions. Yes, these pitiable beings were the survivors — or perhaps the casualties — of the Roman occupation force that had once ruled Britain.

After a time they seemed to become aware of me and attempted variously to command or to entice me into placing myself among them. This I would not do. One legionnaire, armed with Roman shield and spear, hurled the latter upward at me. I leaped aside, not stopping to wonder what effect the weapon would have had. It was, of course, not a physical object, but a psychic one. Yet as a soul, was I not also a psychic being, and might not the spear have inflicted injury or even death upon me?

The legionnaire's conduct furnished me with a clue, however. He had seen me; that I knew because he aimed his throw with such precision that, had I not dodged successfully, I would surely have been impaled on the spear-point. Even as the legionnaire stood shouting and shaking his fist at me, I willed myself to become invisible.

The look of anger on the ancient soldier's face was replaced by one of puzzlement and he began casting his gaze in all directions as if in hopes of locating me. I knew, thus, that I was able to conceal myself from these wretched souls merely by willing myself to be unseen.

Remaining invisible, I proceeded farther along the gray plain. There were many more souls here than I had even imagined. Beyond the Romans I observed a population of early, primitive Britons. Hairy Picts dressed in crude animal skins danced and chanted as if that might do them some good. And beyond the Picts I spied — but suddenly, a wave of panic swept over me.

How long had I been in the turret this night? I looked around, hoping to see the window through which I had entered, but I was too near the gray plain, and all I could in any horizontal direction was a series of encampments of captive souls, the ectoplasmic revenants of men, women, and children somehow drawn to the turret and captured by the gray plain over a period of hundreds or thousands of years.

I turned my gaze upward and realized that the turret room was indeed open to the sky of the Severn Valley, and that night was ending and the morning sky was beginning to turn from midnight blue to pale gray. Soon a rosy dawn would arrive, and in some incomprehensible way I *knew* that it would be disastrous for me still to be in the tower when daylight broke.

Thus I rose as rapidly as I could and sped over the gray plain, past the machines and their attendants, out of the turret and home to my cousin's house.

At work that day I met once again with Nelson MacIvar. He had appeared vaguely familiar to me at our first meeting, and I now realized that this burly, oversized man bore an uncanny resemblance to the great child who had thrown a rock at my car as it carried me from Brichester to Severnford. I came very near to mentioning the incident to him, but decided that no purpose would be served by raising an unpleasant issue.

Rather should I save my verbal ammunition for another attempt to get MacIvar to order tests of the Severn River water used in the Institute. By this time I had come to believe that the water was impregnated with some peculiar *force* that was interfering with the operation of the Zeta/Zed System. This force, I surmised, might be a radioactive contamination, picked up at some point in the river's course, perhaps as a result of the fissure at the foot of the Severn Hills nearby.

When I thought of that fissure and of those hills, a feeling of disquietude filled me, and I had to excuse myself and sip at a glass of water — that same damnable Severn water, I realized too late to stop myself — while I regained my composure. *Why* I should find thoughts of that fissure and of those hills so distressing, I could not recall.

This time MacIvar grudgingly yielded to my request, insisting that nothing would be found, but willing in his burly, overbearing way to humor this troublesome American. I reported this potential break to Alexander Myshkin by Transatlantic telephone, and spent the remainder of the day more or less productively employed.

Again that night I feigned migraine and excused myself from my cousin's company. She expressed concern for my well-being and offered to summon a doctor to examine me, but I ran from her company and locked myself in my room. I stared into the fiery orb of the sun as it fell beneath the Severn Hills, then willed myself across the miles to the turret.

As I approached it tonight I realized that it had changed its form again, assuming the features of a style of architecture unknown and unfamiliar to me, but clearly of the most advanced and elaborate nature imaginable.

I flashed through the window, sped past the machines and their attendants, and hovered above the gray plain. I had reached a decision. Tonight I would pursue my investigation of the plain to its end! I swooped low over the plain, passed rapidly over the Victorian village — for such is the way I now labeled this assemblage of souls — over the Roman encampment, over the rough the Pictish gathering, and on. What would I find, I wondered — Neanderthals?

Instead, to my astonishment, I recognized the ectoplasmic manifestation of an Egyptian pyramid. I dropped toward it, entered an opening near its base, and found myself in a hall of carven obsidian, lined with living statues of the Egyptian hybrid gods — the hawk-headed Horus, the jackal-headed Anubis, the ibis-god Thoth, the crocodile god Sobk — and I knew, somehow, that these, too, were not physical representations created by some ancient sculptors, but the very *souls* of the creatures the Egyptians worshipped!

I did not stay long, although I could see that ceremony was taking place in which worshippers prostrated themselves, making offerings and chanting in honor of their strange deities. I sped from the pyramid and continued along the plain, wondering what next I would encounter.

In Silicon Valley, Alexander Myshkin and I had spent many hours, after our day's work was completed, arguing and pondering over the many mysteries of the world, including the great mystery of Atlantis. Was it a mere legend, a Platonic metaphor for some moral paradigm, a fable concocted to amuse the childish and deceive the credulous? Myshkin was inclined to believe in the literal reality of Atlantis, while I was utterly skeptical.

Alexander Myshkin was right.

The Atlantean settlement was suffused with a blue light all its own. Yes, the Atlanteans *were* the precursors and the inspiration of the Egyptians. Their gods were similar but were mightier and more elegant than the Egyptians'; their temples were more beautiful, their pyramids more titanic, their costumes more fantastic.

And the Atlanteans themselves — I wondered if they were truly human. They were shaped like men and women, but they were formed with such perfection as to make the statues of Praxiteles look like the fumblings of a nursery child pounding soft clay into a rough approximation of the human form.

These Atlanteans had aircraft of amazing grace and beauty, and cities that would make the fancies of Wonderland or of Oz pale by comparison. And yet they had been captured and imprisoned on this terrible gray plain!

I sped beyond the Atlantean settlement, wondering if yet more ancient civilizations might be represented. And they were, they were. People of shapes and colors I could only have imagined, cities that soared to the heavens (or seemed to, in that strange psychic world), wonders beyond the powers of my puny mind to comprehend.

How many ancient civilizations had there been on this puny planet we call Earth? Archaeologists have found records and ruins dating back perhaps 10,000 years, 15,000 at the uttermost. Yet anthropologists tell us that humankind, *homo sap.* or something closely resembling him, has been on this planet for anywhere from two to five *million* years. Taking even the most conservative number, are we to believe that for 1,985,000 years our ancestors were simple fisher-folk, hunters and gatherers, living in crude villages, organized into petty tribes? And that suddenly, virtually in the wink of the cosmic eye, there sprang up the empires of Egypt and Mesopotamia, of ancient China and India, Japan and Southeast Asia and chill Tibet, the Maya and the Aztecs and the Toltecs and the great Incas, the empires of Gambia and of Ghana, the mysterious rock-painters of Australia and the carvers of the stone faces of Easter Island?

This makes little sense. No, there must have been other civilizations, hundreds of them, thousands, over the millions of years of humankind's tenancy of the planet Earth.

But even then, what is a mere 2,000,000 years, even 5,000,000 years, in the history of a planet six *billion* years of age? What mighty species might have evolved in the seas or on the continents of this world, might have learned to think and to speak, to build towering cities and construct great engines, to compose eloquent poems and paint magnificent images...and then have disappeared, leaving behind no evidence that ever they had walked this Earth... or at least, no evidence of which we are aware?

Such races did live on this planet. They had souls, yes, and so much, say I, for human arrogance. This I know because I saw their souls.

How many such races? Hundreds, I tell you. Thousands. Millions. I despaired of ever reaching the end of the gray plain, but I had vowed to fly to its end however long it took. This time, if daylight found me still in the tower, so must it be. My cousin might discover my body, seemingly deep in a normal and restorative slumber, propped up in my easy chair. But she would be unable to awaken me.

Yes. I determined that I would see this thing to its conclusion, and from this objective I would not be swayed. I saw the souls of the great segmented fire-worms who built their massive cities in the very molten mantle of the Earth; I saw submarine creatures who would make the reptilian plesiosaurs look like minnows by comparison, sporting and dancing and telling their own tales of their own watery gods; I saw the intelligent ferns and vines whose single organic network at one time covered nearly one third of the primordial continent of Gondwanaland; I saw the gossamer, feathery beings who made their nests in Earth's clouds and built their playgrounds in Luna's craters.

We humans in our conceit like to tell ourselves that we are evolution's darlings, that millennia of natural selection have led Nature to her crowning creation, *homo sap*. Let me tell you that the opposite is the case. The story of life on Earth is not the story of evolution, but of *de*-volution. The noblest, the most elevated and most admirable of races were the first, not the last.

But still I pursued my flight, past wonder on wonder, terror on terror, until at last I saw the gray plain, the gray *plane* curve upward, rising into the brilliant haze that I recognized as the primordial chaos from which our Solar System emerged. And the souls that were captured by the turret — what was their fate? For what purpose were they caught up in every era of being, and drawn backward, backward toward that primordial haze?

A great mass of soul-force formed before my ectoplasmic eyes. A great seething ball of sheer soul-energy that accreted there in the dawn of time, now burst its bonds and rolled down that great gray plain, sweeping all before it, destroying cities as a boulder would crush an ants' nest, shaking continents to their foundations, causing the globe itself to tremble and to wobble in its orbit around the Sun.

But even this was only the beginning of the havoc wrought by this great ball of soul-energy. From the remote past to the present — our present, yours and mine — it roared, and then on into the future, sweeping planets and suns in its path.

And when the roiling concentration of soul-force reached that unimaginably distant future, when all was dim and silent in the cosmos and infinitesimal granules of existence itself floated aimlessly in the endless void, it reversed it course and swept backward, roiling and rolling from future to past, crushing and rending and growing, always growing, growing.

It reached its beginning point and reversed itself still again, larger and more terrible this time than it had been the first, and as it oscillated between creation and destruction, between future and past, between the beginning of the universe and its end, the very fabric of time-space began to grow weak.

What epochs of history, human and pre-human and, yes, post-human, were twisted and reformed into new and astonishing shapes. Battles were fought and unfought and then fought again with different outcomes; lovers chose one another, then made new and different choices; empires that spanned continents were wiped out as if they had never existed, then recreated in the images of bizarre deities; religions disappeared and returned, transmogrified beyond recognition; species were cut off from the stream of evolution to be replaced by others more peculiar than you can imagine.

A baby might be born, then disappear back into its mother's womb only to be born again a monstrosity unspeakable. A maddened killer might commit a crime, only to see his deed undone and himself wiped out of existence, only to reappear a saintly and benevolent friend to his onetime victim.

And what then, you might wonder, what then? I'll not deny that my own curiosity was roused. Would humankind persist forever? What supreme arrogance to think this would be the case! Mightier species than we, and nobler, had come and gone before *homo sap.* was so much as a gleam in Mother Nature's eye.

In iteration after iteration of the titanic story, humankind disappeared. Destroyed itself with monstrous weapons. Was wiped away by an invisible virus. Gave birth to its own successor race and lost its niche in the scheme of things. Was obliterated by a wandering asteroid, conquered and exterminated by marauding space aliens —

Oh, space aliens. Alexander Myshkin and I had debated that conundrum many a time. Myshkin believed that the universe positively *teemed* with intelligence. Creatures of every possible description, human, human-like, insectoid, batrachian, avian, vegetable, electronic, you name it. Myshkin's version of the cosmos looked like a science fiction illustrator's sample book.

My universe was a lonely place. Only Earth held life, and only human life on Earth was sentient. It was a pessimistic view, I'll admit, but as the mother of the ill-favored baby was wont to say, "It's ugly but it's mine."

Well, Myshkin was right. There were aliens galore. At various times and in various versions of the future — and of the past, as a matter of fact — they visited Earth or we visited their worlds or space travelers of different species met in unlikely cosmic traffic accidents or contact was made by radio or by handwritten notes tossed away in empty olive jars.

One version of post-human Earth was dominated by a single greenish fungus that covered the entire planet, oceans and all, leaving only tiny specks of white ice at the North and South Poles. Another was sterilized, and thank you, weapons industry, for developing a bomb that could kill everything — *everything!* — on an entire planet. But spores arrived from somewhere later on, and a whole new family of living things found their home on Earth.

I saw all of this and more, and I saw the very fabric of space-time becoming feeble and unsure of itself. I saw it tremble and quake beneath the mighty assault of that accumulated and ever-growing soul-force, and I realized what was happening. The cosmos itself was threatened by whatever screaming demons of chaos cavorted beyond its limits.

At length a rent appeared, and I was able to peer into it, but the black, screeching chaos that lay beyond it I will not describe to you. No, I will not do that. But I peered into that swirling orifice of madness and menace and I mouthed a prayer to the God I had abandoned so long ago, and I swore to that God that if one man, if one soul could counter the malignities who populated the fifth dimension, or the fiftieth, or the five millionth, it would be I.

Did I say that the soul is the immaterial and immortal part of a living, sentient being? And did I say that I had realized, in despite of my lifelong skepticism, that God was a living reality? Perhaps I should have said that *gods* were living realities. I do not know how many universes there are, each one created by its own god, each god behaving like a mischievous child.

And that chaotic void beyond the cosmos — was that in fact part of a higher realm of reality, in which *all* the universes drifted like the eggs of some aquatic life-form, within the nourishing fluid of the sea? If my soul should leave our cosmos and enter that chaos, to face the demons — demons that I now realized were the gods of other universes — would it then forfeit its claim to immortality?

Could those demons be stopped? Could I, one man, stand against this infinite army of insanity? There was a single way to learn the answer to that question. I decided that I would take that way.

I —

THE PELTONVILLE HORROR

The Hudson-Terraplane roadster's electric headlights cut twin channels of brilliance through the swirling fog of the Peltonville Turnpike. The hour was late and traffic was almost nonexistent, save for the sporty little car's sleek, bright blue form.

The shrieking voice that had come from the automobile's custom-fitted Stromberg-Carlson radio gave way to the less disturbing and more polished tones of a staff announcer. "Tune in again next week for another Witch's Tale," he urged listeners. "But for now, sit back and relax, put your feet up and enjoy the melodic musical stylings of the Stan Sawyer Orchestra."

"What a relief!" Delia Davis managed a quiet little laugh, tinged with a suggestion of nervousness. "I never did like those spooky programs, Paul darling. If I didn't love you so much I don't think I could ever put up with them."

"But, Delia," Paul Carter reached across the seat to pat his sweetheart's hand, "it's all just make-believe. You don't think there's really an old witch named Nancy who's more than a hundred years old, and lives with a wise black cat named Satan, do you?"

"No." Delia hesitated. Then she repeated, "No. I guess not." Paul released her hand and she tightened the scarf over her head. Her hair was jet black; by candlelight Paul Carter said that it showed bits of midnight blue that matched the color of her eyes. Delia had let her hair grow longer now that the boyish look and the bobbed hair of the previous decade had been abandoned for a more feminine look. "I do so love the feel of the wind and the smell of the fresh air out here in the country. But it's getting awfully cold now that the sun is down. Feels more like winter than spring."

Paul laughed. "Changing the subject, are you?"

"I guess so. When we crossed that bridge over the Beeton River a while ago, I could just imagine we were flying through the stratosphere." Delia reached for the tuning knob on the dashboard. The signal had drifted and she brought it back so the sound of saxophones and trumpets filled the convertible's tonneau. "I guess I just don't enjoy being scared. Well, maybe just a little, like at those frightening movies. But then I know you'll put your arm around me and I feel all safe. I wish we were married, Paul. Then you could put your arm around me all the time and I'd never be frightened again. Oh, Paul, will we ever be married? Can't we even set a date?"

"As soon as this depression is over and the economy picks up again," Paul replied. "You know, I'm lucky to still have a job at all, but since they've been cutting salaries every few months, I can barely pay the rent on a furnished room. There's no way I could afford an apartment and support a wife."

Delia lowered her eyes to the engagement ring on her left hand. "We could sell my ring." She toyed with the narrow band and its tiny, glittering stone. "And we don't really need a car. As much fun as it is, Paul, you could take the streetcar to work at the plant."

Paul shook his head. "I bought the car before the crash. Some timing, wasn't it? I couldn't get a quarter of what it's worth, now. And you'll never sell your ring, Delia, not as long as I can draw breath and do a day's work. Listen — "

Delia interrupted him with a gasp. "Paul — what was that?"

"What, Delia? I didn't see anything."

"Right over there, Paul. I thought I saw something moving in the woods, and then — then there was a flash. I don't know what it was. Something bright, a point of light, two points of light. No, there were more. They kept blinking on and off. I think there were eight of them. I — they were some color I've never seen before. Something like red, I think, but so deep, so powerful — so frightening, oh, Paul, what could it be?"

Paul eased up on the roadster's accelerator and the little car slowed. "I don't see anything, Delia. Through this fog, I don't know how you did. But maybe there was a momentary break. It might have been an electric power line or a radio tower. Or maybe you just caught sight of a couple of stars."

"No, Paul. It was nothing like that. It was — oh, never mind. It's gone now, whatever it was. Let's go on."

A distant flash lit the night sky above the woods to the west. Paul pushed the car to a higher speed. As he did so a low, distant rumble followed the lightning. "Uh-oh. I hope we're not going to get rained on."

"Maybe we should stop and put the top up." Delia looked around them. The fog had largely lifted but the night had actually grown darker than ever. A bright moon struggled to send its light through thick storm clouds, but only an occasional break in the clouds permitted a brief moment of illumination.

Lightning flashed, closer and brighter, a sinister greenish sheet silhouetting dark deciduous vegetation. "Look!" Delia exclaimed, "there it is again!" She pointed toward the east. "Those lights, blinking like terrible, hungry eyes!"

This time Paul pulled the little car onto the shoulder of the road. He turned off the engine, followed Delia's pointing finger with his eyes. "I don't see anything."

"No," Delia shook her head. "They're gone. But wait, Paul, listen." The radio had of course lapsed into silence when the roadster's ignition was cut, and the whisper of the gathering storm sounded through pines and oaks.

There was another flash of lightning. This time Paul counted the seconds until thunder boomed. "What's the saying," he muttered, "a mile a second? That storm is only a few miles away now. In fact, I think I just felt the first raindrops on my face. Help me, Delia, let's get the top up!"

Delia cocked her head, "Listen to that, dear."

Paul frowned. "I hear the wind and rain."

"No, there's another sound. A sort of piping and hissing and scratching. Like some incredibly gigantic — oh, Paul, I don't know. Something horrible. Could there be a spider so huge that it towers above the trees? Is it possible?"

Paul put his arms around her. "No, Delia. It's just the storm. The thunder and lightning and wind. Really, dear, it's just the storm."

Paul fumbled for the three-cell flashlight that he kept in the Hudson-Terraplane. It blazed into light and he used it now as a work-lamp.

It took the effort of a few minutes to raise the canvas top on the little roadster and button it in place. Even so, Paul and Delia were halfway to a good drenching by the time they scrambled back into the car and slammed the side doors that turned it into a snug refuge from the storm.

With the optimism of youth they laughed off their wet condition. Delia undid her scarf and primped her raven curls with a brush she'd carried in her purse.

Paul ran his fingers through his own rust-colored hair. He was overdue for a trim; the hair was beginning to curl over his collar. He turned the ignition key and mashed down on the self-starter switch with his heavy brogan. The Hudson-Terraplane's six-cylinder engine coughed once as if clearing its throat of the falling rain, then purred happily. Paul switched on the headlights. The fog had disappeared now, and twin shafts of raindrops appeared before the roadster.

"What shall it be, darling?" he asked. "Shall we push on or turn back to Springfield?"

Delia hummed for a moment, a habit of hers while considering choices. "I could do with a cup of warm soup beside a friendly fireplace, dear. Isn't there a roadhouse somewhere along the Peltonville Pike?"

Paul's brow furrowed in thought. "I'm pretty sure there is. I've only been to Peltonville a few times, but I think I recall seeing one not far beyond the Beeton River bridge."

"Oh, let's push on then, Paul. It's such a miserable night, the ride home wouldn't be any fun at all with our clothes all clammy and cold as they are."

"No sooner said than done!" He pulled the car back onto the blacktop highway. "It's a good thing they paved over the old dirt road, isn't it!"

The roadster's tires hissed over the rain-swept blacktop. Now a few unseasonable hailstones were mixed with the drops. They clattered and bounced off the Hudson-Terraplane's hood and began to accumulate on the road surface as well. Winds pushed the lightweight car sideways but Paul Carter's skillful hands kept the roadster on a steady course. He reached to switch on the Stromberg-Carlson, but the lightning's interference and the noise of the storm, which had now struck in its full fury, made it impossible to hear anything worthwhile. Paul switched the radio back off.

He felt Delia's head resting on his shoulder and patted her hand with his own. Soon a sign appeared beside the highway, advertising Daniello's Roadhouse two miles ahead. Paul pushed on. Shortly there was another sign. *Daniello's*, it read, *Steaks, Cocktails, Dancing to Willie Moore's African Chili Seven.*

Daniello's Roadhouse was a pleasant-looking establishment built in the popular Tudor Revival style, with cream-colored stucco walls marked by half-timbered beams. At least, that was the way it appeared in the spotlights placed to illuminate its exterior. There was a neon sign on the roof, and the windows of stained diamond-glass showed an inviting amber color.

"We're here, Delia." Paul placed a gentle kiss on his sweetheart's forehead.

Delia smiled up at him sleepily, then leaned away and stretched like a contented kitten.

The roadhouse door was made of heavy wooden planks and swung heavily on old iron hinges. Stepping inside, the couple were enveloped by the pleasant odors of hot, hearty cooking. They made their way to a lounge and found space for themselves on dark leather barstools. They could hear the sound of music coming from another room. Willie Moore's African Chili Seven lived up to their name. A hot version of "Decatur Street Stomp" drifted into the lounge.

A red-jacketed bartender asked for their order. Paul ordered a hot toddy. Delia giggled and asked for a tequila sunset. The lounge was not crowded. A few couples sat at tables. The other barstools were mostly unoccupied. The bartender placed their drinks in front of Paul and Delia and remarked that they were fortunate to make it safely through the storm.

"Why is that?" Paul asked.

The bartender pointed over his shoulder. On the shelf behind him stood a cathedral-topped Capehart radio. "Can't get anything now, but earlier the news said that the bridge was out. Beeton River's rising and the bridge couldn't stand the gaff."

Paul and Delia lifted their glasses in a silent toast. Paul introduced himself and Delia to the bartender.

"Mustafa Cristopolous," the bartender identified himself. Now Paul realized that his speech was unusual, more an oddity of intonation than an actual accent. His voice was deep and sounded like a truckload of gravel. "I am half Greek, half Turkish," the bartender explained, "I was born in Izmir. I don't suppose you've ever heard of that place." His face carried the marks of past experiences. His nose had been broken more than once, an oddly appealing dimple marked the center of his chin and an old scar on one cheek had faded now but looked as if it had once been livid. The absence of hair on his skull was made up for by a huge black moustache.

"In the old country the Greeks hated me because I was Turkish and the Turks hated me because I was Greek. So I come to America. Here, everybody's everything."

"But what about the bridge?" Delia asked.

"Big storm," Cristopolous growled. "The boss don't like me playing the radio when the band is on, but I like to listen to news. I get stations from Springfield, Aurora, Littleton. News on the Springfield station says too much debris coming down the Beeton River, jammed up under the bridge, roadway cracked. They won't even have crews there till after the storm is over."

He looked toward the entrance of the roadhouse as if he could see outside. "How bad is it now?"

Paul said, "It got pretty nasty, Mustafa. Rain turning to hail."

The big bartender nodded his understanding. Paul had finished his drink now, and Delia's glass was mostly empty. Cristopolous asked if they wanted a refill but instead they left the lounge and moved to the dining room. The African Chili Seven were playing "Deep Bayou Blues." Paul and Delia found a table and a waitress took their order. Paul asked for a sirloin steak. Delia asked for chicken. Both requested soup before their entrées.

While they ate, they discussed what to do next. Clearly there was no point in trying to return to Springfield. They would get as far as the bridge and have to wait for repairs to be made.

"I'm afraid we'll have to continue on to Peltonville," Paul announced.

"But then we won't get back to Springfield until tomorrow at the soonest," Delia complained. "What will people think? Mother and Dad will be beside themselves. And all our friends, Paul — do you think it's right?"

He reached across the table and took her hand. "I'm afraid we don't have much choice. Besides, people will just have to think what they choose."

"I don't know." Delia frowned. "It's not as if we were married." Then, "Do you think there's an inn at Peltonville? If we got two rooms it might be all right. And if there's a telephone, I could call Mother and Dad and explain what happened."

"A good idea, darling, but in a storm like this one, if the bridge is out, you can be sure that the telephone lines are down, too. I'm sorry. But if your parents really love you and trust you, they'll stand by you. As for anyone else — well, we'll just have to see it through."

As they were leaving the roadhouse they stopped to speak with Mustafa Cristopolous once again. Paul asked how much farther it would be to Peltonville, and whether Mustafa thought the road would be drivable now. The bartender said it was only another dozen miles, and the road was a good one.

"I'm worried about the hail, though," Paul explained.

Cristopolous shrugged his massive shoulders. "Life is risky." He paused, then added, "But you be careful. Some bad things happen in Peltonville."

"What bad things?"

"Just bad things. There is an old synagogue there, people do not go any more. Good people, I mean. Good people have mostly left Peltonville. You be careful, Paul and Delia."

Cristopolous had remembered their names. Paul found small comfort in that. He asked, "What do you mean by that — about the synagogue, I mean."

A weary smile creased the bartender's battered features. He leaned across the polished mahogany and lowered his voice. "Did I tell you, I am myself a Jew?" He looked around as if worried that he might be overheard. "One more reason I left Europe. Bad enough to be both a Turk and a Greek. Being a Jew as well — that was enough to make everybody hate me. Here in America — well, no place is perfect, is it?" He nodded toward the African Chili Seven. "They still have to struggle. But if they were in Greece or in Turkey, they would have it far worse."

Paul was still concerned about the Peltonville synagogue. He pressed Cristopolous for information. Cristopolous told him that he had once been a member of the congregation. It was called Temple Beth Shalom — the House of Peace. But the old rabbi had been forced to leave and a new leader took control. The old rabbi, Yacoub ben Yitzak, Jacob son of Isaac, replaced by Yeshua ben Yeshua, Joshua son of Joshua.

Ben Yeshua was a kabalist. He introduced ancient Hebrew magic into the synagogue. Its name had been changed to Temple Beth Mogen, House of the Star. The old congregants had all left Peltonville, those who had not mysteriously disappeared before they could get away. Cristopolous was one of the lucky ones, he had avoided Peltonville ever since. Other Jews had come from far away to replace them and fill the ranks of Temple Beth Mogen.

"It's very bad, Paul. If you go to Peltonville, be very careful."

Once they were back in the car and Paul had the engine warming up, Delia turned toward him, the reflected light of the sign on Daniello's Roadhouse showing her worried expression. "Do you think we can make it to Peltonville, Paul?"

"There are other patrons. They didn't look too worried to me."

"But there's something else."

Paul turned and took her in his arms, comforting her. "What, sweetheart? Are you still worried about your reputation? I promise, I'll stand by you whatever they say."

"No, it isn't that, Paul. It's — remember those lights, those eyes, I thought they were. And that weird sound. They were real, you know. I could tell you didn't believe me, I know you too well to be fooled. There was something there."

"Oh, yes. A giant spider, was it?"

"I don't know. Maybe it was. Maybe something else. But there was something there, something alive. Oh, I don't like it. I don't know what it is, but I know it isn't nice at all."

Paul leaned back and looked into Delia's eyes. "If there was a monster loose in these woods, don't you think we'd have heard about it? Wouldn't there be stories in the Springfield *Courier* or reports on the radio? That's just the kind of thing they love to report. It's a nice change from weddings and Rotary Club meetings and high school basketball games. You haven't read anything about a monster, have you?"

"No," she admitted. "But still — I saw those lights and I heard that sound. You don't have to believe me but I know it was real, Paul, I know it!"

"Really, Delia — on a night like this, you were halfway asleep, we'd been listening to that spooky radio program, your imagination was playing tricks on you."

"But what about that evil rabbi? That whole story about the Jewish synagogue in Peltonville. I've been in a synagogue in Springfield. My friend Rebecca was married in a synagogue, I was in the wedding. It was a beautiful service. I don't see how it could be evil, any more than a regular church could be evil, but Mr. Cristopolous didn't seem to be making that up."

Paul shook his head. "Old world superstitions, Delia. Just look at the man. He's had a hard life. Heaven knows what terrible experiences he must have had in Europe. He was lucky to get out of there and come to America, from the things that are going on now. I don't think he was making it up either, but his head is so full of wild folktales, he could believe anything."

He turned on the headlights and backed the Hudson-Terraplane away from the roadhouse. In moments the little car was back on the highway. The storm had passed, the moon was bright and a black sky was dotted with colorful, distant stars that glittered like ice crystals in candlelight. The combination of moonlight, starlight and the roadster's headlamps showed the surface of the roadway, now white with crusted hailstones.

Paul reached to switch on the little car's radio. He twirled the tuning knob. On the Springfield and Aurora frequencies there was only hissing and crackling, but he managed to pick up a signal from Peltonville. He shook his head. "Is that music? Chanting? I can't understand a word of it. And it all sounds so weird."

Delia said, "I think it's Hebrew. The service at Rebecca's wedding was partly in Hebrew. I don't know what it means, of course, but that sounds like the service."

Paul tried to get a stronger signal but the best he could do was a faint chanting in an exotic tongue. He reached to turn off the radio but before he could do so the chanting faded into the background. Over it there came a hissing, piping, scraping noise, followed by the sound of voices exclaiming in ecstasy.

Even though the storm had passed, there was another flash of greenish lightning that seemed to come from all directions at once. The Hudson-Terraplane's engine sputtered into silence that was broken by an ear-shattering boom of thunder. Paul and Delia clutched each other's hands in alarm, then Paul managed a nervous chuckle. He grasped the steering wheel of the roadster and mashed down on the self-starter switch.

The little car's engine coughed once, then roared back to life. The orange light behind the radio's tuning dial glowed but there was no sound so Paul switched it off. He threw in the clutch, put the roadster in gear and set it to moving.

When they passed the Peltonville city limit Paul read the welcoming sign and population figures. Based on his recollection of his last visit he'd thought that Peltonville was bigger than the number indicated. Perhaps the latest census figures had shown a loss of population. Then he thought of Mustafa Cristopolous's words about Peltonville:

Some bad things happen in Peltonville ... Just bad things. There is an old synagogue there, people do not go any more. Good people, I mean. Good people have mostly left Peltonville. You be careful, Paul and Delia.

It was hard for Paul or Delia to tell much about the character of Peltonville as the little roadster rolled into the downtown area. Every building seemed to be dark. Small houses in the style of the previous century loomed to left and right, but apparently Peltonvilliers retired early, for only the jagged silhouettes of the residences could be seen outlined against the backdrop of the night sky.

"Can you tell what time it is?" Paul asked.

Delia found the flashlight they had used earlier and shone its beam against her Elgin wristwatch. "It's 10:30," she announced. "I guess they keep going at Daniello's Roadhouse but people in Peltonville don't stay up."

After a few blocks lined by small retail shops the Hudson-Terraplane's headlamps picked out a building with a darkened marquee extending over the crumbling sidewalk. Paul pulled the car to the curb and Delia shone the flashlight on the sign.

Peltonville Inn, it read.

"Well, that's straightforward enough," Paul commented. "Let's see if they can put us up for the night."

"Paul." Delia took his arm.

He looked at her, waiting to hear what she had to say.

"Paul, you know I love you, dear. You do know that, don't you?"

"Of course, Delia. You shouldn't even have to ask. But — what's the matter?"

"Well — " She looked down. "Well, I'd really love to stay with you tonight. It would be — thrilling, Paul. But I know it would be wrong. I don't want to disappoint you, but would you mind if — if we took two rooms, dear?"

Paul shook his head. "Of course not. What sort of fellow do you think I am?"

He climbed out of the Hudson-Terraplane, walked around the car and opened Delia's door. "Come, darling, let's see what the management has to say to two poor travelers with no luggage to show for themselves!"

As Paul helped Delia from the car he realized that her breath was freezing in the air, as was his own. The wind had reversed its direction and brought the unseasonable storm back over Peltonville, or perhaps this was merely another front in a series. In any case, the wind had begun to howl unpleasantly and hail was battering both travelers.

Paul and Delia hustled to a place of shelter beneath the marquee of the Peltonville Inn. The hotel was dark. Turning back toward the street they observed that the town had not yet converted its street lamps to electric power from the older gas illumination. A few fixtures flickered feebly despite the icy wind that swept the street.

Paul searched his trousers for a coin. He found a silver dollar and used it to rap on the glass panel of the Peltonville Inn's main entrance, but to no avail. He called out but his voice disappeared into the whistling, howling gale.

Stepping to the edge of the sheltered space beneath the marquee he held Delia to him, gazing at the sky. Clouds like shreds of torn black cloth swept overhead; in the breaks between them stars glared down at the couple. Never had Paul seen them so cold and seemingly malevolent. To the east a new constellation appeared, a group of eight stars of a color he had never seen before. If he had needed to name their color he would have called it red, but it was red of a shade and quality he had never previously experienced. The stars danced. Paul shuddered. An eerie auditory amalgam, part whistle, part hiss, part scraping, sounded faintly.

"There's nobody here," he muttered. "I can't tell, Delia, either the inn is out of business or it's closed for the night. Either way, we'll find no shelter here tonight."

"But Paul," she replied. Paul looked into her face. Clearly she was struggling to summon her courage but there were tears in her eyes and the corners of her mouth quivered. "What will we do? Is there any place we can go? We can't just sleep in the car, we'll freeze."

She was right, he realized. The wind whipped through their lightweight garments. Even beneath the marquee of the Peltonville Inn the hailstones bounced from the sidewalk and roadway and stung them like wave after wave of angry ice-hornets.

Across the street a faint light flickered in the windows of an old, two-story building. There was a momentary break in the screaming wind and a low chanting, barely audible, drifted to their ears. Paul stepped out from beneath the marquee, shielding his eyes from the pelting of hailstones as sharp and vicious as a bombardment of granite needles.

Yes, there was a light in the building.

Paul raised his gaze. The sinister constellation had disappeared from its previous location. Now it appeared once again, swooping and gyrating above the lighted building.

"There's somebody over there," Paul exclaimed. "Come on, Delia, they'll have to let us in!"

Hand in hand they ran from the Peltonville Inn to the lighted building across the street. The building loomed above them. The light they had seen flickered through a circular stained glass window. Its pattern was regular in shape, oddly suggestive of a sheriff's badge. Paul found himself wondering crazily if there wasn't a sheriff's station or town police headquarters here in Peltonville, if he and Delia should not have tried to find the authorities and pleaded with them for assistance against the cold and desolation of the darkness and the storm.

But it was too late for that.

Paul pounded on the heavy wooden door and found, to his surprise, that it swung open beneath his blows. He urged Delia in ahead of himself, then stepped into the shelter of the building, drawing the door shut behind them.

Clearly they were in a house of worship. The stained glass window behind them centered around a huge star formed of interlocking equilateral triangles. Paul had seen the pattern before, but there was something wrong with it this time. Each of the star's six points was surmounted by another figure, a clutching claw, a hook, or some other disquieting image. And in the center of the hexagon formed by the major triangles he saw a face such as his most horrifying nightmare had never brought to him, a face whose inhuman features were exceeded in their fearsomeness only by the malevolence of their expression, a face surrounded by dripping tentacles that appeared for all the world to writhe and clutch even as he watched.

Hand in hand Paul and Delia advanced into the sanctuary. The chamber was illuminated by a series of gas mantles mounted on pilasters. There appeared now the massed congregants, robed figures of indeterminate gender. Human they seemed, but somehow and in some incomprehensible way, *wrong*. They stood in a circle, swaying rhythmically and chanting in what had to be Hebrew.

In the center of the circle towered a massive figure, broad-shouldered, bearded, wearing a skull-cap and fringed shawl embroidered with kabalistic symbols and horrifying images. The figure raised his voice and his arms, but where Paul expected to see hands emerging from the sleeves of his robe were frightening claws that clacked angrily, wreathed by tentacles that wove and snapped like miniature whips.

The robed chanters surrounding their foul leader parted ranks. More quickly than Paul could follow they formed themselves into two rows. Those closest to Paul and Delia reached and took them by the hands. Paul's will was frozen. He stumbled forward, Delia at his side, passed from couple to couple of the frightening chanters, until they found themselves standing in the center of the newly reconstituted circle.

The leader loomed over them, far taller and more massive than any human being had the right to be. His arms were still raised, the claws and tentacles still performing their terrible gyrations. Involuntarily Paul raised his eyes, following the direction of the massive arms. Out of the corner of his vision he saw that Delia had done the same, and that even the monstrous figure before them had thrown back its head and was gazing in a state of spiritual rapture into the sky.

Yes, the sky loomed overhead. A retractable panel had been drawn back in the roof of the sanctuary. The hail had ceased to fall, but an icy wind howled through the aperture. The sound of the chanting rose, the leader began a strange and frightening dance, and in the blackness above the building, against the backdrop of faint, distant stars, the foul eight-pointed constellation appeared once more.

Only now Paul realized that the points of illumination were not distant stars but the eyes of a dreadful being, a being something like a huge spider, something like a frightening marine creature, something unholy and infinitely evil.

The eight red eyes drew nearer and the other features of the being became visible, fangs that dripped venom that steamed and sputtered as it struck the sanctuary floor, rope-like excrescencies that writhed and reached for the figures gathered beneath.

The chanting that surrounded Paul and Delia rose in pitch and urgency, the looming clergyman who stood before them lowered his arms and reached for Paul and Delia, seizing one of them in each arm, drawing them to his body that seemed to be more a chitinous shell than mere muscle and bone.

With immense and effortless strength he raised them, Paul in one horrid tentacle-circled claw, Delia in the other. Overhead the monstrous entity nodded and hissed, lowering itself toward the sacrifice that was clearly intended for it.

Paul reached for Delia, hoping in what must surely be the last moments of their lives to clasp her hand, but instead there was a monstrous crash and an icy blast as the massive doors of the building burst open and smashed to the floor. Paul was able to twist in the clergyman's grasp.

Standing in the doorway of the sanctuary was a figure he recognized at once as belonging to Mustafa Cristopolous, the Greek-Turkish-Jewish bartender whom Paul and Delia had met earlier in the evening at Daniello's Roadhouse.

But now Cristopolous was transformed. No longer bent over a mahogany surface, no longer clad in a brass-buttoned, red service jacket, Cristopolous seemed to have grown to a height half-again his previous size. His shoulders bulged with muscles. His features, the broken nose, the cleft chin, had assumed a nobility that Paul had not recognized in them in Daniello's cocktail lounge. The jagged scar on his cheek was no longer a pallid reminder of a long-ago wound, but a blazing talisman of righteous rage.

The low, accented voice that Paul and Delia had heard at Daniello's now roared its challenge in words of ancient Hebrew. Among them Paul recognized a phrase that he had previously heard, *Yeshua ben Yeshua*. The evil clergyman, startled, dropped Paul and Delia. The entity that writhed above the sanctuary hissed and writhed in rage, deprived, at least for the moment, of its sacrificial prey.

The chanting congregants parted in terror, scurrying to cower among the pews and against the walls of the sanctuary.

Cristopolous strode forward, passing between Paul and Delia as he approached the clergyman. Cristopolous reached for the other, his massive hands clutching for the other's throat. The two were of a size and well matched in strength. They bellowed imprecations at each other, both of them growling in the same archaic tongue that Cristopolous had used to issue his first challenge upon entering the sanctuary. But among the alien words of Yeshua ben Yeshua, Paul was sure that he heard the name Yacoub ben Yitzak.

The clergyman and Cristopolous clutched each other in a dreadful parody of a lovers' embrace. The clergyman was clawing at Cristopolous's face and throat; Cristopolous held the other by his waist, lifting him from the floor by main strength.

From above the writhing, seething tangle, a foul cluster of tentacles descended, dripping venom and slime. Ropelike organs wrapped themselves around the two struggling figures, then raised both, slowly, from the floor. Paul reached for Cristopolous's heavy ankles. For a moment he secured a grip on them and felt himself actually lifted from his own feet, but a burning blob of slime spattered on one of his hands. In agony he lost his grasp on Cristopolous's ankle with that hand; the other, alone, had not sufficient strength to maintain its grip.

Paul collapsed back onto the floor. Delia knelt beside him, her arms around him, her tear-stained face pressed against his. Above them Paul saw Cristopolous and the clergyman, now wholly enveloped in a cocoon of writhing, ropelike tentacles, disappear into the gaping maw of the hideous entity that hovered briefly above the sanctuary, then rose with incredible speed until it disappeared once and for all into the starry sky above.

Again a cold wind swept into the sanctuary, and again the clatter of hailstones filled the night, this time pouring unimpeded through the open roof into the ancient building.

Taking Delia by the hand, Paul made his way from the building. The misshapen congregants whose chanting had earlier filled the building and the night had disappeared. Hand in hand, Paul and Delia made their way back to the Hudson-Terraplane.

Together, Paul and Delia turned back for one last sight of the desecrated synagogue. The monstrous creature was nowhere to be seen; it had disappeared along with both Yeshua ben Yeshua and Yacoub ben

Yitzak. But from the swirling clouds overhead a single lurid shaft of shockingly ruddy lightning crackled downward. It must have struck the gas line that fed the mantles in the synagogue. There was a deafening explosion and the building disappeared, fragments clattering down for city blocks in all directions.

"We can't stay in Peltonville," Paul announced. This assertion drew no objection from Delia. "And we can't get back to Springfield until the bridge is repaired. But we can press on. Aurora isn't too much farther, and we can find accommodations there." He paused. Then he added, "Even if we can only find one room."

Delia leaned her head against his shoulder and wrapped her arms around him. "One room is all we'll need, Paul," she murmured.

THE DEVIL'S HOP YARD

It was in the autumn of 1928 that those terrible events which came to be known as the Dunwich Horror transpired. The residents of the upper Miskatonic Valley in Massachusetts, at all times a taciturn breed of country folk never known for their hospitality or communicativeness toward outsiders, became thereafter positively hostile to such few travelers as happened to trespass upon their hilly and infertile region. The people of the Dunwich region in particular, a sparse and inbred race with few intellectual or material attainments to show for their generations of toil, gradually became fewer than ever in number. It was the custom of the region to marry late and to have few children. Those infants delivered by the few physicians and midwives who practiced thereabouts were often deformed in some subtle and undefinable way; it would be impossible for an observer to place his finger upon the exact nature of the defect, yet it was plain that something was frighteningly wrong with many of the boys and girls born in the Miskatonic Valley.

Yet, as the years turned slowly, the pale, faded folk of Dunwich continued to raise their thin crops, to tend their dull-eyed and stringy cattle, and to wring their hard existence from the poor, farmed-out earth of their homesteads.

Events of interest were few and petty; the columns of the Aylesbury *Transcript*, the Arkham *Advertiser*, and even the imposing Boston *Globe* were scanned for items of diversion. Dunwich itself supported no regular newspaper, not even the slim weekly sheet that subsists in many such semi-rural communities.

It was therefore a source of much local gossip and a delight to the scandal-mongers when Earl Sawyer abandoned Mamie Bishop, his common-law wife of twenty years standing, and took up instead with Zenia Whateley. Sawyer was an uncouth dirt farmer, some fifty years of age. His cheeks covered perpetually with a stubble that gave him the appearance of not having shaved for a week, his nose and eyes marked with the red lines of broken minor blood vessels, and his stoop-shouldered, shuffling gait marked him as a typical denizen of Dunwich's hilly environs.

Zenia Whateley was a thin, pallid creature, the daughter of old Zebulon Whateley and a wife so retiring in her lifetime and so thoroughly forgotten since her death that none could recall the details of her countenance or even her given name. The latter had been painted carelessly on the oblong wooden marker that indicated the place of her burial, but the cold rains and watery sunlight of the round of Dunwich's seasons had obliterated even this trace of the dead woman's individuality.

Zenia must have taken after her mother, for her own appearance was unprepossessing, her manner cringing, and her speech so infrequent and so diffident that few could recall ever having heard her voice. The loafers and gossips at Osborn's General Store in Dunwich were hard put to understand Earl Sawyer's motives in abandoning Mamie Bishop for Zenia Whateley. Not that Mamie was noted for her great beauty or scintillating personality; on the contrary: she was known as a meddler and a snoop, and her sharp tongue had stung many a denizen hoping to see some misdemeanor pass unnoticed. Still, Mamie had within her that spark of vitality so seldom found in the folk of the upper Miskatonic, that trait of personality known in the rural argot as gumption, so that it was puzzling to see her perched beside Earl on the front seat of his rattling Model T Ford, her few belongings tied in slovenly bundles behind her, as Sawyer drove her over the dust-blowing turnpike to Aylesbury where she took quarters in the town's sole, dilapidated rooming house.

The year was 1938 when Earl Sawyer and Mamie Bishop parted ways. It had been a decade since the death of the poor, malformed giant Wilbur Whateley and the dissolution — for this word, rather than *death*, best characterizes the end of that monster — of his even more gigantic and even more shockingly made twin brother. But now it was the end of May, and the spring thaw had come late and grudgingly to the hard-pressed farmlands of the Miskatonic Valley this year.

When Earl Sawyer returned, alone, to Dunwich, he stopped in the center of the town, such as it was, parking his Model T opposite Osborn's. He crossed the dirty thoroughfare and climbed onto the porch of old Zebulon Whateley's house, pounding once upon the grey, peeling door while the loafers at Osborn's stared and commented behind his back.

The door opened and Earl Sawyer disappeared inside for a minute. The loafers puzzled over what business Earl might have with Zebulon Whateley, and their curiosity was rewarded shortly when Sawyer reappeared leading Zenia Whateley by one flaccid hand. Zenia wore a thin cotton dress, and through its threadbare covering it was obvious even from the distance of Osborn's that she was with child.

Earl Sawyer drove home to his dusty farm, bringing Zenia with him, and proceeded to install her in place of Mamie Bishop. There was little noticeable change in the routine at Sawyer's farm with the change in its female occupant. Each morning Earl and Zenia would rise, Zenia would prepare and serve a meagre repast for them, and they would breakfast in grim silence. Earl would thereafter leave the house, carefully locking the door behind him with Zenia left inside to tend to the chores of housekeeping, and Earl would spend the entire day working out-of-doors.

The Sawyer farm contained just enough arable land to raise a meager crop of foodstuffs and to support a thin herd of the poor cattle common to the Miskatonic region. The bleak hillside known as the Devil's Hop Yard was also located on Sawyer's holdings. Here had grown no tree, shrub or blade of grass for as far back as the oldest archives of Dunwich recorded, and despite Earl Sawyer's repeated attempts to raise a crop on its unpleasant slopes, the Hop Yard resisted and remained barren. Even so there persisted reports of vague, unpleasant rumblings and cracklings from beneath the Hop Yard, and occasionally shocking odors were carried from it to adjoining farms when the wind was right.

On the first Sunday of June, 1938, Earl Sawyer and Zenia Whateley were seen to leave the farmhouse and climb into Sawyer's Model T. They drove together into Dunwich village, and, leaving the Model T in front of old Zebulon Whateley's drab house, walked across the churchyard, pausing to read such grave markers as remained there standing and legible, then entered the Dunwich Congregational Church that had been founded by the Reverend Abijah Hoadley in 1747. The pulpit of the Dunwich Congregational Church had been vacant since the unexplained disappearance of the Reverend Isaiah Ashton in the summer of 1912, but a circuit-riding Congregational minister from the city of Arkham conducted services in Dunwich from time to time.

This was the first occasion of Earl Sawyer's attendance at services within memory, and there was a nodding of heads and a hissing of whispers up and down the pews as Earl and Zenia entered the frame building. Earl and Zenia took a pew to themselves at the rear of the congregation and when the order of service had reached its conclusion they remained behind to speak with the minister. No witness was present, of course, to overhear the conversation that took place, but later the minister volunteered his recollection of Sawyer's request and his own responses.

Sawyer, the minister reported, had asked him to perform a marriage. The couple to be united were himself (Sawyer) and Zenia Whateley. The minister had at first agreed, especially in view of Zenia's obvious condition, and the desirability of providing for a legitimate birth for her expected child. But Sawyer had refused to permit the minister to perform the usual marriage ceremony of the Congregational Church, insisting instead upon a ceremony involving certain foreign terms to be provided from some ancient documents handed down through the family of the bride.

Nor would Sawyer permit the minister to read the original documents, providing in their place crudely rendered transcripts written by a clumsy hand on tattered, filthy scraps of paper. Unfortunately the minister no longer had even these scraps. They had been retained by Sawyer, and the minister could recall only vaguely a few words of the strange and almost unpronounceable incantations he had been requested to utter: N'gai, n'gha'ghaa, bugg-shoggog, he remembered. And a reference to a lost city "Between the Yr and the Nhhngr."

The minister had refused to perform the blasphemous ceremony requested by Sawyer, holding that it would be ecclesiastically improper and possibly even heretical of him to do so, but he renewed his offer to perform an orthodox Congregational marriage, and possibly to include certain additional materials provided by the couple *if he were shown a translation also,* so as to convince himself of the propriety of the ceremony.

Earl Sawyer refused vehemently, warning the minister that he stood in far greater peril should he ever learn the meaning of the words than if he remained in ignorance of them. At length Sawyer stalked angrily from the church, pulling the passive Zenia Whateley behind him, and returned with her to his farm.

A few nights later the couple were visited by Zenia's father, old Zebulon Whateley, and also by Squire Sawyer Whateley, of the semi-undecayed Whateleys, a man who held the unusual distinction of claiming cousinship to both Earl Sawyer and Zenia Whateley. At midnight the four figures, Earl, Zenia, old Zebulon, and Squire Whateley, climbed slowly to the top of the Devil's Hop Yard. What acts they performed at the crest of the hill are not known with certainty, but Luther Brown, now a fully-grown man and engaged to be married to George Corey's daughter Olivia, stated later that he had been searching for a lost heifer near the boundary between Corey's farm and Sawyer's, and saw the four figures silhouetted against the night constellations as they stood atop the hill.

Luther Brown watched, all four disrobed; he was fairly certain of the identification of the three men, and completely sure of that of Zenia because of her obvious pregnancy. Completely naked they set fire to an altar of wood apparently set up in advance on the peak of the Hop Yard. What rites they performed before Luther fled in terror and disgust he refused to divulge, but later that night loud cracking sounds were heard coming from the vicinity of the Sawyer farm, and an earthquake was reported to have shaken the entire Miskatonic Valley, registering on the seismographic instruments of Harvard College and causing swells in the harbor at Innsmouth.

The next day Squire Sawyer Whateley registered a wedding on the official rolls of Dunwich village. He claimed to be qualified to perform the civil ceremony by virtue of his standing as Chairman of the local Selective Service Board. This claim must surely be regarded as most dubious, but while the Whateleys were not highly regarded in Dunwich, their detractors considered it the better part of valor to hold their criticism to private circumstances, and the marriage of Earl Sawyer and Zenia Whateley was thus officially recognized.

Mamie Bishop, in the meanwhile, had settled into her new home in Aylesbury and began spreading malign reports about her former lover Earl Sawyer and his new wife. Earl, she claimed, had been in league with the Whateleys all along. Her own displacement by Zenia had been only one step in the plot of Earl Sawyer and the Whateley clan to revive the evil activities that had culminated in the events of 1928. Earl and Zenia, with the collaboration of Squire Sawyer Whateley and old Zebulon Whateley, would bring about the ruination of the entire Miskatonic Valley, if left to their own devices, and perhaps might bring about a blight that would cover a far greater region.

No one paid any attention to Mamie, however. Even the other Bishops, a clan almost as numerous and widespread as the Whateleys, tended to discount Mamie's warnings as the spiteful outpourings of a woman scorned. And in any case, Mamie's dire words were pushed from the public consciousness in the month of August, 1938, when Earl Sawyer rang up Dr. Houghton on the party line telephone and summoned him to the Sawyer farm.

Zenia was in labor, and Earl, in a rare moment of concern, had decided that medical assistance was in order.

Zenia's labor was a long and difficult one. Dr. Houghton later commented that first childbirths tended to be more protracted than later deliveries, but Zenia remained in labor for 72 consecutive hours, and barely survived the delivery of the child. Throughout the period of her labor there were small earth temblors centering on the Devil's Hop Yard, and Zenia, by means of a series of frantic hand motions and incoherent mewling sounds, indicated that she wished the curtains drawn back from her window so that she could see the crown of the hill from her bed.

On the third night of her labor, while Zenia lay panting and spent near to death between futile contractions, a storm rose. Clouds swept up the valley from the Atlantic, great winds roared over the houses and through the trees of Dunwich, bolts of lightning flashed from thunderhead to hilltop.

Dr. Houghton, despairing of saving the life of either Zenia or her unborn child, began preparations for a caesarian section. With Earl Sawyer hovering in the background, mumbling semi-incoherent incantations of the sort that had caused the Congregational minister to refuse a church wedding to the couple, the doctor set to work.

With sharpened instruments sterilized over the woodstove that served for both cooking and heat for the Sawyer farmhouse, he made the incision in Zenia's abdomen. As he removed the fetus from her womb there was a terrific crash of thunder. A blinding bolt of lightning struck at the peak of the Devil's Hop Yard. From a small grove of twisted and deformed maple trees behind the Sawyer house, a flock of nesting whippoorwills took wing, setting up a cacophony of sound audible over even the loud rushings and pounding of the rainstorm.

All of Dr. Houghton's efforts failed to preserve the poor, limited life of Zenia Whateley Sawyer, but her child survived the ordeal of birth. The next day old Zebulon Whateley and Squire Sawyer Whateley made their way to the Sawyer house and joined Earl Sawyer in his efforts. He descended the wooden steps to the dank cellar of the house and returned carrying a plain wooden coffin that he himself had surreptitiously built some time before. The three of them placed Zenia's shriveled, wasted body in the coffin and Earl nailed its lid in place.

They carried the wooden box to the peak of the Devil's Hop Yard and there, amid fearsome incantations and the making of signs with their hands unlike any seen for a decade in the Miskatonic Valley, they buried Zenia's remains.

Then they returned to the farmhouse where the child lay in a crude wooden cradle. Squire Whateley tended the infant while its father rang up Central on the party line and placed a call to Mamie Bishop at the rooming house in Aylesbury.

After a brief conversation with his former common-law wife, Earl Sawyer nodded to his father-in-law and to the Squire, and left them with the child. He climbed into his Model T and set out along the Aylesbury Pike to fetch Maine back to Dunwich.

*

The child of Earl Sawyer and Zenia Whateley Sawyer was a girl. Her father, after consultation with his father-in-law and distant cousin Squire Whateley, named his daughter Hester Sawyer. She was a tiny child at birth, and fear was expressed as to her own survival.

Earl contacted the Congregational minister at Arkham, asking him to baptize the infant according to rites specified by Earl. Once more the dispute as to the use of Earl's strange scriptures — if they could be so defined — erupted, and once more the minister refused to lend his ecclesiastical legitimacy to the ceremony. Instead, Earl, Zebulon and Sawyer Whateley carried the tiny form, wrapped in swaddling cloths, to the peak of the Devil's Hop Yard, and on the very ground of her mother's still-fresh grave conducted a ceremony of consecration best left undescribed.

They then returned her to the Sawyer house and the care of Mamie Bishop.

There were comments in Dunwich and even in Aylesbury about Mamie's surprising willingness to return to Sawyer's ménage in the role of nursemaid and guardian to the infant Hester, but Mamie merely said that she had her reasons and refused to discuss the matter further. Under Mamie's ministrations the infant Hester survived the crises of her first days of life, and developed into a child of surprising strength and precocity.

Even as an infant Hester was a child of unusual beauty and — if such a phrase may be used — premature maturity. Her coloring was fair — almost, but not quite, to the point of albinism. Where Hester's distant relative, the long-disappeared Lavinia Whateley, had had crinkly white hair and reddish-pink eyes, little Hester possessed from the day of her birth a glossy poll of the silvery blonde shade known as platinum. Mamie Bishop tried repeatedly to put up the child's hair in miniature curls or scallops as she thought appropriate for a little girl, but Hester's hair hung straight and gracefully to her shoulders, refusing to lie in any other fashion.

The child's eyes showed a flecked pattern of palest blue and the faint pink of the true albino, giving the appearance of being a pale lavender in tint except at a very close range, when the alternation of blue and pink became visible. Her skin was the shade of new cream and was absolutely flawless.

She took her first steps at the age of five months; by this time she had her full complement of baby teeth as well. By the age of eight months, early in the spring of 1939, she began to speak. There was none of the babyish prattle of a normally developing child; Hester spoke with precision, correctness, and a chilling solemnity from the utterance of her first word.

Earl Sawyer did not keep Mamie Bishop imprisoned in his house as he had the dead Zenia Whateley Sawyer. Indeed, Earl made it his business to teach Mamie the operation of his Model T, and he encouraged her — nay, he all but commanded her — to drive it into Dunwich village, Dean's Corners, or Aylesbury frequently.

On these occasions Mamie was alleged to be shopping for such necessities for herself, Earl, or little Hester as the farm did not provide. On one occasion Earl directed Mamie to drive the Model T all the way to Arkham, and there to spend three days obtaining certain items which he said were needed for Hester's upbringing. Mamie spent two nights at one of the rundown hotels that still persisted in Arkham, shabby ornate reminders of that city's more prosperous days.

Mamie's sharp tongue had its opportunities during these shopping expeditions, and she was heard frequently to utter harsh comments about Earl, Zebulon, and Squire Whateley. She never made direct reference to the dead Zenia, but uttered cryptic and unsettling remarks about little Hester Sawyer, her charge, whom she referred to most often as "Zenia's white brat."

As has been mentioned, Dunwich village supported no regular newspaper of its own, but the publications of other communities in the Miskatonic Valley gave space to events in this locale. The Aylesbury Transcript in particular devoted a column in its weekly pages to news from Dunwich. This news was provided by Joe Osborn, the proprietor of Osborn's General Store, in return for regular advertisement of his establishment's wares.

A review of the Dunwich column in the Aylesbury Transcript for the period between August of 1938 and the end of April of 1943 shows a series of reports of rumblings, crackings, and unpleasant odors emanating from the area of Sawyer's farm, and particularly from the Devil's Hop Yard. Two features of these reports are worthy of note.

First, the reports of the sounds and odors occur at irregular intervals, but a check of the sales records of the establishments in Dunwich, Aylesbury, Dean's Corners and Arkham where Mamie Bishop traded, will show that the occurrences at the Devil's Hop Yard coincide perfectly with the occasions of Mamie's absence from Sawyer's farm. Second, while the events took place at irregular intervals, ranging from as close together as twice in one week to as far apart as eight months, their severity increased steadily. The earliest of the series are barely noted in the Dunwich column of the Transcript. By the end of 1941 the events receive lead position in Osborn's writings. By the beginning of 1943 they are no longer relegated to the Dunwich column at all, but are treated as regular news, suggesting that they could be detected in Aylesbury itself — a distance of nearly 15 miles from Dunwich.

It was also noted by the loafers at Osborn's store that on those occasions when Mamie Bishop absented herself from the Sawyer farm, Earl's two favorite in-laws and cronies, Zebulon Whateley and Squire Sawyer Whateley, visited him. There were no further reports of odd goings-on at the Sawyer place such as that made by Luther Brown in 1938.

Perhaps Luther's unfortunate demise in an accident on George Corey's silo roof, where he was placing new shingles, had no connection with his seeing the rites atop the Devil's Hop Yard, but after Luther's death and with the new series of rumblings and stenches, others began to shun the Sawyer place from 1939 onward.

In September of 1942 a sad incident transpired. Hester Sawyer, then aged four, had been educated up to that time primarily by her father, with the assistance of the two elder Whateleys and of Mamie Bishop. She had never been away from the Sawyer farm and had never seen another child.

Mamie Bishop's second cousin Elsie, the maiden sister of Silas Bishop (of the undecayed Bishops), caught Mamie's ear on one of Mamie's shopping expeditions away from the Sawyer place. Elsie was the mistress of a nursery school operated under the auspices of the Dunwich Congregational Church, and she somehow convinced Mamie that it was her duty to give little Hester exposure to other children of her own age. Mamie spoke disparagingly of "Zenia's white brat," but following Elsie's insistence Mamie agreed to discuss the matter with Earl Sawyer.

On the first day of the fall term, Mamie drove Earl's Model T into Dunwich village, little Hester perched on the seat beside her. This was the first look that Hester had at Dunwich — and the first that Dunwich had at Hester.

Although Mamie had bundled the child into loose garments that covered her from neck to ankles, it was obvious that something was abnormal about her. Hester was astonishingly small for a child of four. She was hardly taller than a normal infant. It was as if she had remained the same size in the four years since her birth, not increasing an inch in stature.

But that was only half the strangeness of Hester's appearance, for while her size was the same as a newborn infant's, her development was that of a fully mature and breathtakingly beautiful woman. The sun shone brilliantly on the long platinum hair that hung defiantly around the edges of the bonnet Mamie had forced onto Hester's head. Her strange lavender eyes seemed to hold the secrets of an experienced voluptuary. Her face was mature, her lips full and sensual. And when a sudden gust of wind pressed her baggy dress against her torso this revealed the configuration of a Grecian eidolon.

The loafers at Osborn's, who had clustered about and craned their necks for a look at the mysterious "white brat" were torn between an impulse to turn away from this unnatural sight and a fascination with the image of what seemed a living manikin, a woman of voluptuous bodily form and astonishing facial beauty, the size of a day-old infant, sitting primly beside Mamie Bishop.

Elsie Bishop welcomed her cousin Mamie and her charge, Hester Sawyer, to the nursery school at the Congregational Church. Elsie chose to make no comment on Hester's unusual appearance, but instead introduced her to the children already present. These included her own nephew Nahum Bishop, Silas's five-year-old son. Nahum was a perfectly normal boy, outgoing and playful, one of the few such to appear in the blighted Miskatonic Valley.

He took one look at Hester Sawyer and fell madly in love with her, with the total, enraptured fascination that only a child can feel when first he discovers the magic of the female sex. He lost all interest in the other children in the school and in their games. He wished only to be with Hester, to gaze at her, to hold her miniature woman's hand in his own pudgy boy's fingers. Any word that Hester spoke was as music to his ears, and any favor she might ask, any task that she might set for him, was his bounden duty and his greatest joy to perform.

In a short while the various children of the nursery school were playing happily, some of them scampering up and down the aisle leading between the two banks of pews in the main body of the church. The two cousins, Mamie and Elsie, retired to the chancel kitchen to prepare a pot of tea for themselves. Although they could not see the school children from this position, they could hear them happily playing in the semi-abandoned church.

Suddenly there was a terrible thump from the roof of the church, then a second similar sound from the burying-ground outside, then a series of panic-stricken and terrified screams from the children. Mamie and Elsie ran from the chancel and found nothing, apparently, amiss in the church itself, but the children were clustered at an open window staring into the churchyard, pointing and exclaiming in distress.

The two women shoved their way through the panic-stricken children until they could see. What they beheld was the body of Elsie's nephew Nahum Bishop, grotesquely broken over an old tombstone upon which it had fallen when it bounced from the roof of the church. There was no question that the child was dead, the sightless eyes apparently gazing upward at the steeple of the church.

Before they could even turn away from the window, the two women were able to hear a light tread, one so light that, except for the total hush that had descended upon the church as the children's screams subsided, it would not have been heard at all, calmly descending the wooden staircase from the steeple. In a moment Hester Sawyer emerged from the stairwell, her manner one of complete self-possession, the expression on her beautiful little face one of mockery and amusement.

When the state police arrived Hester explained, with total self-assurance, that she and Nahum had climbed the steeple together, up the narrow wooden staircase that ran from the church's floor to its belfry. Nahum had averred that he would do anything to prove his love for Hester, and she had asked him to fly from the steeple. In attempting to do so he had fallen to the roof, bounced once, then crashed onto the old grave marker in the yard.

The police report listed Nahum's death as accidental, and Hester was returned to the Sawyer farm in charge of Mamie Bishop. Needless to say, the child did not return to the nursery school at the Dunwich Congregational Church; in fact, she was not seen again in Dunwich, or anywhere else away from her father's holdings.

*

The final chapter in the tragedy of the Devil's Hop Yard, if indeed tragedy is the proper designation for such a drama, was played out in the spring of 1943. As in so many years past, the warmth of the equinox had given but little of itself to the upper Miskatonic Valley; winter instead still clung to the barren peaks and the infertile bottomlands of the region, and the icy dark waters of the Miskatonic River passed only few meadows on their way southeasterward to Arkham and Innsmouth and the cold Atlantic beyond.

In Dunwich the bereaved Silas Bishop and his maiden sister Elsie had recovered as best they could from the death of young Nahum. Elsie's work with the nursery school continued and only the boarding-up of the stairwell that led to the steeple and belfry of the Congregational Church testified to the accident of the previous September.

Early on the evening of April 30 the telephone rang in the Bishop house in Dunwich village, and Elsie lifted the receiver to hear a furtive whisper on the line. The voice she barely recognized, so distorted it was with terror, belonged to her second cousin Mamie.

"They've locked me in the house naow," Mamie whispered into the telephone. "Earl always sent me away before, but this time they've locked me in and I'm afeared. Help me, Elsie! I daon't knaow what they're a-fixin' ta do up ta the Hop Yard, but I'm afeared!"

Elsie signaled her brother Silas to listen to the conversation. "Who's locked you in, Mamie?" Elsie asked her cousin.

"Earl and Zeb and Sawyer Whateley done it! They've took Zenia's brat and they've clumb the Hop Yard. I kin see 'em from here! They're all stark naked and they've built 'em a bonfire and an altar and they're throwin' powder into the fire and old Zeb he's areadin' things outen some terrible book that they always keep alocked up!

"And now I kin see little Hester, the little white brat o' Zenia's, and she's clumb onto the altar and she's sayin' things to Zeb an' Earl and Squire Whateley an' they've got down on their knees like they's aworshippin' Hester, and she's makin' signs with her hands. Oh, Elsie, I can't describe them signs, they's so awful, they's so awful what she's adoin', Elsie! Get some help out here, oh please get some help!"

Elsie told Mamie to try and be calm, and not to watch what was happening atop the Devil's Hop Yard. Then she hung up the telephone and turned to her brother Silas. "We'll get the state police from Aylesbury," she said. "They'll stop whatever is happening at Sawyer's. We'd best telephone them now, Silas!"

"D'ye think they'll believe ye, Elsie?"

Elsie shook her head in a negative manner.

"Then we'd best git to Aylesbury ourselves," Silas resumed. "If we go there ourselves they'd more like to believe us than if we jest telephoned."

They hitched up their horse and drove by wagon from Dunwich to Aylesbury. Fortunately the state police officer who had investigated the death of young Nahum Bishop was present, and knowing both Elsie and Silas to be citizens of a responsible nature the officer did not laugh at their report of Mamie's frightened telephone call. The officer started an automobile belonging to the state police, and with the two Bishops as passengers set out back along the Aylesbury Pike to Dunwich, and thence to the Sawyer farm beyond the village center.

As the official vehicle neared Sawyer's place, its three occupants were assailed by a most terrible and utterly indescribable stench that turned their stomachs and caused their eyes to run copiously, and that also, inexplicably, filled each of them with a hugely frightening rush of emotions dominated by an amalgam of fear and revulsion. Sounds of thunder filled the air, and the earth trembled repeatedly, threatening to throw the car off the road.

The state police officer swung the automobile from the dirt road fronting the Sawyer farm onto a narrow and rutted track that ran by the decrepit house and led to the foot of the Devil's Hop Yard. The officer pulled the car to a halt and leaped from its seat, charging up the hill with his service revolver drawn, followed by Silas and Elsie Bishop, who made the best speed they could despite their years.

Before them they could see the altar and the four figures that Mamie Bishop had described to her cousin Elsie. The night sky was cloudless and a new moon offered no competition to the millions of brilliantly twinkling stars. Little Hester Sawyer, her body that of a fully formed woman yet not two feet in height, danced and postured on the wooden altar, the starlight and that of the nearby bonfire dancing lasciviously on her gleaming platinum hair and smooth, cream-colored skin. Her lavender eyes caught the firelight and reflected it like the eyes of a wild beast in the woods at night.

Earl and Zebulon and Sawyer Whateley stood in an equilateral triangle about the altar, and around them there had apparently sprung from the earth itself a perfect circle of slimy, tentacled growths, more animal than vegetable, the only things that had ever been known to grow from the soil of the Devil's Hop Yard. Even as the newcomers watched, too awe-stricken and too revolted to act, the horrid tentacled growths began to lengthen, and to sway in time to the awful chanting of the three naked men and the lascivious posturings of the tiny, four-year-old Hester.

There was the sound of a shrill, reedy piping from somewhere in the air, and strange winds rushed back and forth over the scene.

The voice of Hester Sawyer could be heard chanting, "Ygnaith... ygnaith... thflthkh'ngha... Yog-Sothoth... Y'bthnk... h'ehye-n'grkdl'lh!"

There, was a single, blinding bolt of lightning — an astonishing occurrence as the night sky was entirely clear of any clouds — and the form of Hester Sawyer was bathed in a greenish-yellow glow of almost supernatural electrical display, sparks dancing over her perfect skin, and balls of St. Elmo's fire tumbling from her lips and hands and rolling across the altar, tumbling to the ground and bounding down the slopes of the Devil's Hop Yard.

The eyes of the watchers were so dazzled by the display that they were never certain, afterwards, of what they had seen. But it appeared, at least, that the bolt of lightning had not descended from the sky to strike Hester, but had *originated from her* and struck upward, zigzagging into the wind-swept blackness over Dunwich, streaking upward and upward as if it were eventually going to reach the stars themselves.

And even more quickly than the bolt of lightning had disappeared from before the dazzled eyes of the watchers, the body of Hester Sawyer appeared to rise along its course, posturing and making those terrible shocking signs even as it rose, growing ever smaller as it disappeared above the Hop Yard until the lightning bolt winked out and all sight of Hester Sawyer was lost forever.

With the end of the electrical display the shocked paralysis that had overcome the watchers subsided, and the police officer advanced to stand near the ring of tentacled growths and the three naked men. He ordered them to follow him back to the police vehicle, but instead they launched themselves in snarling, animalistic attacks upon him. The officer stepped back but the three men flew at him growling, clawing, biting at his legs and torso. The police officer's revolver crashed once, again, then a third time, and the three naked men lay thrashing and gesturing on the ground.

They were taken to the general hospital at Arkham, where a medical team headed by Drs. Houghton and Hartwell labored unsuccessfully through the night to save them. By the morning of May 1, all three had expired without uttering a single word.

Meanwhile, back at the Devil's Hop Yard, Silas and Elsie Bishop guided other investigators to the altar that Hester Sawyer had last stood upon. The book that had lain open beside her had been destroyed beyond identification by the lightning bolt of the night of April 30. Agricultural experts summoned from Miskatonic University at Arkham attempted to identify the tentacled growths that had sprung from the ground around the altar. The growths had died within a few hours of their appearance, and only desiccated husks remained. The experts were unable to identify them fully, indicating their complete puzzlement at their apparent resemblance to the tentacles of the giant marine squid of the Pacific Trench near the island of Ponape.

Back at the Sawyer farmhouse, Mamie Bishop was found cowering in a corner, hiding her eyes and refusing to look up or even acknowledge the presence of others when addressed. Her hair had turned completely white, not the platinum white of little Hester Sawyer's hair but the crinkly albino white that had been Lavinia Whateley's so many years before.

Mamie mumbled to herself and shook her head but uttered not a single intelligible word, either then or later, when she too was taken to the general hospital at Arkham. In time she was certified physically sound and transferred to a mental ward where she resides to this day, a harmless, quivering husk, her inward-turned eyes locked forever on whatever shocking sight it was that she beheld that night when she gazed from the window of the Sawyer farmhouse upon the horrid ceremony taking place atop the Devil's Hop Yard.

DOCUMENTS IN THE CASE OF ELIZABETH AKELEY

Surveillance of the Spiritual Light Brotherhood Church of San Diego was initiated as a result of certain events of the mid-and late 1970s. Great controversy had arisen over the conduct of the followers of the Guru Maharaj-ji, the International Society for Krishna Consciousness (the "Hare Krishnas"), the Church of Scientology, and the Unification Church headed by the Reverend Sun Myung Moon.

These activities were cloaked in the Constitutional shield of "freedom of religion," and the cults for the most part resisted suggestions of investigation by grand juries or other official bodies.

Even so, the tragic events concerning the People's Temple of San Francisco aroused government concern which could not be stymied. While debate raged publicly over the question of opening cult records, Federal and local law enforcement agencies covertly entered the field.

It was within this context that interest was aroused concerning the operation of the Spiritual Light Brotherhood, and particularly its leader, the Radiant Mother Elizabeth Akeley.

Outwardly there was nothing secret in the operation of Mother Akeley's church. The group operated from a building located at the corner of Second Street and Ash in a neighborhood described as "genteel shabby," midway between the commercial center of San Diego and the city's tourist — oriented waterfront area.

The building occupied by the Church had been erected originally by a more conventional denomination, but the vicissitudes of shifting population caused the building to be deconsecrated and sold to the Spiritual Light Brotherhood. The new owners, led by their order's founder and then-leader, the Radiant Father George Goodenough Akeley, clearly marked the building with its new identity.

The headline was changed on the church's bulletin board, and the symbol of the Spiritual Light Brotherhood, a shining tetrahedron of neon tubing, was erected atop the steeple. A worship service was held each Sunday morning, and a spiritual message service was conducted each Wednesday evening.

In later years, following the death of the Radiant Father in 1970 and the accession to leadership of the Church by Elizabeth Akeley, Church archives were maintained in the form of tape recordings. The Sunday services were apparently a bland amalgam of non-denominational Judeo-Christian teachings, half-baked and quarter-understood Oriental mysticism, and citations from the works of Einstein, Heisenberg, Shklovskii, and Fermi.

Surviving cassettes of the Wednesday message services are similarly innocuous. Congregants were invited to submit questions or requests for messages from deceased relatives. The Radiant Mother accepted a limited number of such requests at each service. The congregants would arrange themselves in a circle and link their fingers in the classic manner of participants in séances. Mother Akeley would enter a trance and proceed to answer the questions or deliver messages from the deceased, "as the spirits moved her."

Audioanalysis of the tapes of these séances indicates that, while the intonation and accent of the voices varied greatly, from the whines and lisps of small children to the quaverings of the superannuated, and from the softened and westernized pronunciations of native San Diegans to the harsh and barbaric tones of their New Yorker parents, the vocal apparatus was at all times that of Elizabeth Akeley. The variations were no greater than those attainable by an actress of professional training or natural brilliance.

Such, however, was not the case with a startling portion of the cassette for the session of Wednesday, June 13th, 1979. The Radiant Mother asked her congregants if anyone had a question for the spirits, or if any person present wished to attempt contact with some deceased individual.

A number of questions were answered, dealing with the usual matters of marriage and divorce, reassurances of improved health, and counseling as to investments and careers.

An elderly congregant who was present stated that her husband had died the previous week, and she sought affirmation of his happiness "on the other side."

The Radiant Mother moaned. Then she muttered incoherently. All of this was as usual at the beginning of her trances. Shortly the medium's vocal quality altered. Her normally soft, rather pleasant and distinctly feminine voice dropped in register until it suggested that of a man.

Simultaneously, her contemporary Californian diction turned to the twang of a rural New Englander.

While the sound quality of this tape is excellent, the medium's diction was unfortunately not so. The resulting record is necessarily fragmentary. As nearly as it has been transcribed, this is it:

"Wilmarth...Wilmarth...back. Have come...Antares... Neptune, Pluto, Yuggoth. Yes, Wilmarth. Yug —

"Are you... If I cannot receive... Windham County... yes, Townshend... round hill. Wilmarth still alive? Then who... son, son...

"... ever receives... communicate enough Akeley, 176 Pleasant... go, California. Son, see if you can find my old friend Albert Wilmarth... chusetts...

"With wings. Twisted ropes for heads and blood like plant sap... Flying, flying, and all the while a gramophone recordi... must apologize to Wilmarth if he's still alive, but I also have the most wonderful news, the most wonderful tales to tell him...

"... and its smaller satellites, well, I don't suppose anyone will believe me, of course, but not only is Yuggoth there, revolving regularly except in an orbit at right angles to the plane of the ecliptic, no wonder no one believed in it, but what I must describe to you, Albert, the planet glows with a heat and a demoniacal ruby glare that illuminates its own... thon and Zaman, Thog and Thok, I could hardly believe my own...

"... goid beings who cannot... corporeally... Neptune... central caverns of a dark star beyond the rim of the galaxy its...

"... wouldn't call her beautiful, of course... dinary terms... than an arachnid and a cetacean, and yet, could a spider and dolphin by some miracle establish mental communion, who knows what...not really a name as you normally think of names, but... Sh'ch'rrru'a... of Aldebaran, the eleventh, has a constellation of inhabited moons, which... independently, or perhaps at some earlier time, travelling by means simi...

"... ummate in metal canisters, will be necessary to... aid in obtaining... fair exchange, for the donors will receive a far greater boon in the form ..."

At this point the vocal coherence, such as it is, breaks down. The male voice with its New England twang cracks and rises in tone even as the words are replaced by undecipherable mumbles. Mother Akeley recovers from her trance state, and the séance draws quickly to a close. From the internal evidence of the contents of the tape, the Radiant Mother had no awareness of the message, or narration, delivered by the male voice speaking through her. This also is regarded, among psychic and spiritualistic circles, as quite the usual state of affairs with trance mediums.

*

Authorities next became aware of unusual activities through a copy of the *Vermont Unidentified Flying Object Intelligencer*, or Vufoi. Using a variety of the customary cover names and addresses for the purpose, such Federal agencies as the FBI, NSA, Department of Defense, NASA, and National Atmospheric and Oceanographic Agency subscribe regularly to publications of organizations like the Vermont UFO Intelligence Bureau and other self-appointed investigatory bodies.

The President of the Vermont UFO Intelligence Bureau and editor of its *Intelligencer* was identified as one Ezra Noyes. Noyes was known to reside with his parents (Ezra was nineteen years of age at the time) in the community of Dark Mountain, Windham County. Noyes customarily prepared Vufoi issues himself, assembling material both from outside sources and from members of the Vermont UFO Intelligence Bureau, most of whom were former high school friends now employed by local merchants or farmers, or attending Windham County Community College in Townshend.

Noyes would assemble his copy, type it onto mimeograph stencils using a portable machine set up on the kitchen table, and run off copies on a superannuated mimeograph kept beside the washer and dryer in the basement. The last two items prepared for each issue were "Vufoi Voice" and "From the Editor's Observatory," commenting in one case flippantly and in the other seriously, on the contents of the issue. "Vufoi Voice" was customarily illustrated with a crude cartoon of a man wearing an astronaut's headgear, and was signed "Cap'n Oof-oh." "From the Editor's Observatory" was illustrated with a drawing of an astronomical telescope with a tiny figure seated at the eyepiece, and was signed "Intelligencer."

It is believed that both "Cap'n Oof-oh" and "Intelligencer" were Ezra Noyes.

The issue of the *Vermont Unidentified Flying Object Intelligencer* for June, 1979 actually appeared early in August of that year. Excerpts from the two noted columns follow:

From the Editor's Observatory

Of greatest interest since our last issue — and we apologize for missing the March, April and May editions due to unavoidable circumstances — has been the large number of organic sightings here in the northern Vermont region. We cannot help but draw similes to the infamous Colorado cattle mutilizations of the past year or few years, and the ill-conceived Air Farce cover-up efforts *which only draw extra attention to the facts that they can't hide from us who know the Truth*!

Local historians like Mr. Littleton at the High School remember other incidents and the Brattleboro *Reformer* and Arkham *Advertiser* and other Newspapers whose back files constitute an Official Public Record could tell the story of other incidents like this one! It is hard to reconciliate the Windham County sightings and the Colorado Cattle Mutilation Case with others such as the well-known Moth Man sightings in the Southland and especially the batwing creature sightings of as long as a half of a century ago but with a sufficient ingeniusity it is definitely not a task beyond undertaking and the U.S. Air Farce and other cover-up agencies are hear-bye placed on Official notice that such is our intention and we will not give up until success is ours and the Cover-up is blown as Sky-High as the UFO sightings themselves!

Yours until our July issue,

Intelligencer.

Vufoi Voice

Bat-wing and Moth Man indeed! Didn't I read something like that in *Detective Comics* back when Steve Englehart was writing for DC? Or was it in *Mad*? Come to think of it, when it's hard to tell the parody from the original, things are gettin' *mighty* strange.

And there gettin' might strange around here!

We wonder what the ole Intelligencer's been smoking in that smelly meerschaum he affects around Intelligence Bureau meetings. Could it be something illegal that he grows for himself up on the mountainside?

Or is he just playing Sherlock Holmes?

We ain't impressed.

Impressionable, yep! My mom always said I was impressionable as a boy, back on the old asteroid farm in Beta Reticuli, but this is too silly for words.

Besides, she tuck me to the eye dock and he fitted us out with a pair of gen-yew-ine X-ray specs, and that not only cured us of Reticule-eye but now we can see right through such silliness as bat-winged moth men carrying silvery canisters around the skies and the hillsides with 'em.

Shades of a Japanese Sci-Fi Flick! This musta been the stuntman out for lunch!

And that's where we think the old Intelligencer is this month: *Out 2 Lunch* !

Speaking of which, I haven't had mine yet this afternoon, and if I don't hurry up and have it pretty soon it'll be time for dinner and then I'll have to eat my lunch for a bedtime snack and that'll confuse the dickens out of my poor stomach! So I'm off to hit the old Frigidaire (not too hard, I don't want to spoil the shiny finish on my new spaceman's gloves!), and I'll see you-all nextish!

Whoops, here's our saucer now! Bye-bye,

Cap'n Oof-oh.

*

Following the extraordinary spiritual message service of June 13, Mother Akeley was driven to her home at 176 Pleasant Street in National City, a residential suburb of San Diego, by her boyfriend, Marc Feinman. Investigation revealed that she had met Feinman casually while sunning herself and watching the surfers ride the waves in at Black's Beach, San Diego.

Shortly thereafter, Elizabeth had been invited by a female friend of approximately her own age to attend a concert given by a musical group, a member of which was a friend of Akeley's friend. Outside of her official duties as Radiant Mother of the Spiritual Light Brotherhood, Elizabeth Akeley was known to live quite a normal life for a young woman of her social and economic class.

She accompanied her friend to the concert, visited the backstage area with her, and was introduced to the musician. He in turn introduced Elizabeth to other members of the musical group, one of whom Elizabeth recognized as her casual acquaintance of Black's Beach. A further relationship developed, in which it was known that Akeley and Feinman frequently exchanged overnight visits. Elizabeth had retained the house on Pleasant Street originally constructed by her grandfather, George Goodenough Akeley, when he had emigrated to San Diego from Vermont in the early 1920s.

Marc had been born and raised in the Bronx, New York, had emigrated to the West Coast following his college years and presently resided in a pleasant apartment on Upas Street near Balboa Park. From here he commuted daily to his job as a computer systems programmer in downtown San Diego, his work as a musician being more of an avocation than a profession.

On Sunday, June 17, for the morning worship service of the Spiritual Light Brotherhood, Radiant Mother Akeley devoted her sermon to the previous Wednesday's séance, an unusual practice for her. The sexton of the church, a nondescript looking Negro named Vernon Whiteside, attended the service. Noting the Radiant Mother's departure from her usual bland themes, Whiteside communicated with the Federal Agency which had infiltrated him into the Church for precisely this purpose. An investigation of Mother Akeley's background was then initiated.

Within a short time, agent Whiteside was in possession of a preliminary report on Elizabeth Akeley and her forebears, excerpts from which follow.

AKELEY, ELIZABETH — HISTORY AND BACKGROUND

The Akeley family is traceable to one Beelzebub Akeley who traveled from Portsmouth, England, to Kingsport, Massachusetts aboard the sailing caravel Worthy in 1607. Beelzebub Akeley married an indentured servant girl, bought out her indenture papers and moved with her to establish the Akeley dynasty in Townshend, Windham County, Vermont in 1618. The Akeleys persisted in Windham County for more than two centuries, producing numerous clergy, academics, and other genteel professionals in this period.

Abednego Mesach Akeley, subject's great-great grandfather, was the last of the Vermont Akeleys to pursue a life of the cloth. Born in 1832, Abednego was raised in the strict puritanical traditions of the Akeleys and ordained by his father, the Reverend *Samuel Shadrach Solomon Akeley* upon attaining his maturity. Abednego served as assistant pastor to his father until Samuel's death in 1868, at which time he succeeded to the pulpit.

Directly following the funeral of Samuel Akeley, Abednego is known to have traveled to more southerly regions of New England including Massachusetts and possibly Rhode Island. Upon his return to Townshend he led his flock into realms of highly questionable doctrine, and actually transferred the affiliation of his church from its traditional Protestant parent body to that of the new and suspect Starry Wisdom sect.

Controversy and scandal followed at once, and upon the death of Abednego early in 1871 at the age of thirty-nine, the remnants of his congregation moved as a body to Providence, Rhode Island. One female congregant, however, was excommunicated by unanimous vote of the other members of the congregation, and forced to remain behind in Townshend. This female was *Sarah Elizabeth Phillips*, a servant girl in the now defunct Akeley household.

Shortly following the departure of the remnants of Abednego Akeley's flock from Vermont, Sarah Phillips gave birth to a son. She claimed that the child had been fathered by Abednego mere hours before his death. She named the child *Henry Wentworth Akeley*. As the Akeley clan was otherwise extinct at this point, no one challenged Sarah's right to identify her son as an Akeley, and in fact in later years she sometimes used the name Akeley herself.

Henry Akeley overcame his somewhat shadowed origins and built for himself a successful academic career, returning to Windham County in his retirement, and remaining there until the time of his mysterious disappearance and presumed demise in the year 1928.

Henry had married some years earlier, and his wife had given birth to a single child, *George Goodenough Akeley*, in the year 1901, succumbing two days later to childbed fever. Henry Akeley raised his son with the assistance of a series of nursemaids and housekeepers. At the time of Henry Akeley's retirement and his return to Townshend, George Akeley emigrated to San Diego, California, building there a modest but comfortable house at 176 Pleasant Street.

George Akeley married a local woman suspected of harboring a strain of Indian blood; the George Akeleys were the parents of a set of quadruplets born in 1930. This was the first quadruple birth on record in San Diego County. There were three boys and a girl. The boys seemed, at birth, to be of relatively robust constitution, although naturally small.

The girl was still smaller, and seemed extremely feeble at birth so that her survival appeared unlikely.

However, with each passing hour the boys seemed to fade while the tiny girl grew stronger. All four infants clung tenaciously to life, the boys more and more weakly and the girl more strongly, until finally the three male infants -- apparently at the same hour -- succumbed. The girl took nourishment with enthusiasm, growing pink and active. Her spindly limbs rounded into healthy baby arms and legs, and in due course she was carried from the hospital by her father.

In honor of a leading evangelist of the era, and of a crusader for spiritualistic causes, the girl was named *Aimee Semple Conan Doyle Akeley*.

Aimee traveled between San Diego and the spiritualist center of Noblesville, Indiana, with her parents. The George Akeleys spent their winters in San Diego, where George Goodenough Akeley served as Radiant Father of the Spiritual Light Brotherhood, which he founded in a burst of religious fervor after meeting Aimee Semple McPherson, the evangelist whose name his daughter bore; each summer they would make a spiritualistic pilgrimage to Noblesville, where George Akeley became fast friends with the spiritualist leader and sometime American fascist, *William Dudley Pelley*.

Aimee Doyle Akeley married William Pelley's nephew *Hiram Wesley Pelley* in 1959. In that same year Aimee's mother died and was buried in Noblesville. Her father continued his ministry in San Diego.

In 1961, two years after her marriage to young Pelley, Aimee Doyle Akeley Pelley gave birth to a daughter who was named *Elizabeth Maude Pelley*, after two right-wing political leaders, Elizabeth Dilling of Illinois and Maude Howe of England. Elizabeth Maude Pelley was raised alternately by her parents in Indiana and her grandfather in San Diego.

In San Diego her life was relatively normal, centering on her schooling, her home, and to a lesser extent on her grandfather's church, the Spiritual Light Brotherhood. In Indiana she was exposed to a good deal of political activity of a right-wing extremist nature. Hiram Wesley Pelley had followed in his uncle's footsteps in this regard, and Aimee Semple Conan Doyle Akeley Pelley took her lead from her husband and his family. A number of violent scenes are reported to have transpired between young Elizabeth Pelley and the elder Pelleys.

Elizabeth Pelley broke with her parents over political disagreements in 1976, and returned permanently to San Diego where she took up residence with her grandfather. At this time she abandoned her mother's married name and took the family name as her own, henceforth being known as *Elizabeth Akeley*. Upon the death of George Goodenough Akeley, Elizabeth succeeded to the title of Radiant Mother of the Spiritual Light Brotherhood and the pastorhood of the Church, as well as the property on Pleasant Street and a small income from inherited securities.

*

Vernon Whiteside read the report carefully. Through his position as sexton of the Spiritual Light Brotherhood Church he had access, as well, to most church records, including the taped archives of the Sunday worship services and Wednesday message services. He followed the Radiant Mother's report to the congregation, in which she referred heavily to the séance of June 13, by borrowing and listening carefully to the tape of the séance itself.

He also obtained a photocopy from Agency headquarters, of the latest issues of the *Vermont UFO Intelligencer*. These he read carefully, seeking to correlate any references in the newsletter with the Akeley family, or with any other name connected with the Akeleys or the content of the séance tape. He mulled over the Akeleys, Phillipses, Wilmarths, Noyeses, and all other references. He attempted also to connect the defunct (or at least seemingly-defunct) Starry Wisdom sect of the New England region, with the San Diego-based Spiritual Light Brotherhood.

At this time it appears also that Elizabeth Akeley began to receive additional messages outside of the Spiritual Light message services. During quiet moments she would lapse involuntarily into her trance or trance-like state. Because she was unable to recall the messages received during these episodes, she prevailed upon Marc Feinman to spend increasing amounts of time with her. During the last week of June and July of 1979 the two were nearly inseparable. They spent every night together, sometimes at Elizabeth's house in National City, sometimes at Marc's apartment on Upas Street.

It was at this time that Vernon Whiteside recommended that Agency surveillance of the San Diego cult be increased by the installation of wiretaps on the church and the Pleasant Street and Upas Street residences. This recommendation was approved and recordings were obtained at all three locations. Transcripts are available in Agency files. Excerpts follow:

July 25, 1979 (Incoming)
Voice #1 (Definitely identified as Marc Feinman): Hello.
Voice #2 (Tentatively identified as Mrs. Sara Feinman, Marc's mother, Bronx, New York): Marc.
Voice #1: (Pause.) Yes, Ma.
Voice #2: Markie, are you all right?
Voice #1: Yeah, Ma.
Voice #2: Are you sure? Are you really all right?
Voice #1: Ma, I'm all right.
Voice #2: Okay, just so you're all right, Markie. And work, Markie? How's your work? Is your work all right?
Voice #1: It's all right, Ma.
Voice #2: No problems?
Voice #1: Of course, problems, Ma. That's what they pay me to take care of.
Voice #2: Oh my God, Markie! What kind of problems, Markie?
Voice #1: (Pauses, sighs or inhales deeply) We're trying to integrate the 2390 remote console control routines with the sysgen status word register and every time we run it against —
Voice #2: (Interrupting) Markie, you know I don't understand that kind of —
Voice #1: (Interrupting) But you asked me —
Voice #2: (Interrupting) Marc, don't contradict your mother. Are you still with that shicksa? She's the one who's poisoning your mind against your poor mother. I'll bet she's with you now, isn't she, Marc?
Voice #1: (Sighs or inhales deeply) No, Ma, it's Wednesday. She's never here Wednesdays. She's at church every Wednesday. They have these services every Wedn —
Voice #2: That isn't what I called about. I don't understand, Markie, for the money that car must have cost you could have had an Oldsmobile at least, even a Buick like your father. Markie, it's your father I phoned about. Markie, you have to come home. Your father isn't well, Markie. I

phoned because he isn't home now but the doctor said he's not a well man. Markie, you have to come home and talk to your father. He respects you, he listens to you God knows why. Please, Markie. (Sound of soft crying.)

Voice #1 What's wrong with him, Ma?

Voice #2 I don't want to say it on the telephone.

*

July 25, 1979 (Outgoing)

Voice #3: (Definitely identified as Vernon Whiteside): Spiritual Light Brotherhood. May the divine light shine upon your path.

Voice #1: Vern, this is Marc. Is Liz still at the church? Is the service over?

Voice #3: The service ended a few minutes ago, Mr. Feinman. The Radiant Mother is resting in the sacristy.

Voice #1: That's what I wanted to know. Listen, Vern, tell Lizzie that I'm on my way, will you? I had a long phone call from my mother and I don't want Liz to worry. Tell her I'll give her a ride home from the church.

*

Feinman left San Diego by automobile, driving his Ferrari Boxer eastward at a top speed in the 140 MPH range, and arrived at the home of his parents in the Bronx, New York, sometime during the night of July 27-28.

In the absence of Marc Feinman, Akeley took agent Whiteside increasingly into her confidence, asking him to remain in her presence day and night. He set up a temporary cot in the living room of the Pleasant Street house during this period. His instructions were to keep a portable cassette recorder handy at all times, and to record anything said by Mother Akeley during spontaneous trances. On the first Saturday of August, following a lengthy speech in the now — familiar male New England twang, Akeley asked agent Whiteside for the tape. She played it back, then made the following long — distance telephone call:

August 4, 1979 (Outgoing)

Voice #4 (Tentatively identified as Ezra Noyes): Vermont Bureau. May we help you?

Voice #5 (Definitely identified as Elizabeth Akeley): Is this Mr. Noyes?

Voice #4: Oh, I'm sorry, Dad isn't home. This is Ezra. Can I give him a —

Voice #5 (Interrupting): Oh, I wanted to speak with Ezra Noyes. The editor of the *UFO Intelligencer.*

Voice #4: Oh, yes, right. Yes, that's me. Ezra Noyes.

Voice #5: Mr. Noyes, I wonder if you could help me. I need some information about, ah, recent occurrences in or around Townshend.

Voice #4: That's funny, what did you say your name was?

Voice #5: Elizabeth Akeley.

Voice #4: I thought I knew all my subbers.

Voice #5: Oh, I'm not a subscriber, I got your name from — well, that doesn't matter. Mr. Noyes, I wonder if you could tell me if there have been any unusual UFO sightings in your region lately.

Voice #4 (Suspiciously): Unusual?

Voice #5: Well, these wouldn't be your usual run-of-the-mill flying objects. Flying saucers. I hope that phrase doesn't offend you. These would be more like flying creatures.

Voice #4: Creatures? You mean birds?

Voice #5: No. No. Intelligent creatures.

Voice #4: People, then. You mean Buck Rogers and Wilma Deering with their rocket flying belts.

Voice #5. Please don't be sarcastic, Mr. Noyes. (Pauses.) I mean intelligent, possibly hominoid but non-human creatures. Their configuration may vary, but some of them, at least, I believe would have large, membranous wings, probably stretched over a bony or veinous framework in the fashion of bats' or insects' wings. Also, some of them may be carrying artifacts such as polished metallic cylinders of a size capable of containing a — of containing, uh, a human — a human — brain. (Sounds of distress, possible sobbing.)

Voice #4: Miss Akeley? Are you all right, Miss Akeley?

Voice #5: I'm sorry. Yes, I'm all right.

Voice #4: I didn't mean to be so hard on you, Miss Akeley. It's just that we get a lot of crank calls. People wanting to talk to the little green men and that kind of thing. I had to make sure that you weren't —

Voice #5: I understand. And you *have* had —

Voice #4: I'm reluctant to say too much on the phone. Miss Akeley, do you think you could get here? There have been sightings. And there are older ones. Records in the local papers. A rash of incidents about fifty years ago. And others farther back. There was a monograph by an Eli Davenport over in New Hampshire back in the 1830s, I've got a Xerox of it...

*

Shortly after her telephone conversation with Ezra Noyes, Elizabeth Akeley appealed to Vernon Whiteside for assistance. "I don't want to go alone," she is reported as saying. "If only Marc were here, I know he'd help me. He'd go with me. But he's with his family and I can't wait till he gets back. We'll have to close the church. No, no we won't. We can have a lay reader conduct the worship services. We can suspend the message services 'til I get back. Will you help me, Vernon?"

Whiteside, maintaining his cover as the sexton of the Brotherhood, assured Akeley. "Anything the Radiant Mother wishes, ma'am. What would you like me to do?"

"Can you get away for a few days? I have to go to Vermont. Would you book two tickets for us? There are church funds to cover the cost."

"Yes, ma'am." Whiteside lowered his head. "Best way would be via Logan International in Boston, then a Boston and Maine train to Newfane and Hardwick."

Akeley made no comment on the sexton's surprising familiarity with transcontinental air routes or with the railroad service between Boston and upper New England. She was obviously in an agitated state, Whiteside reported when he checked in with his superiors prior to their departure from San Diego.

Two days later the Negro sexton and the Radiant Mother climbed down from B & M train #5508 at Hardwick, Vermont. They were met at the town's rundown and musty-smelling station by Ezra Noyes. Noyes was driving his parents' 1959 Nash Ambassador station wagon and willingly loaded Akeley's and Whiteside's meager baggage into the rear cargo deck of the vehicle.

Ezra chauffeured the visitors to his parents' home. The house, a gambrel — roofed structure of older design, was fitted for a larger family than the two senior Noyeses and their son Ezra; in fact, an elder son and daughter had both married and departed Windham County for locales of greater stimulation and professional opportunity, leaving two surplus bedrooms in the Noyes home.

Young Noyes proposed that he invite the full membership of the Vermont UFO Intelligence Bureau to attend an extraordinary meeting, to convene without delay at his home. Both Elizabeth Akeley and Vernon Whiteside demurred, pleading fatigue at the end of their transcontinental flight as well as the temporary debilitation of jet lag.

Noyes agreed reluctantly to abandon his plan for the meeting, but was eager to offer his own services and assistance to Akeley and Whiteside. Elizabeth informed Ezra Noyes that she had received instructions to meet a visitor at a specific location near the town of Passumpsic in neighboring Caledonia County. She did not explain to Noyes the method of her receiving these instructions, but Vernon's later report indicated that he was aware of them, the instructions having been delivered to Miss Akeley in spontaneous trance sessions, the tapes of which he had also audited.

It must be again emphasized at this point that the voice heard on the spontaneous trance tapes was, in different senses, both that of Miss Akeley and of another personage. The pitch and accent, as has been stated, were those of an elderly male speaking in a semi-archaic New England twang while the vocal apparatus itself was unquestionably that of Elizabeth Akeley, neé Elizabeth Maude Pelley.

Miss Akeley's instructions were quite specific in terms of geography, although it was found odd that they referred only to landmarks and highway or road facilities known to exist in the late 1920s. Young Noyes was able to provide alternate routes for such former roadways as had been closed when superseded by more modern construction.

Before retiring, Elizabeth Akeley placed a telephone call to the home of Marc Feinman's parents in the Bronx. In this call she urged Feinman to join her in Vermont. Feinman responded that his father, at the urging of himself and his mother, had consented to undergo major surgery. Marc promised to travel to Vermont and rendezvous with Akeley at the earliest feasible time, but indicated that he felt obliged to remain with his parents until the surgery was completed and his father's recovery assured.

The following morning Elizabeth Akeley set out for Passumpsic. She was accompanied by Vernon Whiteside and traveled in the Nash Ambassador station wagon driven by Ezra Noyes.

Her instructions had contained very specific and very emphatic requirements that she keep the rendezvous alone, although others might provide transportation and wait while the meeting took place. The party who had summoned Elizabeth Akeley to the rendezvous had not, to this time, been identified, although it was believed to be the owner of the male voice and New England twang who had spoken through Elizabeth herself in her trances.

Prior to their departing Windham County for Caledonia County, a discussion took place between Akeley and Whiteside. Whiteside appealed to Elizabeth Akeley to permit him to accompany her to the rendezvous.

That would be impossible, Akeley stated.

Whiteside pointed out Elizabeth's danger, in view of the unknown identity of the other party. When Akeley remained adamant, Whiteside gave in and agreed to remain with Ezra Noyes during the meeting. It must be pointed out that at this time the dialog was not cast in the format of a highly trained and responsible agent of the Federal establishment, and an ordinary citizen; rather, the façade which Whiteside rightly although with difficulty maintained was that of a sexton of the Spiritual Light Brotherhood acting under the authority of and in the service of the Radiant Mother of the Church.

Akeley was fitted with a concealed microphone which transmitted on a frequency capable of being picked up by a small microcassette recorder which Whiteside was to keep with him in or near the Nash station wagon; additionally, an earphone ran from the recorder so that Whiteside was enabled to monitor the taped information in real time.

The Nash Ambassador crossed the county line from Windham into Caledonia on a two-lane county highway. This had been a dirt road in the 1920s, blacktopped with Federal funds administered by the Works Progress Administration under Franklin Roosevelt, and superseded by a nearby four-lane asphalt highway built during the Eisenhower Presidency. The blacktop received minimal maintenance, and only pressure from local members of the Vermont legislature, this brought in turn at the insistence of local residents who used the highway for access to Passumpsic, South Londonderry, and Bellows Falls, prevented the State from declaring the highway closed and striking it from official roadmaps.

Reaching the town of Passumpsic, Akeley, who had never previously traveled farther east than Indianapolis, Indiana, told Ezra to proceed 800 yards, at which point the car was to be halted. Ezra complied. At the appointed spot, Akeley left the car and opened a gate in the wooden fence fronting the highway.

Noyes pulled the wagon from the highway through the gate and found himself on a narrow track that had once been a small dirt road, long since abandoned and overgrown.

This track led away from the highway and into hilly farm country, years before abandoned by the poor farmers of the region that lay between Passumpsic and Lyndonville.

Finally, having rounded an ancient dome-topped protuberance that stood between the station wagon and any possible visual surveillance from the blacktop highway or even the overgrown dirt road, the Nash halted, unable to continue. The vegetation hereabouts was of a peculiar nature. While most of the region consisted of thin, played-out soil whose poor fertility was barely adequate to sustain a covering of tall grasses and undersized, gnarly-trunked trees, in the small area set off by the dome-topped hill the growth was thick, lush and luxuriant.

However, there was a peculiar quality to the vegetation, a characteristic which even the most learned botanist would have been hard pressed to identify, and yet which was undeniably present. It was as if the vegetation were *too* vibrantly alive, as if it sucked greedily at the earth for nourishment and by so doing robbed the countryside for a mile or more in every direction of sustenance.

Through an incongruously luxuriant copse of leafy trees a small building could be seen, clearly a shack of many years' age and equally clearly of long abandonment. The door hung angularly from a single rusted hinge, the windows were cracked or missing altogether and spiders had filled the empty frames with their own geometric handiwork. The paint, if ever the building had known the touch of a painter's brush, had long since flaked away and been blown to oblivion by vagrant tempests, and the bare wood beneath had been cracked by scores of winters and bleached by as many summers' suns.

Elizabeth Akeley looked once at the ramshackle structure, nodded to herself and set out slowly to walk to it. Vernon Whiteside placed himself at her elbow and Ezra Noyes set a pace a short stride behind the others, but Akeley halted at once, turned and gestured silently but decisively to them both to remain behind. She then resumed her progress through the copse.

Whiteside watched Elizabeth Akeley proceeding slowly but with apparently complete self-possession through the wooded area. She halted just outside the shack, leaned forward and slightly to one side as if peering through a cobwebbed window frame, then proceeded again. She tugged at the door, managed to drag it open with a squeal of rusted metal and protesting wood and disappeared inside the shack.

"Are you just going to let her go like that?" Ezra Noyes demanded of Whiteside. "How do you know who's in there? What if it's a Beta Reticulan? What if it's a Moth Man? What if there's a whole bunch of aliens in there? They might have a tunnel from the shack to their saucer. The whole thing might be a front. Shouldn't we go after her?"

Whiteside shook his head. "Mother Akeley issued clear instructions, Ezra. We are to wait here." He reached inside his jacket and unobtrusively flicked on the concealed microcassette recorder. When he pulled his hand from his pocket be brought with it the earphone. He adjusted it carefully in his ear.

"Oh, I didn't know you were deaf," Noyes said.

"Just a little," Whiteside replied.

"Well, what are we going to do?" Ezra asked him.

"I shall wait for the Radiant Mother," Whiteside told him. "There is nothing to fear. Have faith in the Spiritual Light, little brother, and your footsteps will be illuminated."

"Oh." Ezra made a sour face and climbed onto the roof of Ambassador. He seated himself there cross-legged to watch for any evidence of activity at the shack.

Vernon Whiteside also kept watch on the shack, but chiefly he was listening to the voices transmitted by the cordless microphone concealed behind Elizabeth Akeley's lapel. Excerpts from the transcript later made of these transmissions follow.

Microcassette, August 8, 1979

Voice #5 (Elizabeth Akeley): Hello? Hello? Is there —

Voice #6 (Unidentified voice; oddly metallic intonation; accent similar to male New England twang present in San Diego trance tapes): Come in, come in, don't be afraid.

Voice #5: It's so dark in here.

Voice #6: I'm sorry. Move carefully. You are perfectly safe but there is some delicate apparatus set up.

(Sounds of movement, feet shuffling, breathing, a certain vague buzzing sound. Creak as of a person sitting in an old wooden rocking chair.)

Voice #5: I can hardly see. Where are you?

Voice #6: The cells are very sensitive. My friends are not here. You are not Albert Wilmarth.

Voice #5: No, I don't even —

Voice #6: (Interrupting) Oh, my God! Of course not. It's been so — tell me, what year is this?

Voice #5: 1979.

Voice #6: Poor Albert. Poor Albert. He could have come along. But of course he — what did you say your name was, young woman?

Voice #5: Akeley. Elizabeth Akeley.

(Silence. Buzzing sound. A certain unsettling sound as of wings rustling, but wings larger than those of any creature known to be native to Vermont.)

Voice #6: Do not taunt me, young woman!

Voice #5: Taunt you? Taunt you?

Voice #6: Do you know who I *am*? Does the name Henry Wentworth Akeley mean nothing to you?

(Pause…buzzing…rustling.)

Voice #5: Yes! Yes! Oh, oh, this is incredible! This is wonderful! It means — Yes, my grandfather spoke of you. If you're really — My grandfather was George Akeley. He — we —

Voice #6: (Interrupting) Then I am your great-grandfather, Miss Akeley. I regret that I cannot offer you my hand. George Akeley was my son. Tell me, is he still alive?

Voice #5: No, he — he died. He died in 1971, eight years ago. I was a little girl, but I remember him speaking of his father in Vermont. He said you disappeared mysteriously. But he always expected to hear from you

139

again. He even founded a church. The Spiritual Light Brotherhood. He never lost faith.

I have continued his work. Waiting for word from — beyond. That's why I came when I — when I started receiving messages.

Voice #6: Thank you. Thank you, Elizabeth. Perhaps I should not have stayed away so long, but the vistas, my child, the vistas! How old did you say you were?

Voice #5: Why — why — 18. Almost 19.

(Buzzing.)

Voice #6: You have followed my directions, Elizabeth? You are alone? Yes? Good. The cells are very sensitive. I can see you, even in this darkness, even if you cannot see me. Elizabeth, I have been gone from Earth for half a century, yet I am no older than the day I — departed — in the year 1928. The sights I have seen, the dimensions and the galaxies I have visited! Not alone, my child. Of course not alone. Those ones who took me — ah, child! Human flesh is too weak, too fragile to travel beyond the earth.

Voice #5: But there are spacesuits. Rockets. Capsules. Oh, I suppose that was after your time. But we've visited the moon. We've sent instruments to Venus and Mars and the moons of Jupiter.

Voice #6: And what you know is what Columbus might have learned of the New World, by paddling a rowboat around the port of Cadiz! Those ones who took me, those Old Ones! They can fly between the worlds on their great ribbed wings! They can span the very aether of space as a dragonfly flits across the surface of a pond! They are the greatest scientists, the greatest naturalists, the greatest anthropologists, the greatest explorers in the universe! Those whom they select to accompany them, if they cannot survive the ultimate vacuum of space, the Old Ones discard their bodies and seal their brains in metal canisters and carry them from world to world, from star to burning, glittering star!

(Buzzing, loud sound of rustling.)

Voice #5: Then — you have been to other worlds? Other planets, other physical worlds. Not other planes of spiritual existence. Our congregants believe —

Voice #6: (Interrupting) Your congregants doubtlessly believe poppycock. Yes, I have been to other worlds. I have seen all the planets of the solar system, from little, sterile Mercury to giant, distant Yuggoth.

Voice #5: Distant Yu — Yuggoth?

Voice #6: Yes, yes. I suppose those fool astronomers have yet to find it, but it is the gem and the glory of the solar system, glowing with its own ruby-red glare. It revolves in its own orbit, turned ninety degrees from the plane of the ecliptic. No wonder they've never seen it. They don't know where to look. Yet it perturbs the paths of Neptune and Pluto. That ought to be clue enough! Yuggoth is very nearly a sun. It possesses its own corps of worldlets, Nithon, Zaman, the miniature twins Thog and Thok! And there is life there! There is the Ghooric Zone where bloated shoggoths splash and spawn!

Voice #5: I can't — I can't believe all this! My own great-grandpa! Planets and beasts...

Voice #6: Yuggoth was merely the beginning for me. Those Ones carried me far away from the sun. I have seen the worlds that circle Arcturus and Centaurus, Wolf and Barnard's Star and Beta Reticuli. I have seen creatures whose physical embodiment would send a sane man mad into screaming nightmares of horror that never ends and whose minds and souls would put to shame the proudest achievements of Einstein and Schopenhauer, Confucius and Plato, the Enlightened One and the Anointed One! And I have known love, child, love such as no earthbound mortal has ever known.

Voice #5: Lo — love, great-grandfather?

(Sound of buzzing, loud and agitated rustling of wings.)

Voice #6: You know about love, surely, Elizabeth. Doesn't your church preach a gospel of love? In fifty-seven years on this planet I never came across a church that didn't claim that. And have you known love? A girl your age, surely you've known the feeling by now.

Voice #5: Yes, great-grandfather.

Voice #6: Is it merely a physical attraction, Elizabeth? Do you believe that souls can love? Or do you believe in such things as souls? Can *minds* love one another?

Voice #5: All three. All three of those.

Voice #6: Good. Yes, all three. And when two beings love with their minds and their souls, they yearn also for bodies with which to express their love. Hence the physical manifestation of love. (Pause.) Excuse me, child. In a way I suppose I'm nothing but an old man rambling on about abstractions. You have a young man, have you?

141

Voice #5: Yes.

Voice #6: I would like to meet him. I would like very much to meet him, my child.

Voice #5: Great-grandfather. May I tell the people about you?

Voice #6: No, Elizabeth. The time is not ripe.

Voice #5: But this is the most important event since — since — (Pause.) Contact with other beings, with other races, not of the earth. Proof that there is intelligent life throughout the universe. Proof of visits between the worlds and between the galaxies.

Voice #6: All in time, child. Now I am tired. Please go now. Will you visit me again?

Voice #5: Of course. Of course.

*

Elizabeth Akeley emerged from the shack, took one step and staggered.

At the far side of the copse of trees, Vernon Whiteside and Ezra Noyes watched. They saw Elizabeth. Ezra scrambled from the roof of the station wagon. Whiteside started forward, prepared to assist Mother Akeley.

But she had merely been blinded, for the moment, by the bright sunlight of a Vermont August. Whiteside and Ezra Noyes saw her returning through the glade. Once or twice she stopped and leaned against a strangely spongy tree. Each time she started again, to all appearances further debilitated rather than restored.

She reached the station wagon and leaned against its drab metalwork. Whiteside said, "Are you all right, Radiant Mother?"

She managed a wan smile. "Thank you, Vernon. Yes, I'm all right. Thank you."

Ezra Noyes was beside himself.

"Who was in there? What was going on? Were there really aliens in that shack? Can I go? Oh, darn it, darn it!" He pounded one fist into the palm of his other hand. "I should never have left home without my camera! Kenneth Arnold himself said that back in '47. It's the prime directive of all Ufologists and I went off without one, me of all people. Oh, darn, darn, darn!"

Vernon Whiteside said, "Radiant Mother, do you wish to leave now? May I visit the shack first?"

"Please, Vernon, don't. I asked him" — She drew Whiteside away from Noyes — "I asked him if I could reveal this to the world and he said, not yet."

"I monitored the tape, Reverend Mother."

"Yes."

"What does it mean, Reverend Mother?"

She passed her hand across her face, tugging soft bangs across her eyes to block out the bright sunlight. "I feel faint. Vernon. Ask Ezra to drive us back to Dark Mountain, would you?"

He helped her climb into the station wagon and signaled to Ezra. "Mother Akeley is fatigued. She must be taken back at once."

Ezra sighed and started the Ambassador's straight-six engine.

Elizabeth Akeley telephoned Marc Feinman from the Noyes house in Dark Mountain. A message had been transmitted surreptitiously by agent Whiteside in time for monitoring arrangements to be made. Neither Akeley nor Feinman was aware of the monitoring system.

Excerpts from the call follow:

August 9, 1979 (outgoing)

Voice #2 (Sara Feinman): Yes.

Voice #5 (Elizabeth Akeley): Mrs. Feinman?

Voice #2: Yes, who is this?

Voice #5: Mrs. Feinman, this is Elizabeth Akeley speaking. I'm a friend of Marc's from San Diego. Is Marc there, please?

Voice #2: I know all about Marc's friend, Elizabeth darling. Don't you know Marc's father is in the hospital? Should you be bothering Marc at such a time?

Voice #5: I'm very sorry about Mr. Feinman, Mrs. Feinman. Marc told me before he left California. Is he all right?

Voice #2: Don't ask.

(Pause.)

Voice #5: Could I speak with Marc? Please?

Voice #2: (Off line, pick-up is very faint) Marc, here, it's your little goyishe priestess. Yes. On the telephone. No, she didn't say where. No, she didn't say.

Voice #1 (Marc Feinman):Lizzy? Lizzy baby, are you okay?

Voice #5: Yes, I'm okay. Is your father —

Voice #1: (Interrupting) They operated this morning. I saw him after. He's very weak, Liz. But I think he's going to make it. Lizzy, where are you? Pleasant Street?

Voice #5: Vermont.

Voice #1: What? *Vermont?*

Voice #5: I couldn't wait, Marc. You were on the road, and there was another trance. I couldn't wait till you arrived in New York. Vernon came with me. We're staying with a family in Dark Mountain. Marc, I met my great-grandfather. Yesterday. I tried to call you last night but —

Voice #1: I was at the hospital with Ma, visiting my father. We couldn't just —

Voice #5: Of course, Marc. You did the right thing. (Pause) How soon can you get here?

Voice #1: I can't leave now. My father is still — they're not sure. (Lowering voice.) I don't want to talk too loud. The doctor said it's going to be touch and go for at least forty-eight hours. I can't leave Ma.

Voice #5: (Sobs.) I understand, Marc. But — but — my great-grandfather…

Voice #1: How old is the old coot? He must be at least ninety.

Voice #5: He was born in 1871. He's 108.

Voice #1: My God! Talk about tough old Yankee stock!

Voice #5: It isn't that, Marc! It has to do with the trance messages. Don't you understand? All of that strange material about alien beings, and other galaxies? That was no sci-fi trip —

Voice #1: I never said you were making it up, Lizzy! Your subconscious, though, I mean, you see some TV show or a movie and —

Voice #5: But that's just it, Marc! Those are real messages. Not from my subconscious. My great-grandpa was sending, oh, call them spirit messages or telepathic radiations or anything you like. He's here. He's back. Aliens took him away, they took his brain in a metal cylinder and he's been travelling in outer space for fifty years and now he's back here in Vermont and —

Voice #1: Okay, Lizzy, enough! Look, I'll drive up there as soon as I can get away. As soon as my father's out of danger. I can't leave my ma now but as soon as I can. What's this place…

*

Late on the afternoon of August 9th Ezra Noyes rapped on the door of Elizabeth Akeley's room. She admitted him and he stood in the center of the room, nervously wondering whether it would be proper to sit in her presence. Akeley urged him to sit. The conversation which ensued was recalled by young Noyes in a deposition taken later at an Agency field office. Excerpts from the deposition follow.

"Well, you see, I told her that I was really serious about UFOs and all that stuff. She didn't know much about Ufology. She'd never heard about the men in black, even, so I told her all about them so she'd be on the lookout. I asked her who this Vernon Whiteside was, and she said he was the sexton of her church and completely reliable and I shouldn't worry about him.

"I showed her some copies of the *Intelligencer* and she said she liked the mag a lot and asked if she could keep them. I said sure. Anyway, she wanted to know how long the Moth Man sightings had been going on. I told her, only about six months ago over at Townshend or around here. Then she asked me what I knew about a rash of similar sightings about fifty years ago.

"That was right up my alley. You know, I did a lot of research. I went down and read a lot of old newspaper files. They have the old papers on microfilm now, it kills your eyes to crouch over a reader all day looking at the old stuff, but it's really interesting.

"Anyway, there were some odd sightings back in the '20s, and then when they had those floods around here in November of '27, there were some really strange things. They found some bodies, parts of bodies that is, carried downstream in the flood. There were some in the Winooski River over near Montpelier, and some right in the streets of Passumpsic. The town was flooded, you know.

"Strange bodies. Things like big wings. Not like moth wings, though. More like bat wings. And there seems to have been some odd goings on with Miss Akeley's great — grandfather, Henry Akeley. He was a retired prof, you know. And something about a friend of his, a guy called Al Wilmarth. But it was all hushed up.

"Well, I told Miss Akeley everything I knew and then I asked her who was in the cabin over at that dirt road near Lyndonville. I think she must have got mixed up, because she said it was Henry Akeley. He disappeared in 1927 or '28. Even if he turned up, he couldn't be alive by now. She said he said something to her about love, and about wanting a young man's body and a young woman's body so he could make love with some woman from outer space, he said from Aldebaran. I guess you have to be a sci-fi nut to know about Aldebaran. I'm a sci-fi nut. I don't say too much about it in UFO circles — they don't like sci-fi, they think the sci-fi crowd put down UFOs. They're scared of 'em. They want to keep it all nice and safe and imaginary, you ought to read Sanderson and Earley on that some time.

"Well, how could a human and an alien make love? I guess old Akeley must have thought something like mind-transfer, like one partner could take over the body of a member of the other partner's species, you know. Only be careful, don't try it with those spiders where the female eats the male after they mate. Ha — ha — ha! Ha-ha!

"But Miss Akeley kept asking about lovemaking, you know, and I started to wonder if maybe she wasn't hinting at something, you know. I mean, there we were in this room. And it was my own parents' house and all, but it *was* a bedroom, and I didn't want her to think that she could just walk in there and, uh, well, you know.

"So I excused myself then. But she seemed upset. She kept running her hand through her hair. Pulling it down, those strips, what do women call them, bangs, over her forehead. I told her I had to get to work on the next ish of my mag, you know, and she'd have to excuse me but the last ish had been late and I was trying to get the mag back on schedule. But I told her, if she wanted a lift over to Passumpsic again, I'd be glad to give her a ride over there any time, and I'd like to meet her great-grandfather if he was living in that old shack. Then she said he wasn't exactly living in the shack, but he sort of was, sort of was there and sort of was living there. It didn't make any sense to me, so I went and started laying out the next issue of the *Intelligencer* 'cause I wanted to get it out on time for once, and show those guys that I can get a mag out on time when I get a chance.

"Anyway, Miss Akeley said her great-grandfather's girlfriend was named something like Sheera from Aldebaran. I told her that sounded like something out of a bad 50s sci-fi flick on the TV. There's a great channel in Montreal, we get it on the cable, they show sci-fi flicks every week. And that sure sounded like a sci-fi flick to me.

"Sheera from Aldebaran! Ha — ha — ha! Ha-ha!"

*

Marc Feinman wheeled his Ferrari up to the Noyes home. His sporty driving cap was cocked over one ear. Suede jacket, silk shirt, Gucci jeans and Frye boots completed his outfit.

The front door swung in as Fienman's boot struck the bottom wooden step. Elizabeth Akeley was across the whitewashed porch and in Feinman's arms before he reached the top of the flight. Without releasing his embrace of Akeley, Feinman extended one hand to grasp that of Vernon Whiteside.

They entered the house. Ezra Noyes greeted them in the front parlor. Elizabeth and Vernon briefed Marc on the events since their arrival in Vermont. When the narrative was brought up to date, Feinman asked simply, "What do you want to do?"

Ezra started to blurt out an ambitious plan for gaining the confidence of the aliens and arranging a ride in their saucer, but Whiteside, still maintaining the role of sexton of the Spiritual Light Church, cut him off. "We will do whatever the Radiant Mother asks us to do."

All eyes turned to Akeley.

After an uncomfortable interval she said, "I was — hoping that Marc could help. It's so strange, Marc. I know that I'm the one who always believed in — in the spirit world. The beyond. What you always call the supernormal."

Feinman nodded.

"But somehow," Elizabeth went on, "this seems more like your ideas than mine. It's so — I mean, this is the kind of thing that I've always looked for, believed in. And you haven't. And now that it's true, it doesn't seem to have any spiritual meaning. It's just — something that you could explain with your logic and your computers."

Feinman rubbed his slightly blue chin with his free hand. "This great-grandpa of yours, this Henry Akeley ..."

He looked into her eyes.

"You say, he was talking about some kind of mating ritual?"

Liz nodded.

Feinman said, "What did he look like? Did you ever *see* your great-grandfather before? Even a picture? Maybe one that your grandfather had in San Diego?"

She shook her head. "No. At least, I don't remember ever seeing a photo at home. There might have been one. But I hardly saw anything in the shack, Marc."

Ezra Noyes was jumping up and down in his chair. "Yes, you never told us, Lizzy — Miss Akeley. What did you see? What did he look like?"

"I hardly saw anything!" Liz covered her face with her hands, dropped one to her lap, tugged nervously at her bangs with the other. "It was pitch dark in there. Just a little faint light seeping between the cracks in the walls, through those broken windows. The windows that weren't broken were so filthy they wouldn't let any light in."

"So you couldn't tell if it was really Henry Akeley."

"It was the same voice," Vernon Whiteside volunteered. "We, ah, we bugged the meeting, Mr. Feinman. The voice was the same as the one on the trance tapes from the church."

Feinman's eyes widened. "The same? But the trance tapes are in Lizzy's voice!"

Whiteside back-pedaled. "No, you're right. I don't suppose they were the same vocal chords. But the timbre. And the enunciation. Everything. Same person speaking. I'd stake my reputation on it!"

Feinman stroked his chin again. "All right. Here's what I'd like to do. Lizzy, Henry Akeley said he'd see you again, right? Okay, let's surprise him. Suppose Whiteside and I head out there. Can you find the shack again, Vernon? Good! Okay, we'll take the Ferrari out there."

"But it's nearly dark out."

"No difference if it's so damned dark inside the shack! I've got a good five-cell torch in the emergency kit in the Ferrari."

"I ought to come along," Ezra Noyes put in. "I *do* represent the Vermont UFO Intelligence Bureau, you know!"

"Right," Feinman nodded. "And we'll need your help later. No, we'll need you, Ezra, but not right now. Whiteside and I will visit Henry Akeley — or whoever or whatever is out there claiming to be Henry Akeley. Give us a couple of hours' head start. And then, you come ahead."

"Can I get into the shack this time?" Ezra jumped up and paced nervously, almost danced, back and forth. "The other time, I had to wait at the car. If I can get into the shack, I can get some photos. I'll rig up a flash on my Instamatic. I want to get some shots of the inside of that cabin for the *Intelligencer*."

"Yes, sure." Feinman turned from Ezra Noyes and took Elizabeth Akeley's hand. "You don't mind, do you, Lizzy? I'm worried that your ancestor there — or whoever it is — has some kind of control over you. Those trances — what if he puts you under some kind of hypnotic influence while we're all out there together?"

"How do you know he's evil? You seem to — just assume that Henry Akeley wants to harm me."

"I don't know that at all." Feinman frowned. "I just have a nasty feeling about it. I want to get there first. I think Whiteside and I can handle things, and then you can arrive in a while. Please, Lizzy. You did call me to help. You didn't have to, you could just have gone back and never said anything to me until it was over."

Elizabeth looked very worried. "Maybe I should have."

"Well, but you didn't. Now, can we do it my way? Please?"

"All right, Marc."

Feinman turned to Vernon Whiteside. "Let's go. How long a ride is it out there?"

Whiteside paused. "Little less than an hour."

Feinman grunted. "Okay. Vernon and I will start now. We'll need about another hour once we're there, I suppose — call it two to be on the safe side. Lizzy and Ezra, if you'll follow us out to the shack in two hours, just come ahead in, we'll be there."

Ezra departed to check his camera. Vernon accompanied Marc. Shortly the Ferrari Boxer disappeared in a cloud of yellow Vermont dust, headed for Passumpsic.

As soon as they had pulled out of sight of the house, Vernon spoke. "Mr. Feinman, I've been helping Radiant Mother on this trip."

"I know that, Vernon. Lizzy mentioned it several times. I really appreciate it."

"Mr. Feinman, you know how concerned Radiant Mother is about Church archives. The way she records her sermons and the message services. Well, she was worried about her meeting with old Mr. Akeley. So I helped her to rig a wireless mike on her jacket, so we got a microcassette of the meeting."

Feinman said he knew that.

"Well, if you don't mind, I'd like to do the same again." Whiteside held the tiny microcassette recorder for Feinman to see. The Ferrari's V-12 purred throatily, loafing along the Passumpsic road in third gear.

"Sure. That's a good idea. But you needn't rig me up. I want you along. You can just mike yourself."

Vernon Whiteside considered. "Tell you what ..." He reached into his pocket, pulled out a pair of enamel ladybugs. "I'll mike us both. If we happen to pick up the same sounds there'll be no harm. In fact, it'll give us a redundancy check. If we get separated — "

"I don't see why we should."

"Just in case." He pinned a ladybug to Feinman's suede jacket, attached the second bug to his own. He made a minor adjustment to the recorder.

"There." He slipped the recorder back into his pocket. "I separated the input circuits. Now we'll record on two channels. We can mix the sound if we record the same events or keep it separate if we pick up different events. In fact, just to be on the safe side, suppose I leave the recorder here in the car when you and I go to the shack."

Feinman assented and Whiteside peeled the sealers from a dime-sized disk of double-adhesive foam. He stuck it to the recorder and stuck the recorder to the bottom of the Ferrari's dashboard.

"You're the sexton of the Spiritual Light Church," Feinman said. "You know a hell of a lot about electronics."

"My sister's boy, Mr. Feinman. Bright youngster. It's his hobby. Started out with a broken Victrola. Got his science teacher to helping. Going to San Diego State next term. I couldn't be prouder if he was my own boy. He builds all sorts of gadgets."

Feinman tooled the Ferrari around the dome-topped hill and pulled to a halt where the Noyes station wagon had parked on the earlier visit. The sun was setting and the somehow too-lush glade was filled with murk.

Vernon Whiteside reached under the dashboard and flicked the microcassette recorder to automatic mode. He climbed from the car.

Feinman went to the rear of the Ferrari and extracted a long-handled electric torch. He pulled his sports cap down over his eyes and touched Whiteside's elbow. The men advanced.

The events that transpired following this entrance to the sycamore copse were captured on the microcassette recorder, and a transcript of these sounds appears later in the report.

In the meanwhile, Elizabeth Akeley and Ezra Noyes waited at the Noyes home in Dark Mountain.

Two hours to the minute after the departure of Marc Feinman and Vernon Whiteside in Feinman's Ferrari Boxer, the Noyes station wagon, its aged suspension creaking, pulled out of the driveway.

Ezra pushed the Nash to the limit of its tired ability, chattering the while to Elizabeth. Preoccupied, she responded with low monosyllables. At the turning-point from the PassumpsicLyndonville road onto the old farm track, she waited in the station wagon while Ezra climbed down and opened the fence gate.

The Nash's headlights picked a narrow path for the car, circling the dome-topped hill that blocked the copse of lush vegetation from the sight of passers-by. The Ferrari Boxer stood silently at the edge of the copse.

Ezra lifted his camera-bag from the floor and slung it over his shoulder. Elizabeth waited in the car until Ezra walked to her side, opened the door and offered his hand.

They started through the copse. Noyes testified later that this was his first experience with the unusual vegetation. He claimed that, even as he set foot beneath the overhanging branches of the first sycamore a strange sensation passed through him. The day had been hot and even in the hours of darkness the temperature did not drop drastically. Even so, with his entry into the copse Noyes felt an unnatural and debilitating heat, as if the trees were adapted to a different climate than that of northern Vermont and were actually emitting heat of their own.

He began to perspire.

Elizabeth Akeley led the way through the wooded area, retracing the steps of her previous visit to the wooden shack.

Noyes found it more and more difficult to continue. With each pace he felt drained of energy and will. Once he halted and was about to sit down for a rest but Akeley grasped his hand and pulled him along.

When they emerged from the copse the dome-topped hill stood directly behind them, the rundown shack directly ahead.

Ezra and Elizabeth crossed the narrow grassy patch between the sycamore copse and the ramshackle cabin. Ezra found a space where the glass had fallen away and there was a small opening in the omnipresent cobwebs. He peered in, then lifted his camera and poked its lens through the opening. He shot a picture.

"Don't know what I got, but maybe I got something," he said.

Elizabeth Akeley pulled the door open. She stepped inside the cabin, closely followed by young Noyes.

The room, Ezra could see, was far larger than he'd estimated. Although the shack contained but a single room, that was astonishingly deep, its far corners utterly lost in shadow. Near to him were a rocking chair, a battered overstuffed couch and a dust-laden wooden table of a type often found in old New England homes.

Ezra later reported hearing odd sounds during these minutes. There was a strange buzzing sound. He couldn't tell whether it was organic — a sound such as a flight of hornets might have made, or such as might have been made by a single insect magnified to a shocking gigantism — or whether the sound was artificial, as if an electrical generator were running slightly out of adjustment.

The modulation was its oddest characteristic. Not only did the volume rise and fall, but the pitch, and in some odd way, the very tonal quality of the buzzing, kept changing. "It was as if something was trying to talk to me. To us. To Miss Akeley and me. I could almost understand it, but not quite."

Noyes stood, paralyzed, until he heard Elizabeth Akeley scream. Then he whirled, turning his back to the table from whence the buzzing sounds were coming. He saw Elizabeth standing before the rocking chair, her hands to her face.

The chair was rocking slowly, gently. The cabin was almost pitch black, its only illumination coming from an array of unfamiliar machinery set up on the long wooden table. Ezra could see now that a figure was seated, apparently unmoving, in the rocker.

It spoke.

"Elizabeth, my darling, you have come," the figure said. "Now we shall be together. We shall know the love of the body as we have known the love of the mind and of the soul."

Strangely, Noyes later stated, although the voice in which the figure spoke was that of Marc Feinman, the accent and intonation were those of a typical New England old-timer. Noyes testified also that his powers of observation played a strange trick on him at this moment. Although the man sitting in the chair was undoubtedly Marc Feinman — the clothing he wore, even to the sporting cap pulled low over his eyes, as if he were driving his Ferrari in bright sunlight — what Ezra noticed most particularly was a tiny red-and-black smudge on Feinman's jacket.

"It looked like a squashed lady bug," the youth stated later.

From somewhere in the darker corners of the cabin there came a strange rustling sound, like that of great leathery wings opening and folding again.

Noyes shot a quick series of pictures, one of the figure in the rocking chair, one of the table with the unusual mechanical equipment on it, and one of the darker corners of the cabin, hoping vaguely that he would get some results. The rocking chair tilted slowly backward, slowly forward. The man sitting in it finally said to Ezra, "You'll never get anything from there. You'd better get over to the other end of the shack and make your pictures."

As if hypnotized, Noyes walked toward the rear of the cabin. He stated later that as he passed a certain point, it was as if he had penetrated a curtain of total darkness. He tried to turn and look back at the others, but could not move. He tried to call out but could not speak. He was completely conscious, but seemingly had plunged into a state of total paralysis and of sensory deprivation.

What transpired behind him, in the front end of the cabin, he could not tell. When he recovered from his paralysis and loss of sensory inputs, it was to find himself alone at the rear of the shack. It was daylight outside and sunshine was pushing through the grimy windows and open door of the shanty. He turned around and found himself facing two figures. A third was at his side.

"Ezra!" The third figure said.

"Mr. Whiteside." Noyes responded.

"Well, I'm glad to see that you two are all right," a voice came to them from the other end of the cabin. It was the old New England twang that Ezra had heard from the man in the rocking chair, and the speaker was, indeed, Marc Feinman. He stood, wooden-faced, his back to the doorway. Elizabeth Akeley, her features similarly expressionless, stood at his side. Feinman's sporting cap was pulled down almost to the line of his eyebrows. Akeley's bangs dangled over her forehead.

Noyes claimed later that he thought he could see signs of a fresh red scar running across Akeley's forehead beneath the bangs. He claimed also that a corner of red was visible at the edge of the visor of Feinman's cap. But of course this is unverified.

"We're going now," Feinman said in his strange New England twang. "We'll take my car. You two go home in the other."

"But — but, Radiant Mother," Whiteside began.

"Elizabeth is very tired," Feinman said nasally. "You'll have to excuse her. I'm taking her away for a while."

He started out the door, guiding Elizabeth by the elbow. She walked strangely, yet not as if she were tired, ill, or even injured. Rather, she had the tentative, uncertain movements that are associated with an amputee first learning to maneuver on prosthetic devices.

They left the cabin and walked to the Ferrari. Feinman opened the door on the passenger side and guided Akeley into the car. Then he circled the vehicle, climbed in and seated himself at the wheel. Strangely, he sat for a long time staring at the controls of the sports car, as if he were unfamiliar with its type.

Vernon Whiteside and Ezra Noyes followed the others from the cabin. Both were still confused from their strange experience of paralysis and sensory deprivation; both stated later that they felt only half-awake, half-hypnotized. "Else," agent Whiteside later deposed, "I'd have stopped 'em for sure. Warrant or no warrant, I had probable cause that something fishy was going on, and I'd have grabbed the keys out of that Ferrari, done anything it took to keep those two there. But I could hardly move, I could hardly even think.

"I *did* manage to reach into that car and grab out my machine. My microcassette recorder. Then I looked at my little bug mike and saw that it was squashed, like somebody'd just squeezed it between his thumb and his finger, only he must have been made out of iron 'cause those bug-mikes are ruggedized. They can take a wallop with a sledgehammer and not even know it. So who squashed my little bug?

"Then Feinman finally got his car started and they pulled away. I looked at the Noyes kid and he looked at me, and we headed for his Nash wagon and we went back to his house. Nearly cracked up half a dozen times on the way home, he drove like a drunk. When we got to his place we both passed out for twelve hours while Feinman and Akeley were going God-knows-where in that Ferrari.

"Soon as I got myself back together I phoned in to Agency field HQ and came on in."

When agent Whiteside reported to Agency field HQ he turned over the microcassette which he and Feinman had made at the shack. Excerpts from the tape follow.

(Whiteside's Channel)

(All voices mixed): Yeah, this is the place all right... I'll — got it open, okay... Sheesh, it's dark in here. How'd she see anything? Well... (Buzzing sound.) What's that? What's that? Here, I'll shine my — what the hell? It looks like... Shining cylinder. No, two of 'em. Two of 'em. What the hell, some kind of futuristic espresso machines. What the hell...

(Buzzing sound becomes very loud, dominates tape. Then volume drops and a rustling is heard.)

Voice #3 (Vernon Whiteside): Here, lend me that thing a minute. No, I just gotta see what's over there. Okay, you stay here a minute, I gotta see what's...

(Sound of walking. Buzzing continues in background but fades, rustling sound increases.)

Voice #3: Jesus God! That can't be! No, no, that can't be! It's too...

(Sound of thump, as if microphone were being struck and then crushed between superhard metallic surfaces. Remainder of Whiteside channel is silent.)

(Feinman Channel)

(Early portion identical to Whiteside channel; excerpts begin following end of recording on Whiteside channel.)

Voice #1 (Marc Feinman): Vernon? Vernon? What —

Voice #6 (Henry Wentworth Akeley): He is unharmed.

Voice #1: Who's that?

Voice #6: I am Henry Wentworth Akeley.

Voice #1: Lizzy's great-grandfather.

Voice #6: Precisely. And you are Mr. Feinman?

Voice #1: Where are you, Akeley?

Voice #6: I am here.

155

Voice #1: Where? I don't see... what happened to Whiteside? What's going on here? I don't like what's going on here.

Voice #6: Please, Mr. Feinman, try to remain calm.

Voice #1: Where are you, Akeley? For the last time...

Voice #6: Please, Mr. Feinman, I must ask you to calm yourself. (Rustling sound.) Ah, that's better. Now, Mr. Feinman, do you not see certain objects on the table? Good. Now, Mr. Feinman, you are an intelligent and courageous young man. I understand that your interests are wide and your thirst for knowledge great. I offer you a grand opportunity. One which was offered to me half a century ago. I tried to decline at that time. My hand was forced. I never regretted having... let us say, gone where I have gone. But I must now return to earthly flesh, and as my own integument is long destroyed, I have need of another.

Voice #1: What — where — what are you talking about? If this is some kind of...

(Loud sound of rustling, sound of thumping and struggle, incoherent gasps and gurgles, loud breathing, moans.)

(At this point the same sound that ended the Whiteside segment of the tape is heard. Remainder of Feinman channel is blank.)

*

When agent Whiteside and young Ezra Noyes woke from their exhausted sleep, Whiteside identified himself as a representative of the Agency. He obtained the film from young Noyes's camera. It was promptly developed at the nearest Agency facility. The film was subsequently returned to Noyes and the four usable photographs, in fuzzily screened and mimeographed form, appeared in the *Vermont UFO Intelligencer*.

A description of the four photographs follows:

Frame 1: (Shot through window of the wooden shack) A dingy room containing a rocking chair and a large wooden table.

Frame 2: (Shot inside room) A rocking chair. In the chair is sitting a man identified as Marc Feinman. Feinman's sporting cap is pulled down covering his forehead. His eyes are barely visible and seem to have a glazed appearance, but this may be due to the unusual lighting conditions. A mark on his forehead seems to be visible at the edge of the cap, but is insufficiently distinct for verification.

Frame 3: (Shot inside room) Large wooden table holding unusual mechanical apparatus. There are numerous electrical devices, power units, what appears to be a cooling unit, photoelectric cells, items which appear to be microphones, and two medium-sized metallic cylinders estimated to contain sufficient space for a human brain, along with compact life-support paraphernalia.

Frame 4: (Shot inside room) This was obviously Noyes's final frame, taken as he headed toward the darkened rear area of the cabin. The rough wooden flooring before the camera is clearly visible. From it there seems to rise a curtain or wall of sheer blackness. This is not a black *substance* of any sort, but a curtain or mass of sheer negation. All attempts at analysis by Agency photoanalysts have failed completely.

*

Elizabeth Akeley and Marc Feinman were located at — of all places — Niagara Falls, New York. They had booked a honeymoon cottage and were actually located by representatives of the Agency returning in traditional yellow slickers from a romantic cruise on the craft *Maid of the Mist* .

Asked to submit voluntarily to Agency interrogation, Feinman refused. Akeley, at Feinman's prompting, simply shook her head negatively. "But I'll tell you what," Feinman said in a marked New England twang, "I'll make out a written statement for you if you'll settle for that."

Representatives of the Agency considered this offer unsatisfactory, but having no grounds for holding Feinman or Akeley and being particularly sensitive to criticism of the Agency for alleged intrusion upon the religious freedoms of unorthodox cults, the representatives of the Agency were constrained to accept Feinman's offer.

The deposition provided by Feinman — and co-sworn by Akeley — represented a vague and rambling narrative of no value. Its concluding paragraph follows.

All we want is to be left alone. We love each other. We're here now and we're happy here. What came before is over. That's somebody else's concern now. Let them go. Let them see. Let them learn. Vega, Aldebaran, Ophiuchi, the Crab Nebula. Let them see. Let them learn. Someday we may wish to go back. We will have a way to summon those Ones. When we summon those Ones they will respond.

*

A final effort by representatives of the Agency was made, in an additional visit to the abandoned shack by the sycamore copse off the Passumpsic-Lyndonville road. A squad of agents wearing regulation black outfits were guided by Vernon Whiteside. An additional agent remained at the Noyes home to assure noninterference by Ezra Noyes.

Whiteside guided his fellow agents to the sycamore copse. Several agents remarked at the warmth and debilitating feeling they experienced as they passed through the copse. In addition, an abnormal number of small cadavers — of squirrels, chipmunks, one gray fox, a skunk, and several whippoorwills — were noted, lying beneath the trees.

The shack contained an aged wooden rocking chair, a battered overstuffed couch, and a large wooden table. Whatever might have previously stood upon the table had been removed.

There was no evidence of the so-called wall or curtain of darkness. The rear of the shack was vacant.

*

In the months since the incidents above reported, two additional developments have taken place, note of which is appropriate herein.

First, Marc Feinman and Elizabeth Akeley returned to San Diego in Feinman's Ferrari Boxer. There, they took up residence at the Pleasant Street location. Feinman vacated the Upas Street apartment; he returned to his work with the computer firm. Inquiries placed with his employers indicate that he appeared, upon returning, to be absent-minded and disoriented, and unexpectedly to require briefings in computer technology and programming concepts with which he had previously been thoroughly familiar.

Feinman explained this curious lapse by stating that he had experienced a head injury while vacationing in Vermont, and still suffered from occasional lapses of memory. He showed a vivid but rapidly fading scar on his forehead as evidence of the injury. His work performance quickly returned to its previous high standard. "Marc's as smart as the brightest prof you ever studied under," his supervisor stated to the Agency. "But that Vermont trip made some impression on him! He picked up this funny New England twang in his speech, and it just won't go away."

Elizabeth Akeley went into seclusion. Feinman announced that they had been married, and that Elizabeth was, at least temporarily, abandoning her position as Radiant Mother of the Spiritual Light Church, although remaining a faithful member of the Church. In Feinman's company she regularly attends Sunday worship services, but seldom speaks.

The second item of note is of questionable relevance and significance, but is included here as a matter of completing the appropriate documentation. Vermont Forestry Service officers have reported that a new variety of sycamore tree has appeared in the Windham County - Caledonia County section of the state. The new sycamores are lush and extremely hardy. They seem to generate a peculiarly *warm* atmosphere, and are not congenial to small forest animals. Forestry officers who have investigated report a strange sense of lassitude when standing beneath these trees, and one officer has apparently been lost while exploring a stand of the trees near the town of Passumpsic.

Forestry Service agents are maintaining a constant watch on the spread of the new variety of sycamores.

BRACKISH WATERS

Delbert Marston, Jr., Ph.D., D.Sc., was the youngest tenured professor on the faculty of the University of California. He was widely regarded as a rising academic star, not only on the University's premiere campus at Berkeley but throughout the huge multi-campus system and, if the truth be known, throughout the national and international community of scholars.

Tall and dark-haired with a touch of premature gray at the temples, he was regarded as a catch by female faculty members who competed vigorously for his attention. He dressed conservatively, held his tongue in matters of both public and campus politics, drank single-malt scotch whiskey exclusively, and drove an onyx-black supercharged 1937 Cord Phaeton. Perhaps it was Marston's otherwise thoroughly conventional lifestyle that caused his vehicular preference to be regarded as a sign of high taste and acceptable self-indulgence rather than one of eccentricity.

He had the Cord serviced regularly at an exclusive garage on the island of Alameda, the owner of which establishment catered to fanciers of the three marques formerly built in Auburn, Indiana — the Auburn, the stately Duesenberg, and the tragically short-lived Cord. The Auburn Motor Car Company, or what was left of it, was now producing Lycoming aircraft engines and B-24 Liberator bombers for the Army Air Forces. Once the war was over there was no predicting the future of the discontinued automobiles but in Marston's estimation their prospects were poor.

On the night in question — the night, at any rate, that would initiate the series of events destined to lead to Delbert Marston's apotheosis — the sky above the San Francisco Bay Area was black with a cold storm that had swept down from the Gulf of Alaska and attacked the Pacific Coast with fierce winds and a series of hammering downpours of pelting rain laced with occasional hints of sleet. Such weather was not uncommon in Northern California during the winter months, and the winter of 1943-44 was no exception; the onslaught of wind and water was regarded as anything but freakish. The Bay Bridge was swept by an icy gale but the

Cord held the roadway with a steadiness unmatched by vehicles of lesser quality.

Professor Marston was accompanied by an older colleague, one Aurelia Blenheim, Ph.D. Gray-haired and dignified, Professor Blenheim had served for some years as Marston's mentor and sponsor. It was her spirited championing of his cause that had persuaded the Tenure Committee to grant him its seal of approval despite what was regarded as his almost scandalous youth. Marston's intellectual equal, Aurelia Blenheim had found in the younger academic the friendship and platonic camaraderie that her lifelong celibacy had otherwise denied her.

"I don't know why I let you talk me into spending an evening with this squad of eccentrics, Aurelia." Marston braked to keep his distance behind a superannuated Model A Ford that looked ready to topple over in the gale.

"Why, for the sheer pleasure and mental stimulation of bouncing off some people with unconventional ideas. Besides, the semester's over, most of the kiddies who have managed to stay out of the service have gone home to Bakersfield or Beloit or wherever they came from. What else did you have to do?"

"You've got to be kidding. The Oakland Symphony is doing an all-Mahler program, the San Francisco Ballet has a Berlioz show, and the opera is offering *The Marriage of Figaro*. And we're going to meet a bunch of wackos who think — if you can call it thinking — as a matter of fact, Aurelia, what in the world is it that they think?"

Aurelia Blenheim shook her head. "Come now, Delbert. They have a lot of different ideas. That's the fun of it. They don't have a body of fixed beliefs. Attending one of their meetings is like sitting in on a First Century council of bishops and listening to them debate the nature of the mystical body of Christ."

"I can't think of anything less interesting."

They had reached the San Francisco end of the bridge now and Marston maneuvered the Cord through merging traffic and headed south. A rattletrap Nash sedan full of high school kids pulled alongside the Cord. The driver lowered his window and yelled at Aurelia, "Why don't you put that submarine back in the water where it belongs, grandma?"

Aurelia Blenheim turned to face the heckler and mouthed some words that remained unheard and unknown to Delbert Marston. The expression on the face of the heckler changed suddenly. He raised his window and floored his gas pedal. The Nash sped away. Three kids in the backseat stared openmouthed at the gray-haired professor.

"Aurelia," Marston asked, "what did you say to them?"

"I just gave them a little warning, Delbert. Best keep your eyes on the road. I'll get us a little music." She reached for the radio controls on the Cord's dashboard. Although the radio had added to the price of Marston's Cord he had ordered it installed when he purchased the phaeton.

The sounds of Franz Liszt's *Mephisto Waltz* filled the Cord's tonneau.

A particularly dense sheet of rain mixed with a seeming bucketful of hailstones crashed against the Cord's roof and engine hood, adding the sound of an insane kettle drum concerto to the music.

"There's our exit sign," Aurelia Blenheim shouted above the din.

Delbert Marston edged into the exit lane and guided the Cord off the highway and onto a local thoroughfare. Aurelia Blenheim navigated for him, giving instructions until she finally said: "There it is. You can park in the driveway."

The house stood out like an anomaly. Curwen Street and its environs — still known as Curwen Heights — had once been among San Francisco's more fashionable neighborhoods. Victorian homes had reared their turrets and cupolas against the chilly air and damply cloying fog. Families who claimed the status of municipal pioneers, direct descendants of the leaders of the Gold Rush and survivors of the earthquake and fire of 1906, had erected gingerbread-encrusted mansions and filled them with children and servants. Carriage-houses and stables were discreetly placed behind the family establishments.

But the passing decades had brought changes to Curwen Street and Curwen Heights. Urban crowding had driven the wealthiest families to Palo Alto, Burlingame and other lush, roomy suburbs. The construction of the Golden Gate Bridge and Bay Bridge in the 1930's had opened the unspoiled territories and sleepy villages of Marin and Alameda Counties for the use of daily commuters. Key Route trains brought workers from Oakland and Berkeley into the city each day.

Marston switched off the engine and half-blackened headlights, and climbed from behind the steering wheel. He exited the car and helped Aurelia Blenheim to do the same. He carefully locked the vehicle's doors and escorted her to the front entrance of the house. In the darkened street and with storm clouds blackening the sky it was difficult to see anything. Even so, the house had the appearance of a onetime showplace, long since fallen into disrepair. Blackout curtains made the windows look like shrouded paintings. Marston searched for a doorbell and found none. Instead, a heavy cast-iron knocker shaped like a gargoyle signaled their arrival.

The door swung open and they were greeted by a rotund individual wearing thick, horn-rimmed glasses. He peered owlishly at Marston, then dropped his gaze to Aurelia Blenheim.

"Dr. Blenheim!" He took her hand in both of his and pumped it enthusiastically. After he released her she introduced Marston. The rotund youth identified himself as Charlie Einstein, "No relation," subjected Marston's hand to the same treatment Aurelia Blenheim's had received, and ushered them into the house.

Voices were emerging from another room, as was the odor of fried food. In the background a radio added to the din.

Charlie Einstein led Marston and Aurelia Blenheim to a high-ceilinged parlor. Men and women sat on worn furniture, each of them holding a plate of snack food or a beverage or both.

Einstein clapped his hands for attention and conversations wound down. The radio continued to play. Einstein said, "Ben, would you mind?" He gestured toward a Philco console. "You're the closest."

A painfully thin and painfully young-looking man in a navy uniform reached for the Philco and switched it off. "Nobody was paying attention anyhow," he said. He turned toward Marston and Aurelia Blenheim. "Aurelia, hello. And you must be Professor Marston."

Del Marston nodded.

"Ben Keeler," the sailor said. His spotless winter blues bore the eagle-and-chevron insignia of a petty officer. He shook Marston's hand. "We've been hearing about you for weeks now, sir. I'm so pleased that you could finally make it to a meeting."

Charlie Einstein set out to fetch beverages for Marston and Aurelia Blenheim. Keeler pointed out the others in the room, giving their names. Marston nodded to each.

One of them was a thirtyish woman whose mouse-brown sweater was a perfect match for her stringy hair. She was sitting next to the fireplace, where a log smoldered fitfully. "This is Bernice," Keeler announced. "Bernice Sanderson."

The woman looked up at Marston and Aurelia Blenheim. It was obvious that she knew Blenheim; they exchanged silent nods. "So you're the famous professor." She glared at Marston. "The skeptic who doesn't believe in anything he can't see for himself. You've got a lot to learn, professor."

She turned away.

Keeler took Marston by the elbow and steered him away. "Sorry about that, sir."

Marston interrupted. "Please, just call me Del."

"Fine." The sailor grinned. You know, I was an undergrad at Cal until we got into this war. I'm accustomed to calling professors, *Sir*." He reddened. "Or, *Ma'am*," Professor Bleinheim."

"Aurie."

"Yes." Keeler turned a brighter shade of red. "Anyway, once the war is over I plan to go back and finish up my degree."

Marston nodded. He saw that Keeler wore an engineer's rating on his uniform sleeve. "Good for you," he said. "There will be plenty of need for good engineers in the postwar world."

Keeler said, "Yes, sir. In fact — " He was interrupted by Charlie Einstein carrying a tray with two steaming cups on it. "I know Aurie likes these things and she told me that you did, too, Professor."

"Del."

"Right. Hot rum toddies. Good for a night like this."

When Einstein went on his way, Ben Keeler resumed. "I'd hoped to have you as my faculty adviser when I get to grad school. If I'm not being too pushy, that is."

Marston shook his head. "I'm flattered. Sure, come and see me when the war's over. I envy you, Ben, serving in the Navy. You just went down and enlisted when Pearl Harbor was attacked?"

"I thought it was the right thing to do. In fact, I'd have thought that a man with your credentials would have a commission. If you don't mind my saying so, Professor. Del."

Marston sipped at his rum toddy. "They turned me down. Said I couldn't march right, and besides, they wanted me to hang around and lend my expertise when they had problems for me to play with. Said I was more valuable as a civilian than I would be in the Navy."

Keeler nodded sympathetically.

Marston breathed a sigh of relief. The rum couldn't be that strong and fast-acting, it was just careless of him to mention not being able to march right. He'd been born with minor deformities of both feet. They'd never kept him from normal activities, in fact he felt that they helped him as a swimmer. But the navy doctors had taken one look at his feet and told him to go home and find a way to contribute to the war effort as a civilian.

Still, the Navy had accepted him as a consultant, calling upon his expertise as a marine geologist and hydrologist. He'd received a high security clearance and worked with naval personnel whenever he wasn't busy teaching. He looked around, observing that nearly everyone in the room was young. Aurelia Blenheim had persuaded Marston to attend a meeting, but this looked more like a party. There were plates of snack foot scattered around the room and bottles of soft drinks. There was a low, steady hum of conversation. Marston spotted only two girls among the crowd, discounting the acerbic Miss Sanderson. Outnumbered as they were by males, they were twin centers of constant attention and maneuvering.

A fireplace dominated one end of the room. A young man of neurasthenic appearance wearing a baggy suit and hand-painted necktie had stationed himself in front of it. He held a brass bell and miniature hammer above his head and sounded the bell.

"The twelfth regular meeting of the New Deep Ones Society of the Pacific will come to order." He looked around, clearly pleased with himself. Conversation had ceased and he was the target of all eyes. "We have a distinguished guest with us tonight, Professor Marston of the University of California. If anyone can shed light on the problem of the Deep Ones, I'm sure Professor Marston can."

Now attention shifted from the young man to Del Marston. What a farce this was turning into. Marston mulled over suitable forms of revenge against Aurelia Blenheim.

"Professor Marston," the young man was babbling on, "perhaps you'll be willing to address our little group."

Marston was holding a thick sandwich in one hand and a soft drink in the other. He put them on a table and said, "I'm afraid I'm not quite prepared for that. Maybe you'll tell me a little bit about your group, starting with your name."

"Albert Hartley, Dr. Marston. I'm the President of the New Deep Ones Society of the Pacific. Our members are dedicated to unraveling the mystery of the Deep Ones. Hence our name." He giggled nervously, then resumed.

"And Dr. Blenheim says that you're the leading marine geologist in the region."

"Dr. Blenheim flatters me. But tell me about your New Deep Ones Society. Does the name refer to the fact that you're all deep thinkers?"

"Now you flatter us," Hartley replied. They had settled onto chairs and sofas by now, the boys clustering around the girls while Albert Hartley tried to hold their attention. "The Deep Ones," (Marston could almost hear the capital letters) "are strange creatures who live on the sea-bottoms of the world. People have known about them for thousands of years. They're in Greek mythology, Sumerian mythology, African mythology. And in modern times authors keep writing about them. But nowadays they have to disguise their books as fiction."

"Why?"

Hartley looked startled. The room was silent.

Then somebody else made an ostentatious demand for the floor. Del Marston recognized the new speaker as Charlie Einstein. The ponderous Einstein blew out a breath. "There are people in the government who don't want us to know about the Deep Ones. People in every government. You wouldn't think that the Nazis in Germany and the Reds in Russia and the Democrats in Washington could agree on anything while they're fighting this huge war and all, but they have secret meetings in Switzerland, you know. The Japs are there, too."

"You mean the war is a front for something else?" Marston asked. "Cities getting blown up, soldiers dying in foxholes, aerial and naval battles, people suffering all over the world — it's all a put-up job?"

Einstein shook his head, his too-long, dirty-blonde hair falling across his face. "Oh, the war is real enough, okay. My brother is in the Army, he was at Tobruk in North Africa and was wounded and he's back in England now, in the hospital. The war is real, you bet, Dr. Marston. But the big shots who are running things still have their secret agreements. You'll see, when it ends, nothing much will change. And they really don't want us to know about the Deep Ones. Lovecraft wrote about them, too. In fact, he was writing about them even before that Czech guy, Karel Capek, wrote his book *War with the Newts*. They're everywhere. Lovecraft was a New Englander and he knew about them, they have a big base at Innsmouth, in Massachusetts."

"But that was just fiction." Marston tried to calm the excited youngsters. "Foolish stories about monsters. As silly as Orson Welles' radio play about Martians. There are problems enough in this world without having to invent more."

"Oh, no. Oh, no." Einstein shook his head. His fleshy jowls shook with emotion. "And another thing. There's the 1890 Paradox."

"The what?" Marston could barely keep from laughing.

"The 1890 Paradox," Einstein repeated. "Karel Capek was born in 1890 in Bohemia, in what is now Czechoslovakia. Howard Phillips Lovecraft was born in Rhode Island. And Adolf Hitler was born in Linz, Austria. You can't call that a coincidence, can you?"

"Of course I can." Marston frowned. "Millions of people are born every year. You can pick any year out of history and find musicians, authors, politicians, scientists, generals, philosophers, all born that year. Of course it's a coincidence."

After a moment he added, "Besides, I'm pretty sure that Hitler was born in 1889, not 1890. Do you have an encyclopedia here? Let's look it up."

Einstein looked pained. "Well, 1890, 1889, those records aren't exactly reliable. It's close enough, Dr. Marston."

Marston smiled and waited for Einstein to go on.

"Then what about their deaths? Lovecraft and Capek both wrote about the Deep Ones, both exposed their intentions, and both died within a matter of months! Explain that for me, if you can, Dr. Marston."

"I can't explain it. There's no explaining to do. Out of all the millions of people born in 1890, I imagine that tens or hundreds of thousands would have died in — what year was it that your two writers passed on?"

"Lovecraft died in 1937, Capek in 1938."

"And Hitler?"

"You know he's still alive. That's because the stars were right for those births in 1889 and 1890, and they were right for the two deaths in 1937 and '38. As for Hitler — he's no menace to the Deep Ones. It wouldn't surprise me if he's in league with them. Malignant beings have a long history of making alliances with humans willing to sell out their species for personal gain, like vampires offering their sort of undead immortality to their human servants. And the Deep Ones have a lot to offer their allies. Long, long life for one thing. And incredible pleasures obtained through their unspeakable rites. That's what the Deep Ones have to offer."

"And we believe they're here, Dr. Marston." This from Albert Hartley, taking back the center of attention. He was interrupted by a middle aged woman who entered the room wearing a housedress and apron. "There's coffee and cocoa on the stove for anybody who wants them," she announced.

Hartley looked exasperated. "Thanks, Mom. Not right now, please."

The woman withdrew.

"They're out in the Bay, even as we speak," Hartley resumed. "They have a whole city down there. When people disappear, when you hear about people jumping off the new bridge to Marin, the Deep Ones are involved in that."

Marston frowned. It was hard to take these kids seriously but he had promised Aurelia Blenheim and he was going to do his best. "I think the jumpers are suicides."

"That's what you're supposed to think. The Deep Ones, they're amphibians. Lovecraft said so in his writings. They look like regular people at first. They grow up among us, they could be anybody. Then as they get older they start to show their true nature. It's called the Innsmouth Look. They start to resemble frogs or toads. Eventually they have to go back to the sea, to live with their own people."

Marston picked up his abandoned sandwich and took a bite. Mom Hartley made good snacks, anyway. The sandwich was spiced salami and crisp lettuce with a really sharp mustard, served on hard-crusted sourdough. Marston had a good appetite, and besides, chewing earnestly away at Mom Hartley's salami sandwich gave him an excuse not to answer young Albert Hartley's wild assertions.

Now a girl sitting surrounded by boys spoke up. "My name is Narda Long, Dr. Marston."

Del Marston nodded.

"We don't think that there has to be war with the Deep Ones." Narda wore her medium brown hair in curls. Her face would be pretty, Marston decided, in a few years when she shed her baby fat. It would help her figure, too. For now, she filled her pink blouse and plaid skirt a bit more amply than she might, but in this crowd anyone young and female would get all the attention she wanted.

The room was filled with a buzz. Apparently the New Deep Ones Society was divided between those who thought they could make league with the wet folk and those who considered the amphibians the implacable enemies of land-dwellers.

"If we'd just make friends with them, I'm sure they'd leave us alone. Or even help us. Who knows what treasures there are in the sea, on the sea bottom, and we probably have things here on land that would help them."

"That's right." The boy sitting next to Narda Long agreed. "We have these battles and we go shooting torpedoes around and we set off depth charges, we're probably ruining their cities. No wonder they're mad at us."

"What can you tell us about the Deep Ones, Dr. Marston?" The only other non-hostile girl in the room, a freckled redhead, asked.

Marston shook his head. "I think you invited the wrong person to your meeting. You need a folklorist or maybe a mystic. Somebody from the Classics Department might be good. I'm just a marine geologist. I study things like underwater volcanism and seismology, and their effect on shore structures and the way bodies of water behave. It's all pretty dry stuff."

Nobody got the joke.

The debate went on, the let's-be-friends-with-the-frogs group versus the it's-a-fight-to-the-finish group. Finally Del Marston looked at his watch and exchanged a signal with Aurelia Blenheim.

"I'm sorry but I have to teach an early class tomorrow," she announced. "You know, we old folks can't stay up as late as we used to, not if we're going to go to work in the morning."

*

"Thanks for getting us out of there," Marston addressed Aurelia Blenheim. "Another five minutes and I was about ready to take a couple of those young blockheads and knock their skulls together."

Aurelia Blenheim laughed. "They weren't that bad, Delbert. They're young, they can't help that, and a certain amount of foolish passion goes with the territory."

"I suppose so," Marston grumbled. "And a couple of them even seemed moderately intelligent. The only one who seemed sensible was the young sailor — what was his name?"

"Ben Keeler. You weren't just impressed by his hero-worshipping attitude, by any chance."

"Not in the least. Sincere and merited admiration is never misplaced and is always appreciated."

"What a lovely aphorism." Aurelia Blenheim leaned forward and switched on the Cord's radio. The phaeton had cleared the Bay Bridge, the structural steel and giant cables of which would have interfered with reception. A late-night broadcaster was rhapsodizing about the progress of General Clark's forces in Italy and the successes of Admiral Nimitz's fleet against the Japanese. The announcer must have been local because he went on to talk about Nimitz's pre-war connection with the University of California in Berkeley.

When the news broadcast ended Marston switched to a station playing a Mozart clarinet piece. "You don't really think those kids have something, do you?" he asked his companion.

"I try to keep an open mind."

Marston asked, not for the first time, how his friend had first encountered the New Deep Ones. As usual she referred to a vague relationship between herself and Mrs. Hartley. "We went to school together a million years ago. I was in her wedding. Poor Walter, her husband, was on a sub that went down in the Pacific. She carries on and I try to keep her spirits up."

"And you really do have a class in the morning," Marston commented. He drove through Berkeley, dropped her at her home on Garber Street and returned to his home on Brookside Drive.

He refused further invitations to attend meetings of the New Deep Ones. His feet were bothering him and walking had become difficult and uncomfortable if not downright painful. And he was having problems with his jaw and teeth. He consulted his dentist and his medical doctor alternately. Each reported that he could find no source for Marston's difficulties and referred him to the other.

Marston worked at his office on campus, solving problems brought to him from local naval installations. He reduced his social schedule until he was a near recluse, moving between his bachelor's bungalow and his office on the university campus. He met requests for his company with increasingly abrasive refusals until the day he realized he was excluded from faculty cocktail parties and all but the most compulsory of campus events.

The conversation he had in part overheard, in part contributed to, at the meeting of the New Deep Ones preyed on his mind. Several times he sought out Aurelia Blenheim, by now not only his longest-enduring acquaintance but virtually his only friend. Over a cup of coffee or a glass of wine he queried her about Selena Hartley, young Albert's mother. At least Aurelia Blenheim had revealed her friend's first name.

Her maiden name had been Curwen. She was a native San Franciscan, descended from the founder of Curwen Heights. She had married Walter at the height of the tumultuous Roaring Twenties and had struggled at his side through the years of the Depression to preserve their relationship and to keep the old house, built by the original Eben Curwen in the previous century, in the family.

Beyond that, Aurelia Blenheim had no information to share with Delbert Marston.

Naval Intelligence had ferreted out Japanese plans to send submarines against the West Coast of the United States. To Marston this made no sense. Earlier in the war, after the Japanese had decimated the US Pacific Fleet at Pearl Harbor and had conquered the Philippines and Wake Island, it would have made sense. But the Japanese were being forced back by General MacArthur's island hopping campaign and General LeMay's fire-bombing of the home islands.

An antisubmarine net had been strung across the Golden Gate in 1942, when a direct attack by Admiral Yamamoto's forces seemed imminent. The attack had never come, but the Navy had been spooked by their intelligence and Marston was called on to help design a new and improved underwater defense line. Knowing the Navy, the war would be over before the new defenses were built and the defenses would be outdated before another war could make them useful, but Marston was not one to shirk his duty.

He spent his days touring the Bay and the Golden Gate in naval motor launches, alternating the excursions with long days at the desk calculator and the drawing board. His nights he spent in his living room, looking out over Brookside Drive, listening to music, and drinking scotch whiskey. It was almost impossible to find good single malt nowadays, far more difficult than it had been during the laughably ineffective Prohibition of Marston's youth. He shuddered at the thought of having to switch to blended swill.

As walking became increasingly painful he spent more hours in the University pool. Even sitting in an easy chair or lying in bed he had to deal with discomfort, and the ongoing changes in his jaw and teeth made eating a nasty chore. He was losing his teeth one by one, and new ones were emerging in their place. He'd heard of people getting a third set of teeth, it was a rare but not-unknown phenomenon. His own new teeth were triangular in shape and razor-sharp. Only when he had slipped into the waters of the pool did the pain in his extremities ease, and even his mouth felt less discomfort.

Yet he was drawing unwelcome glances in the changing area at the pool. He altered his routine, suiting up at home and wearing baggy clothing over his trunks until he reached the locker room. There he would doff his outer costume and plunge into the water, staying beneath the surface as long as he could before rising for air. As time passed he found himself able to stay under for longer periods. He ascribed this to the practice of almost daily swims.

One day he stayed under for a period that must have set his personal record. When he surfaced he was the center of attention. One of the other swimmers muttered, "Say, you must have been down there for five or six minutes. How do you do that?"

Marston growled an answer, then hastened to his locker, pulled his baggy clothing on over his wet body and dripping suit, and headed for home.

That night he drove to the Berkeley Marina. He parked his Cord, looked around and ascertained that he was alone. He walked to the water's edge, disrobed, and slipped into the Bay. The water was icy but somehow it eased the now-constant ache in his legs and feet. His hands, too, seemed to be changing their shape in some small, subtle way. They were uncomfortable, as well. He wondered if he was developing arthritis.

He swam out toward Angel Island. He had no way of knowing just how far he had gone or how long he had remained submerged, but he felt that it must have been fifteen or twenty minutes. He broke surface and realized that he was not out of breath. In fact, he had to force himself to inhale the fog-drenched night air. His neck itched and he rubbed it with his hands, feeling horizontal ridges of muscle that he had never noticed before.

He looked around, searching for landmarks, but the enforced wartime blackout precluded the use of bright lights in the cities that lined San Francisco Bay. He made out the silhouette of the Bay Bridge against the sky, then that of the Golden Gate Bridge. He turned in the water, recognizing the forbidding fortifications of Alcatraz. Without inhaling again he ducked beneath the surface and swam back toward the Berkeley shoreline. In time he waded from the cold, brackish waters of the Bay. By contrast, the night air felt warm against his body. He shook like a dog to rid himself of water, pulled on his clothing, and drove home.

In the Brookside Drive cottage he drew a polished captain's chair to an open window. Through the window he could hear the soft gurgle of the nearby stream that gave the thoroughfare its name. Odd, Marston thought, that he had never noticed this before. The sound brought with it a melancholy, pleasant feeling. He thought of putting a record on the turntable, had even selected Handel's *Music for the Royal Fireworks*, and pouring himself a scotch while he listened to the recording, but instead brought a pillow from his bedroom and placed it on the living room carpet.

He lay down in darkness and closed his eyes, letting the sound of the stream fill his consciousness. He fell asleep and dreamed of dark waters, strange creatures and ancient cities beneath the sea. He awoke the following morning and staggered to the mirror in his bedroom. He brushed water from his hair.

By the end of May, in normal times, the university's spring semester would have ended and the students departed, leaving Berkeley a quiet suburb of Oakland instead of the bustling community of scholars it became during the academic year. But in wartime the military had set up accelerated programs for the education of junior officers, and the University of California was on a year-round schedule.

Delbert Marston's assignments from his naval superiors had changed as well. The computations and design of the antisubmarine defenses were completed and construction was well under way. The data provided to Marston now was peculiar and the requested analytical reports were more peculiar than ever. In Europe the long-anticipated cross-channel invasion had taken place and Allied forces were pushing the Wehrmacht back toward Germany. In the Pacific Japanese troops were resisting with fanatical dedication, whole units dying to the last soldier rather than raise the flag of surrender.

But as the Office of War Information reminded the American public, the conflict was far from over. The Germans had developed flying bombs and rocket weapons and were using them against Allied forces in France and Belgium, and sending them to wreak havoc in England. If they could develop longer-range models, even the US would be in danger. A Nazi super-scientist named Heisenberg was rumored to be developing a weapon of unprecedented power that could be delivered to New York by a jet-propelled flying wing bomber. The whole thing seemed like a scenario from a Fritz Lang movie.

Still, Marston made his way to his office each morning, laboring on feet that sent agony lancing up his increasingly deformed legs. Once at work he found it hard even to hold a pencil, relying on an assistant to take dictation rather than try to write up his own notes. He seldom spoke with anyone save his naval superiors and assistants.

His only pleasures were his solitary, nocturnal excursions beneath the surface of the Bay. He no longer bothered with the fiction of breathing air once he entered the Bay, relying on water inhaled through his now wide mouth and expelled through the gill slits in his neck once his body had extracted its oxygen content.

He saw shapes beneath the water now, sometimes dark, sometimes sickly luminescent. At first he avoided them, then he began to pursue them. He couldn't make out their shapes well, either, although as time passed he began to develop more acute vision in the dark medium. From time to time one of the shapes would swim toward him, then flash aside when he reached out to touch it.

One night he found one of the creatures drifting aimlessly a few feet beneath the surface. He swam to it and saw that it was more or less human in shape but clearly not human. He reached for it and it did not flash away. Once he grasped it he realized that it was dead, its flesh horribly torn as if it had been caught in the propeller of a passing ship. Even as he studied the strange cadaver two more shapes flashed into sight and snatched it from his grasp, moving first out of his reach and then out of his sight.

But he had touched the remains. The flesh was white and stringy, the skin as smooth and slick as that of a giant frog.

Despite the changes he was undergoing he managed to maintain the pretense of normality, taking his meals, filling his Cord Phaeton with precious, rationed gasoline, sending his laundry out to be done, keeping his modest lodgings in order.

Late one Saturday afternoon he nearly collided with Aurelia Blenheim while pushing a shopping cart in the aisle of the grocery store nearest his home. He was shocked at her haggard appearance. How long had it been since their last meeting? How could she have aged so badly? He thought of his own changed appearance and wondered if he looked as worrisome to Aurelia as she to him.

The expression on Aurelia Blenheim's face showed shock and deep concern. "Delbert," the elderly woman exclaimed, "are you all right?"

"Of course I am."

"But you look so — are you certain?"

"Yes," he growled. He should have turned and left the store the instant he spotted Blenheim, but he had failed to act and now he was caught. "I'm just a little tired," he explained. "Very tired, in fact. The war. So much work."

"I'm coming to your house," Blenheim asserted. "I'm going to make dinner for you. You're not taking care of yourself. You're headed for the hospital if you don't get yourself together. You should be ashamed!"

When they reached Marston's cottage he turned his key in the door lock and stood aside to let Aurelia Blenheim enter first. Marston carried the bag of groceries Blenheim had helped him select. She had even loaned him a few ration stamps and tokens to complete his purchase.

The selection of foodstuffs was far more extensive than the Spartan diet Marston had been living on in recent months. In fact he occasionally supplemented his nourishment during his nocturnal swims in the Bay. That body was densely populated with marine species that throve in its cold, brackish waters. Marston became ravenous when he came upon the abalone, eels, crabs, clams and small octopods that lurked in the silted seabed. When he came upon one he would devour it raw, fresh, and sometimes living. His new teeth could pierce the shell of a living crab as if it were paper.

Just inside the doorway Aurelia Blenheim bent over and picked up a buff-colored envelope. "Here's a telegram for you, Delbert."

He took the envelope from her and opened it. The message was typed in capital letters on strips of buff paper and glued to the message form. The telegram came from a Captain Kinne, commanding officer of the Naval Weapons Station at Port Chicago, a village on the shore of Suisun Bay, an extension of San Francisco Bay fed by the Sacramento River.

The message itself was terse. It directed Marston to report to the commanding officer's headquarters first thing Monday morning. In traditional naval fashion Marston was told to show up at or about 0600 hours, on or about 3 July 1944. Marston had never heard of anyone in the Navy arriving after the designated time and date with the excuse that he had arrived "about" the indicated time.

Aurelia Blenheim steered Marston into an easy chair and carried the bag of groceries into his kitchen. She had visited the Brookside Drive cottage before, although months had passed since her last visit. Marston put some light music on the turntable, an RCA Red Seal 12-inch recording of *Vltava* by the tragic Bohemian madman Bedrich Smetana.

With astonishing speed Blenheim produced a tempting bouillabaisse. The odor coming from the kitchen was mouthwatering and the flavor of the marine stew proved delicious. The only problem, for Marston, was that everything seemed overdone. He would have preferred to consume the aquatic creatures uncooked.

After dinner they relaxed in Marston's living room with glasses of prewar brandy. Jokingly, Aurelia Blenheim asked why Marston's mother hadn't taught him to take better care of himself. When he reacted to the question with frowning silence the older woman set down her glass and took his free hand between both of hers. "I'm sorry. I didn't mean to upset you."

Marston drew away. Of late his arthritis had become worse. The last joints of his fingers and toes had curled downwards and his finger- and toenails seemed to be turning into claws. He worked to keep them trimmed but they grew back rapidly. The small triangles of flesh between the bases of his digits were growing, also, a change that proved helpful in water but embarrassing in public.

Desperate to draw attention away from his increasing physical abnormalities, Marston said, "No, I'm afraid she didn't."

Blenheim frowned, "Who didn't what?"

"My mother. She never taught me to take care of myself. She never taught me anything. I never knew her. My father told me that she loved to swim. They lived in Chicago and she would swim in Lake Michigan all year round. She joined a group, they called themselves the Polar Bear Club, and they would plunge into the lake every New Year's Day, no matter how cold it was, even if it was snowing. But that was just a stunt. They used to get their picture in the Chicago *Times* and the *Tribune* and the *Sun*. But Mother took it all very seriously. The photographers loved her, she was the only female Polar Bear."

He took a deep draught of golden liqueur.

"She was an immigrant," he resumed. "I never knew where she was born. Father just said it was a cold country. I was born on December 25, you know," he changed the subject. "I was a Christmas baby." He said it with bitterness. "Father brought Mother and me home from the hospital on New Year's Eve. The next day Mother insisted on her annual plunge with the other Polar Bears. They used to run out into the lake, throw themselves into the surf, frisk for a few minutes and then come running back out of the water. But Mother swam out. Snow was falling, Father told me, and visibility was poor. Mother just swam out into the lake. They sent search parties after her but they never found her."

"I'm so sorry," Aurelia Blenheim said. She started again to reach for his hand, then drew back, avoiding a repetition of his previous withdrawal. After a moment she said, "Did your father ever remarry?"

Marston shook his head. "He raised me alone, as best he could, until he was gunned down when I was six. I had no other relatives and I wound up bouncing from one orphanage to another until I went out on my own."

"But you've made such a success of yourself, Delbert. I never know about your childhood. How sad. But look at you now, a tenured professor, a respected member of the community. I'm so proud of you, and you should be proud of yourself."

She insisted on clearing the dishes and cleaning up Marston's kitchen. She returned to the living room and said, "You know I live nearby. I'll just walk home, it's such a warm evening. Please promise me you'll take better care of yourself. And let me know how things work out at Port Chicago. As much as the Navy lets you tell me, of course."

He stood on his lawn and watched until she disappeared. He returned to his house and filled another snifter of brandy, then sipped until it was gone. The summer evening was long and he was in agony by the time full darkness descended. Then he left the house and drove to the marina. He parked, disrobed at the water's edge and slipped into the Bay.

Monday morning he rose early and drove to Port Chicago. The naval base consisted mainly of warehouses and barracks. A railroad spur ran onto a pier that extended into the Bay. Even at this early hour he could see crews of colored stevedores in navy fatigues working to move munitions from railroad cars to the hold of a ship moored to the side of the pier. The stevedores were supervised by white men in officers' uniforms.

A guard had demanded to see Marston's identification and the telegram summoning him to the base. Once satisfied, the guard directed Marston to the headquarters building, a wood-frame structure badly in need of fresh paint. Once inside he was escorted by a smartly-uniformed WAVE into the commander's office.

Captain Kinne looked as if he had stepped out of a bandbox. Every crease in his uniform was knife-sharp, every button glistened.

Marston of course wore civilian garb, the academic uniform of tweed jacket, flannel slacks and button-down shirt. He had replaced his customary striped necktie with a scarf that concealed his gill-slits and added a pair of oversized dark glasses. He stood in front of Captain Kinne's desk wondering whether he was expected to salute or shake hands. The WAVE introduced him and Kinne looked up at him. "You're Marston, eh?"

He said, "I am."

"All right, I just wanted to get a look at you. Tell a lot about a man with one look. You'll do. What happened to your hands, Marston? Some kind of tropical disease? Jungle rot?"

Marston started to answer but Kinne went on.

"Jaspers," he addressed the WAVE, "take Mr. Marston down the hall. Give him to Keeler." He turned back to Marston and nodded curtly. "Go with Jaspers. Keeler will tell you what to do. Thanks for coming."

The WAVE, obviously Jaspers, led Marston to another office. She halted and knocked at the door, then turned the knob and opened the door a few inches. "Mr. Marston is here, sir."

She gestured and Marston stepped past her into the office. He heard Jaspers close the door behind him. He found himself in a smaller office now, surrounded by charts and manuals. The man who stood up to greet him wore a set of summer khakis with the twin tracks of a Navy lieutenant on the collar.

"A real pleasure to see you again, Dr. Marston. After that little party in Curwen Heights I was afraid you wouldn't want anything to do with us."

"Ben Keeler?" Marston said. "You've certainly risen fast. You were a junior petty officer the last time I saw you."

Keeler grinned. "Petty Officer Third Ben Keeler, Lieutenant Benjamin Keeler, same fellow. ONI put me in that EM's uniform to check out the New Deep Ones Society. They were pretty worried at one point, those kids were getting too close to the truth and Naval Intelligence wanted them steered off. That was my job. I still attend their meetings, by the way. If you ever want to come by again, I'd love some moral support. Just don't blow my cover."

"All right," Marston smiled. "I wouldn't want to get you in trouble with Naval Intelligence."

"And they're just a bunch of harmless eccentrics, you know," Keeler added. He walked around the desk and put his arm on Marston's shoulders. "Take a walk with me, Dr. Marston. There are some things you need to see, and then some questions I'll want to ask you."

Marston acceded, determined not to show the pain that he knew he was in for. At Keeler's side he made his way along the pier. A freighter stood in the middle of Suisun Bay, black smoke pouring from its stacks. It would clear the Golden Gate before noon, Marston knew, *en route* to the soldiers and marines fighting the Japanese in the Pacific. An empty ship had already taken the place of the freighter on one side of the pier, while another, opposite it, received pallets and crates of munitions.

As they moved past work gangs Keeler took salutes from ensigns and petty officers supervising the stevedores. The latter continued to work as Marston and Keeler passed.

At the end of the pier they halted. A breeze had kicked up and the surface of Suisun Bay had turned choppy.

Marston gestured back toward the work gangs they had passed. "All of the stevedores are Negroes, all of the officers are white," he commented. The question was implicit.

"That's Navy policy," Keeler said. "Not very long ago the Navy was trying to get rid of all its Negroes, even though they were just mess-men and laundry workers. Filipinos make better workers. But there's too much pressure from Washington, finally the service gave in. And these colored stevedores are pretty good, as long as you keep a close eye on them."

They turned to face the buildings of Port Chicago. "What we're concerned about, Del, is a very special cargo that we're going to ship out this month."

Marston nodded, then waited for Keeler to continue.

"It's a very special bomb. It's coming in by train next week, and Captain Kinne wanted to get your help in handling it."

Marston shook his head. "What do I know about bombs?"

"Oh, we have plenty of people who know about bombs," Keeler grinned. "We need somebody who knows hydrology and submarine geology to keep this baby safe."

"What is it, something bigger than the ones LeMay is dropping on Japan? The closer we get to the home islands, the easier it's going to be to hit 'em."

"No," Keeler shook his head. "This is something different. Look, everybody knows that we're close to finishing off the European war. Ike took a big risk with the Normandy landings but that was a big success and Patton and Montgomery are rolling through France. Italy's out of the game. And the Russians are closing in on the Nazis from the East. It's just a matter of time now."

"And in the Pacific, too, don't you agree, Benjamin?"

"But we're taking terrible losses. The President is up for reelection this November and those casualties are going to hurt him. He's put pressure on the War Department and the Navy Department to give him this bigger, better bomb. We figure once we drop a couple of these babies on Japan, maybe one on Tokyo and one on Kobe, even the fanatical Nips will cave in. Washington doesn't want to have to invade the home islands, don't you see. That's what this is all about, Del."

There was a moment of silence as a zephyr swept in from the Bay, bringing the smell of brine and brackish waters with it. Then the wind shifted and the clatter of tools, the sound of voices, the roar of donkey engines came to them from the ships and the railroad cars.

"And there's another thing," Keeler added. "You know Uncle Sam didn't much care for the Bolshies when they first took over Russia twenty-five years ago. President Wilson even sent some troops over there. The government doesn't like to talk about that any more now that Joe Stalin is our buddy but you know we took sides in their civil war and we picked a loser."

"That was a long time ago," Marston put in.

The combination of the choppy Bay and the increasingly brisk breeze whipped up a spray of salt-flavored water that pelted onto the pier and onto Keeler and Marston. Keeler pulled a bandanna from his uniform trousers pocket and wiped his face, frowning. Marston licked his lips. He felt hugely refreshed.

"The US wouldn't even recognize the new government in Russia until Roosevelt came in, and there are still a lot of powerful men in Washington who don't trust Stalin and his gang. They want to get this new bomb and use it before the war is over as a warning to the Reds not to get too big for their britches."

He hooked his arm through Marston's and the two men strolled back along the pier, returning finally to Keeler's office. Keeler said, "Will you get to work on this, Del? Captain Kinne has already worked it out with his counterparts, you'll be excused from your other duties until the special bomb is safely out on the ocean, on its way to a bomber base in the islands. We need your analysis and your recommendations about the seabed and waters from here to the Farralons. And we need your report before that ship moves. The bomb is coming in next week, and we need to get it out of here on the *Quinalt Victory*. Our Negroes will be working on the *Bryan* most of the time; that will serve as cover for the bomb going out on the *Quinalt*."

Keeler opened a safe and extracted a pass for Marston. "This will get you anywhere on the base," he said. "Guard it, Del, it could be dangerous if it got away from you."

Marston accepted the pass, slipped it into his pocket and left.

He spent the next few days alternating between Port Chicago and the University campus in Berkeley, studying the physical layout at Suisun Bay and existing charts and studies of the area. He could hardly hold himself back from examining the seabed in person, but he resisted the temptation until he felt ready.

Then he drove from Berkeley to Port Chicago after dark, parked the Cord, and walked out to the pier. The work here went on around the clock, seven days a week. There was no way he could use the pier without being observed, so he informed the young officer supervising the loading work of his intentions.

At the end of the pier he left his clothing, climbed down a ladder, and slipped into the water.

The Bay water was cold and dark and as it welcomed him he felt the aches leave his body and limbs. He had always been a strong swimmer; now, the webbing between his fingers and between his toes turned him into a virtual amphibian. His eyes, too, had developed a sensitivity that permitted him to maneuver in the dark, brackish water.

He spotted a huge dark-green crab scuttling toward a large rock on the seabed. The creature didn't have a chance. Marston's new, powerful jaw and strong, triangular teeth crunched through its shell. The living meat was sweet and the juices of the crab were more delicious than the finest liquor.

Marston saw human-like forms swimming nearby and pursued them. Ever since his encounter with the dead creature he had wondered about these beings. They might be a species of giant batrachian hitherto unknown to science, far larger than any recorded frog or toad; perhaps they were survivors of a species of amphibian that had evolved eons ago only to disappear from most of the world.

He swam after them and they permitted him to approach them but not to establish direct contact. They swam with the current created by the waters of the Sacramento River as it emptied into Suisun Bay. They looked back from time to time as if to encourage Marston to follow them, but the speed and stamina with which they swam far exceeded even his enhanced abilities.

Finally he gave up and swam back toward the loading pier and the two ships at Port Chicago.

He climbed the ladder, then drew himself onto the pier. The young ensign he had spoken with earlier greeted him with a shake of his head. "I was getting pretty worried," the ensign said. "Do you know how long you were gone, sir? And do you realize how cold the Bay is, and how tricky the currents can be?"

Marston didn't feel like talking with this youngster but he managed a few polite words. Yes, he knew exactly what he was doing, he had never been in danger, there was nothing to worry about but he appreciated the ensign's concern.

During the brief conversation he had been pulling his clothing back on. He had purchased new shoes, as wide as he could find, to accommodate his newly altered feet. Even so, it was fiercely painful to force his feet into them.

He repeated his activities each night. The underwater creatures gradually grew accustomed to him, permitting him to approach ever more closely, permitting him to accompany them farther and farther from Port Chicago. It was clear to Marston that they communicated with one another, mainly by means of subtle gestures made with their broad, webbed, clawed hands. Marston inferred that they had a language as sophisticated and complex as any spoken by land-dwellers.

Now that he was affiliated with the Port Chicago base Marston had discontinued all contacts with his former associates in Berkeley. He did not worry about running into Aurelia Blenheim at the grocery as he now relied entirely on a diet of creatures he encountered during his nocturnal explorations of the Bay's waters.

He maintained a relationship with Lieutenant Keeler and though him with Captain Kinne, furnishing reports and recommendations as required of him. He resented every meeting he had to attend, every conversation he had to conduct; in fact, he found himself living for his submarine excursions and suffering through each hour he spent walking on land, breathing with his gradually atrophying lungs instead of his gills.

On Friday, July 14, Keeler demanded that Marston attend a meeting with Captain Kinne. Also present were two high-ranking officers, one from the Navy and the other from the Army, the latter with Army Air Force insignia on his uniform blouse, and the commanders of the Negro stevedoring gangs.

Captain Kinne's WAVE secretary, Jaspers, ushered Marston into the commanding officer's area. When the meeting participants were assembled they were joined by a pair of armed shore patrolmen and the doors securely locked.

"The bomb will arrive in forty-eight hours," the army officer announced. A major general's paired silver stars glittered on his uniform shoulders. "We will deliver it to the loading pier, then we need a sign-off from the Navy and our job is finished."

"And ours begins," the naval officer took over. His uniform sleeves bore the broad gold stripes of a rear admiral. "Captain Kinne, are your men ready to get the bomb stowed in *Quinalt Victory* Monday evening? ONI insists that we do the loading at night, but it must be finished in time to catch the late tide out of the Golden Gate." The admiral cast a sharp look at Marston. "Dr. Marston has provided all the information we'll need to get *Quinalt Victory* safely out of the Bay and on her way by midnight?"

The utterance was worded as a statement but spoken as a question.

"We have everything, sir," Keeler furnished.

"All right. Let's go over the complete plan again," The admiral growled. "There must be no slip-ups, I can't emphasize that too much."

They spent the rest of the day going over the details of unloading the special bomb from its railroad car and loading it into the hold of the *Quinalt Victory* without a hitch. A squad of white-jacketed mess-men served coffee and rolls at midmorning and a full meal at noon. No one left the meeting for any reason. Marston was able to pass up the coffee and rolls but by lunch time he was forced to consume a few sips of beverage and half a sandwich. This disgusted him.

When the meeting ended he drove into Port Chicago. He had seen the town fleetingly each day but today for the first time he parked his Cord and walked through the town. He found a motion picture theater and purchased a ticket. They were running a long program, the dramatic film *Lifeboat* with Tallulah Bankhead and Canada Lee, the lightweight *Bathing Beauty* with Esther Williams, a newsreel and a chapter of "Crash" Corrigan's old serial, *Undersea Kingdom*.

Once inside he settled into a seat and unlaced his shoes, finding a modicum of relief for his aching feet. He leaned back and studied the neon-ringed clock mounted high on one wall of the auditorium. Most of the patrons were servicemen in uniform, whiling away their off-duty hours. None of them were colored, of course. Negroes were excluded from the theater and from the town's plain restaurants. They had to find their own entertainment, or make it.

Marston ignored the images on the screen and closed his eyes. Images of undersea life swam through his mind, the peace and serenity of the submarine world contrasting with the pain and violence that dominated the world of the land-dwellers.

After a while he opened his eyes and glanced at the illuminated clock-face. Even in the long July evening, darkness would have fallen by now.

He drove back to the naval base, showed his pass to the gate-guard, and parked as near to the water's edge as he could. He carefully locked the Cord and walked to the base of the pier. A special guard had been placed there, and even Marston's special pass could not gain him access to the pier.

Instead he walked back to his car, unlocked the door and climbed inside. He disrobed, left the car again, and walked undiscovered to the edge of the Bay. He slipped into the Bay and swam away from the shore.

He made his way to the cold, flowing water that he knew came from the Sacramento River. The river water had less flavor than the Bay water. With a start Marston realized that he had never experienced the richness of the Pacific. He turned to swim with the current. His anticipation of the new experience filled him with an almost sexual excitement.

When he reached the submarine net at the mouth of San Francisco Bay he paused briefly, then pulled himself through it into the ocean. He was terrified but soon calmed himself. He had undergone a rite of passage, he felt, had experienced a sea change. He would explore farther in later days, he decided, but for now he felt emotionally drained and physically exhausted.

He turned and began the long swim back to Suisun Bay.

He had seen fewer of the human-like creatures than usual on this night, but as he approached Port Chicago they became more numerous. He was beginning to learn their language and felt eager to converse with them, find out who or what they were, but they kept their distance from him this night, and instead of joining them he continued on his solitary way.

In time he recognized the submerged landmarks that told him he was at his destination. He had been swimming along the sea bottom, insulated by fathoms of brackish water from the world of men, immune from the noisome companionship of air breathers and land dwellers. He rose slowly toward the top of the water. He was shocked as he breached to realize that he had spent the entire night under water. The brilliant sun now blasted down from a bright blue sky.

He made his way to his Cord, drove home and slept around the clock. He awoke Sunday morning and spent the day in seclusion, sustaining himself with alcohol and music. After dark he made his way to the nearby stream and stood in it, letting its waters soothe his feet. He went home and slept, dreaming once more of an undersea city, and rose late on Monday. He hadn't realized how far he had swum on Friday night, or how exhausted the effort had left him. Still, the experience had been an exhilarating one and he looked forward to spending even more time beneath the surface, to travelling farther into the ocean.

When he reached Port Chicago on Monday the transfer of the bomb from railroad freight car to the hold of *Quinalt Victory* was well under way. Marston's expertise had been of immense value, he would be told. He encountered Captain Kinne himself on the pier and the usually stern Kinne recognized him and thanked him for his assistance.

Powerful electric vapor-lights had been rigged to illuminate the operation once the sun had set and their peculiar glare gave the faces of the men on the pier, both white and colored, a ghostly look.

Marston walked to the end of the pier. When he turned back toward the center of activity he saw that all eyes were fixed on the delicate work at the *Quinalt Victory*. He checked his wristwatch and saw that it was ten o'clock. Bright moonlight was reflected off the surface of the Bay.

Instead of climbing down the ladder to the water's surface, Marston left his clothing in its usual neat pile, stood on the edge of the pier, and dived into the Bay. He swam to the seabed, taking delicious water in and passing it through his gills, letting his eyes grow accustomed to the faint phosphorescence that provided illumination in this world.

He turned to observe the hull of the *Quinalt Victory*. He was astonished at the number of human-like forms moving around the ship, gesturing meaningfully to one another, attaching something, something, to the metal hull of the *Quinalt Victory*.

Marston swam toward the ship, curious as to what the creatures were doing. This was the first time he had seen them using anything that looked like machinery. As he drew closer several of the creatures turned and swam toward him. As they approached he realized that they were like him in every way. The wide mouth and triangular teeth, the splayed limbs, the webbed hands and feet, the hooked claws, the oversized eyes and flattened noses.

How had he managed to pass among men until now? How had his alienness gone undetected? The scarf and dark glasses had helped but surely he would be caught out soon if he tried to continue his masquerade as human. He raised a hand and gestured, showing these aquatic beings that he was one of them, telling them in their own language, a language which he was just beginning to comprehend, that he was not a human, not a land-dweller.

He was not the enemy.

He was shocked by a brilliant flash from the *Quinalt Victory*, a glare that seemed as bright as the sun. Marston felt a shock wave, felt its unimaginable, crushing pressure as it reached him. Then, even before he could react, there was a second flash, this one brighter than a thousand suns, and a second shock wave infinitely greater than the first. But he felt it for only the most fleeting of moments, and then he felt nothing more.

*

Historic Note

At 10:20 PM, Monday, July 17, 1944, a huge explosion occurred at Port Chicago, California. Two ships were moored at the loading pier of the naval station there. The *E. A. Bryan* was fully loaded and ready to leave for the Pacific theater of operations with a huge cargo of high explosives and military equipment. The *Quinalt Victory*, a brand new vessel built at the Kaiser Shipyard in nearby Richmond, California, was preparing to take on its own cargo.

Some 320 individuals were killed in the explosion, most of them African-American stevedores. An additional 400 persons were injured. A common form of injury was blindness caused by flying splinters of window-glass in naval barracks. The main explosion was preceded by a rumble or smaller explosion, reports differing, which drew many off-duty stevedores to the windows to see what had caused the sound.

The brilliant flash, the roar of the explosion, and the shaking of the earth that resulted, were seen, heard, and felt as far away as the cities of Berkeley, Oakland, and San Francisco.

The *Bryan*, the *Quinalt Victory*, the loading pier, the railroad spur running along the pier, and the ammunition train that was parked on the pier at the time, were all totally destroyed. The town of Port Chicago was obliterated and a visitor to its site today will find only a few forlorn street markers to show where once a community thrived.

While official statements about the disaster aver only to the high explosives which had been loaded in the *E. A. Bryan*, critics in later years suggested that the explosion was nuclear in nature. In the summer of 1944 the atomic bomb was top secret and the very existence of the Manhattan Project was shrouded in layers of security. But once the bomb was dropped on Hiroshima and Nagasaki, speculation began that more than dynamite had been involved in the Port Chicago disaster.

If the Port Chicago explosion was indeed nuclear in nature, further speculation is divided between those who believe the explosion was accidental in origin, or was in fact a test by the United States government to measure the effects of a nuclear bomb. Certainly the weapons base at Port Chicago would have made a fine test subject, with ships, a railroad spur, temporary and permanent buildings, and many hundreds of expendable human subjects.

Perhaps the Port Chicago explosion was a nuclear accident. If so, it represented a major setback to the American nuclear weapons project. The successful Alamogordo test did not take place until July 16, 1945, one day short of a year after the Port Chicago explosion. Nuclear weapons were exploded in the air over Hiroshima and Nagasaki the following month, bringing about the end of the Second World War and providing an object lesson for Josef Stalin.

Where the Port Chicago naval weapons depot once stood, there is now the Concord Naval Weapons Station, a major loading area for the United States Pacific Fleet. The storage of nuclear weapons in barrow-like bunkers at the naval weapons station, while not officially acknowledged by the US government, is one of the most ill-kept secrets of our era.

THE ADVENTURE OF THE VOORISH SIGN

It was by far the most severe winter London had known in human memory, perhaps since the Romans had founded their settlement of Londinium nearly two millennia ago. Storms had swept down from the North Sea, cutting off the Continent and blanketing the great metropolis with thick layers of snow that were quickly blackened by the choking fumes of ten thousand charcoal braziers, turning to a treacherous coating of ice when doused with only slightly warmer peltings of sleet.

Even so, Holmes and I were snug in our quarters at 221B Baker Street. The fire had been laid, we had consumed a splendid dinner of meat pasties and red cabbage served by the ever-reliable Mrs. Hudson, and I found myself dreaming over an aged brandy and a pipe while Holmes devoted himself to his newest passion.

He had raided our slim exchequer for sufficient funds to purchase one of Mr. Emile Berliner's new gramophones, imported by Harrods of Brompton Road. He had placed one of Mr. Berliner's new disk recordings on the machine, advertised as a marked improvement over the traditional wax cylinders. But the sounds that emerged from the horn were neither pleasant nor tuneful to my ears. Instead they were of a weird and disquieting nature, seemingly discordant yet suggestive of strange harmonies which it would be better not to understand.

As I was about to ask Holmes to shut off the contraption, the melody came to an end and Holmes removed the needle from its groove.

Holmes pressed an upraised finger against his thin lips and sharply uttered my name. "Watson!" he repeated as I lowered my pipe. The brandy snifter had very nearly slipped from my grasp, but I was able to catch it in time to prevent a disastrous spill.

"What is it, Holmes?" I inquired.

"Listen!"

He held one hand aloft, an expression of intense concentration upon his saturnine features. He nodded toward the shuttered windows which gave out upon Baker Street.

"I hear nothing except the whistle of the wind against the eaves," I told him.

"Listen more closely."

I tilted my head, straining to hear whatever it was that had caught Holmes's attention. There was a creak from below, followed by the sound of a door opening and closing, and a rapping of knuckles against solid wood, the latter sound muffled as by thin cloth.

I looked at Holmes, who pressed a long finger against his lips, indicating that silence was required. He nodded toward our door, and in a few moments I heard the tread of Mrs. Hudson ascending to our lodging. Her sturdy pace was accompanied by another, light and tentative in nature.

Holmes drew back our front door to reveal our landlady, her hand raised to knock. "Mr. Holmes!" she gasped.

"Mrs. Hudson, I see that you have brought with you Lady Fairclough of Pontefract. Will you be so kind as to permit Lady Fairclough to enter, and would you be so good as to brew a hot cup of tea for my lady. She must be suffering from her trip through this wintry night."

Mrs. Hudson turned away and made her way down the staircase while the slim young woman who had accompanied her entered our sitting room with a series of long, graceful strides. Behind her, Mrs. Hudson had carefully placed a carpetbag valise upon the floor.

"Lady Fairclough." Holmes addressed the newcomer. "May I introduce my associate, Dr. Watson. Of course you know who I am, which is why you have come to seek my assistance. But first, please warm yourself by the fire. Dr. Watson will fetch a bottle of brandy with which we will fortify the hot tea that Mrs. Hudson is preparing."

The newcomer had not said a word, but her face gave proof of her astonishment that Holmes had known her identity and home without being told. She wore a stylish hat trimmed in dark fur and a carefully tailored coat with matching decorations at collar and cuffs. Her feet were covered in boots that disappeared beneath the lower hem of her coat.

I helped her off with her outer garment. By the time I had placed it in our closet, Lady Fairclough was comfortably settled in our best chair, holding slim hands toward the cheerily dancing flames. She had removed her gloves and laid them with seemingly careless precision across the wooden arm of her chair.

"Mr. Holmes," she said in a voice that spoke equally of cultured sensitivity and barely repressed terror, "I apologize for disturbing you and Dr. Watson at this late hour, but — "

"There is no need for apologies, Lady Fairclough. On the contrary, you are to be commended for having the courage to cross the Atlantic in the midst of winter, and the captain of the steamship *Murania* is to be congratulated for having negotiated the crossing successfully. It is unfortunate that our customs agents delayed your disembarkation as they did, but now that you are here, perhaps you will enlighten Dr. Watson and myself as to the problem which has beset your brother, Mr. Philip Llewellyn."

If Lady Fairclough had been startled by Holmes's recognizing her without introduction, she was clearly amazed beyond my meager powers of description by this statement. She raised a hand to her cheek, which showed a smoothness of complexion and grace of curve in the flattering glow of the dancing flames. "Mr. Holmes," she exclaimed, "how did you know all that?"

"It was nothing, Lady Fairclough, one need merely keep one's senses on the alert and one's mind active." A glance that Holmes darted in my direction was not welcome, but I felt constrained from protesting in the presence of a guest and potential client.

"So you say, Mr. Holmes, but I have read of your exploits and in many cases they seem little short of supernatural," Lady Fairclough replied.

"Not in the least. Let us consider the present case. Your valise bears the paper label of the Blue Star Line. The *Murania* and the *Lemuria* are the premiere ocean liners of the Blue Star Line, alternating upon the easterly and westerly transatlantic sea-lanes. Even a fleeting glance at the daily shipping news indicates that the *Murania* was due in Liverpool early this morning. If the ship made port at even so late an hour as ten o'clock, in view of the fact that the rail journey from Liverpool to London requires a mere two hours, you should have reached our city by noon. Another hour at most from the rail terminus to Baker Street would have brought you to our door by one o'clock this afternoon. And yet," concluded Holmes, glancing at the ormolu clock that rested upon our mantel, "you arrive at the surprising hour of ten o'clock *post meridian*."

"But, Holmes," I interjected, "Lady Fairclough may have had other errands to perform before coming to us."

"No, Watson, no. I fear that you have failed to draw the proper inference from that which you have surely observed. You did note, did you not, that Lady Fairclough has brought her carpetbag with her?"

I plead guilty to the charge.

"Surely, had she not been acting in great haste, Lady Fairclough would have gone to her hotel, refreshed herself, and left her luggage in her quarters there before traveling to Baker Street. The fact that she has but one piece of luggage with her gives further testimony to the urgency with which she departed her home in Canada. Now, Watson, what could have caused Lady Fairclough to commence her trip in such haste?"

I shook my head. "I confess that I am at a loss."

"It was but eight days ago that the *Daily Mail* carried a dispatch marked Marthyr Tydhl, a town situated on the border of England and Wales, concerning the mysterious disappearance of Mr. Philip Llewellyn. There would have been time for word to reach Lady Fairclough in Pontefract by transatlantic cable. Fearing that delay in traveling to the port and boarding the *Murania* would cause intolerable delay, Lady Fairclough had her maid pack the fewest possible necessities in her carpetbag. She then made her way to Halifax, whence the *Murania* departed, and upon reaching Liverpool this morning would have made her way at once to London. Yet she arrived some nine hours later than she might have been expected to do. Since our rail service remains uninterrupted in even the most severe of climatic conditions, it can only have been the customs service, equally notorious for their punctilio and their dilatory conduct, which could be responsible."

Turning once more to Lady Fairclough, Holmes said, "In behalf of Her Majesty's Customs Service, Lady Fairclough, I tender my apologies."

There was a knock at the door and Mrs. Hudson appeared, bearing a tray with hot tea and cold sandwiches. This she placed upon the table, then took her leave.

Lady Fairclough looked at the repast and said, "Oh, I simply could not."

"Nonsense," Holmes insisted. "You have completed an arduous journey and face a dangerous undertaking. You must keep up your strength." He rose and added brandy to Lady Fairclough's tea, then stood commandingly over her while she consumed the beverage and two sandwiches.

"I suppose I was hungry after all," she admitted at last. I was pleased to see some color returning to her cheeks. I had been seriously concerned about her well-being.

"Now, Lady Fairclough," said Holmes, "it might be well for you to go to your hotel and restore your strength with a good night's slumber. You do have a reservation, I trust."

"Oh, of course, at Claridge's. A suite was ordered for me through the courtesy of the Blue Star Line, but I could not rest now, Mr. Holmes. I am far too distraught to sleep until I have explained my need to you, and received your assurance that you and Dr. Watson will take my case. I have plenty of money, if that is a concern."

Holmes indicated that financial details could wait, but I was pleased to be included in our guest's expression of need. So often I find myself taken for granted, while in fact I am Holmes's trusted associate, as he has himself acknowledged on many occasions.

"Very well." Holmes nodded, seating himself opposite Lady Fairclough. "Please tell me your story in your own words, being as precise with details as possible."

Lady Fairclough drained her cup and waited while Holmes filled it once again with brandy and a spot of Darjeeling. She downed another substantial draught, then launched upon her narrative.

"As you know, Mr. Holmes — and Dr. Watson — I was born in England of old stock. Despite our ancient Welsh connections and family name, we have been English for a thousand years. I was the elder of two children, the younger being my brother, Philip. As a daughter, I saw little future for myself in the home islands, and accepted the proposal of marriage tendered by my husband, Lord Fairclough, whose Canadian holdings are substantial and who indicated to me a desire to emigrate to Canada and build a new life there, which we would share."

I had taken out my notebook and fountain pen and begun jotting notes.

"At about this time my parents were both killed in a horrendous accident, the collision of two trains in the Swiss Alps while vacationing abroad. Feeling that an elaborate wedding would be disrespectful of the deceased, Lord Fairclough and I were quietly married and took our leave of England. We lived happily in Pontefract, Canada, until my husband disappeared."

"Indeed," Holmes interjected, "I had read of Lord Fairclough's disappearance. I note that you refer to him as your husband rather than your late husband still, nor do I see any mourning band upon your garment. Is it your belief that your husband lives still?"

Lady Fairclough lowered her eyes for a moment as a flush rose to her cheeks. "Although ours was somewhat a marriage of convenience, I find that I have come to love my husband most dearly. There was no discord between us, if you are concerned over such, Mr. Holmes."

"Not in the least, Lady Fairclough."

"Thank you." She sipped from her teacup. Holmes peered at it, then refreshed its contents once again. "Thank you," Lady Fairclough repeated. "My husband had been corresponding with his brother-in-law, my brother, and later, after my brother's marriage, with my brother's wife, for some time before he disappeared. I saw the envelopes as they came and went, but I was never permitted to so much as lay eyes on their contents. After reading each newly delivered letter, my husband would burn it and crush the ashes beyond recovery. After receiving one very lengthy letter — I could tell it was lengthy by the heft of the envelope in which it arrived — my husband summoned carpenters and prepared a sealed room which I was forbidden to enter. Of course I obeyed my husband's command."

"A wise policy," I put in. "One knows the story of Bluebeard."

"He would lock himself in his private chamber for hours at a time, sometimes days. When he disappeared, in fact, I half expected him to return at any moment." Lady Fairclough put her hand to her throat. "Please," she said softly, "I beg your pardon for the impropriety, but I feel suddenly so warm." I glanced away, and when I looked back at her I observed that the top button of her blouse had been undone.

"My husband has been gone now for two years, and all have given him up for dead save myself, and I will concede that even my hopes are of the faintest. During the period of correspondence between my husband and my brother, my husband began to absent himself from all human society from time to time. Gradually the frequency and duration of his disappearances increased. I feared I knew not what — perhaps that he had become addicted to some drug or unspeakable vice for the indulging of which he preferred isolation. I inferred that he had caused the construction of the sealed room for this purpose, and determined that I should learn its secret."

She bowed her head and drew a series of long, sobbing breaths, which caused her graceful bosom visibly to heave. After a time she raised her face. Her cheeks were wet with tears. She resumed her narrative.

"I summoned a locksmith from the village and persuaded him to aid me in gaining entry. When I stood at last in my husband's secret chamber I found myself confronting a room completely devoid of feature. The ceiling, the walls, the floor were all plain and devoid of ornament. There were neither windows nor fireplace, nor any other means of egress from the room."

Holmes nodded, frowning. "There was nothing noteworthy about the room, then?" he asked at length.

"Yes, Mr. Holmes, there was." Lady Fairclough's response startled me so, I nearly dropped my fountain pen, but I recovered and returned to my note taking.

"At first the room seemed a perfect cube. The ceiling, floor, and four walls each appeared absolutely square and mounted at a precise right angle to one another. But as I stood there, they seemed to — I suppose, *shift* is the closest I can come to it, Mr. Holmes, but they did not actually move in any familiar manner. And yet their shape seemed to be different, and the angles to become peculiar, obtuse, and to open onto other — how to put this? — *dimensions*."

She seized Holmes's wrist in her graceful fingers and leaned toward him pleadingly. "Do you think I am insane, Mr. Holmes? Has my grief driven me to the brink of madness? There are times when I think I can bear no more strangeness."

"You are assuredly not insane," Holmes told her. "You have stumbled upon one of the strangest and most dangerous of phenomena, a phenomenon barely suspected by even the most advanced of mathematical theoreticians and spoken of even by them in only the most cautious of whispers."

He withdrew his arm from her grasp, shook his head, and said, "If your strength permits, you must continue your story, please."

"I will try," she answered.

I waited, fountain pen poised above notebook.

Our visitor shuddered as with a fearsome recollection. "Once I had left the secret room, sealing it behind myself, I attempted to resume a normal life. It was days later that my husband reappeared, refusing as usual to give any explanation of his recent whereabouts. Shortly after this a dear friend of mine living in Quebec gave birth to a child. I had gone to be with her when word was received of the great Pontefract earthquake. In this disaster a fissure appeared in the earth and our house was completely swallowed. I was, fortunately, left in a state of financial independence, and have never suffered from material deprivation. But I have never again seen my husband. Most believe that he was in the house at the time of its disappearance, and was killed at once, but I retain a hope, however faint, that he may somehow have survived."

She paused to compose herself, then resumed.

"But I fear I am getting ahead of myself. It was shortly before my husband ordered the construction of his sealed room that my brother, Philip, announced his engagement and the date of his impending nuptials. I thought the shortness of his intended period of engagement was unseemly, but in view of my own marriage and departure to Canada so soon after my parents' death, I was in no position to condemn Philip. My husband and I booked passage to England, on the *Lemuria* in fact, and from Liverpool made our way to the family lands in Marthyr Tydhl."

She shook her head as if to free it of an unpleasant memory.

"Upon arriving at Anthracite Palace, I was shocked by my brother's appearance."

At this point I interrupted our guest with a query.

"Anthracite Palace? Is that not an unusual name for a family manse?"

"Our family residence was so named by my ancestor, Sir Llewys Llewellyn, who built the family fortune, and the manor, by operating a network of successful coal mines. As you are probably aware, the region is rich in anthracite. The Llewellyns pioneered modern mining methods which rely upon gelignite explosives to loosen banks of coal for the miners to remove from their native sites. In the region of Marthyr Tydhl, where the Anthracite Palace is located, the booming of gelignite charges is heard to this day, and stores of the explosive are kept at the mine heads."

I thanked her for the clarification and suggested that she continue with her narrative.

"My brother was neatly barbered and clothed, but his hands shook, his cheeks were sunken, and his eyes had a frightened, hunted look to them," she said. "When I toured my childhood home I was shocked to find its interior architecture modified. There was now a sealed room, just as there had been at Pontefract. I was not permitted to enter that room. I expressed my concern at my brother's appearance but he insisted he was well and introduced his fiancée, who was already living at the palace."

I drew my breath with a gasp.

"Yes, Doctor," Lady Fairclough responded, "you heard me correctly. She was a woman of dark, Gypsyish complexion, glossy sable hair, and darting eyes. I disliked her at once. She gave her own name, not waiting for Philip to introduce her properly. Her maiden name, she announced, was Anastasia Romelly. She claimed to be of noble Hungarian blood, allied both to the Habsburgs and the Romanovs."

"Humph," I grunted, "Eastern European nobility is a ha'penny a dozen, and three-quarters of them aren't real even at that."

"Perhaps true," Holmes snapped at me, "but we do not know that the credentials of the lady involved were other than authentic." He frowned and turned away. "Lady Fairclough, please continue."

"She insisted on wearing her native costume. And she had persuaded my brother to replace his chef with one of her own choosing, whom she had imported from her homeland and who replaced our usual menu of good English fare with unfamiliar dishes reeking of odd spices and unknown ingredients. She imported strange wines and ordered them served with meals."

I shook my head in disbelief.

"The final straw came upon the day of her wedding to my brother. She insisted upon being given away by a surly, dark man who appeared for the occasion, performed his duty, and then disappeared. She — "

"A moment, please," Holmes interrupted. "If you will forgive me — you say that this man disappeared. Do you mean that he took his leave prematurely?"

"No, I do not mean that at all." Lady Fairclough was clearly excited. A moment earlier she had seemed on the verge of tears. Now she was angry and eager to unburden herself of her tale.

"In a touching moment, he placed the bride's hand upon that of the groom. Then he raised his own hand. I thought his intent was to place his

197

benediction upon the couple, but such was not the case. He made a gesture with his hand, as if making a mystical sign."

She raised her own hand from her lap, but Holmes snapped, "Do not, I warn you, attempt to replicate the gesture! Please, if you can, simply describe it to Dr. Watson and myself."

"I could not replicate the gesture if I tried," Lady Fairclough said. "It defies imitation. I cannot even describe it accurately, I fear. I was fascinated and tried to follow the movement of the dark man's fingers, but I could not. They seemed to disappear and reappear most shockingly, and then, without further warning, he was simply gone. I tell you, Mr. Holmes, one moment the dark man was there, and then he was gone."

"Did no one else take note of this, my lady?"

"No one did, apparently. Perhaps all eyes were trained upon the bride and groom, although I believe I did notice the presiding official exchanging several glances with the dark man. Of course, that was before his disappearance."

Holmes stroked his jaw, deep in thought. There was a lengthy silence in the room, broken only by the ticking of the ormolu clock and whistling of the wind through the eaves. Finally Holmes spoke.

"It can be nothing other than the Voorish Sign," he said.

"The Voorish Sign?" Lady Fairclough repeated inquiringly.

Holmes said, "Never mind. This becomes more interesting by the moment, and also more dangerous. Another question, if you please. Who was the presiding official at the wedding? He was, I would assume, a priest of the Church of England."

"No." Lady Fairclough shook her head once again. "The official was neither a member of the Anglican clergy nor a *he*. The wedding was performed by a woman."

I gasped in surprise, drawing still another sharp glance from Holmes.

"She wore robes such as I have never seen," our guest resumed. "There were symbols, both astronomical and astrological, embroidered in silver thread and gold, green, blue, and red. There were other symbols totally unfamiliar to me, suggestive of strange geometries and odd shapes. The ceremony itself was conducted in a language I had never before heard, and I am something of a linguist, Mr. Holmes. I believe I detected a few words of Old Temple Egyptian, a phrase in Coptic Greek, and several suggestions of Sanskrit. Other words I did not recognize at all."

Holmes nodded. I could see the excitement growing in his eyes, the excitement that I saw only when a fascinating challenge was presented to him.

He asked, "What was this person's name?"

"Her name," Lady Fairclough voiced through teeth clenched in anger, or perhaps in the effort to prevent their chattering with fear, "was Vladimira Petrovna Ludmilla Romanova. She claimed the title of Archbishop of the Wisdom Temple of the Dark Heavens."

"Why — why," I exclaimed, "I've never heard of such a thing! This is sheer blasphemy!"

"It is something far worse than blasphemy, Watson." Holmes leaped to his feet and paced rapidly back and forth. At one point he halted near our front window, being careful not to expose himself to the direct sight of anyone lurking below. He peered down into Baker Street, something I have seen him do many times in our years together. Then he did something I had not seen before. Drawing himself back still farther, he gazed upward. What he hoped to perceive in the darkened winter sky other than falling snowflakes, I could hardly imagine.

"Lady Fairclough," he intoned at length, "you have been remarkably strong and courageous in your performance here this night. I will now ask Dr. Watson to see you to your hotel. You mentioned Claridge's, I believe. I will ask Dr. Watson to remain in your suite throughout the remainder of the night. I assure you, Lady Fairclough that he is a person of impeccable character, and your virtue will in no way be compromised by his presence."

"Even so, Holmes," I objected, "the lady's virtue is one thing, her reputation is another."

The matter was resolved by Lady Fairclough herself. "Doctor, while I appreciate your concern, we are dealing with a most serious matter. I will accept the suspicious glances of prudes and the smirks of servants if I must. The lives of my husband and my brother are at stake."

Unable to resist the lady's argument, I followed Holmes's directions and accompanied her to Claridge's. At his insistence I even went so far as to arm myself with a large revolver, which I tucked into the top of my woolen trousers. Holmes warned me, also, to permit no one save himself entry to Lady Fairclough's suite.

Once my temporary charge had retired, I sat in a straight chair, prepared to pass the night in a game of solitaire. Lady Fairclough had donned camisole and hair net and climbed into her bed. I will admit that my cheeks burned, but I reminded myself that in my medical capacity I was accustomed to viewing patients in a disrobed condition, and could surely assume an avuncular role while keeping watch over this courageous lady.

There was a loud rapping at the door. I jerked awake, realizing to my chagrin that I had fallen asleep over my solitary card game. I rose to my feet, went to Lady Fairclough's bedside and assured myself that she was unharmed, and then placed myself at the door to her suite. In response to my demand that our visitor identify himself, a male voice announced simply, "Room service, guv'nor."

My hand was on the doorknob, my other hand on the latch, when I remembered Holmes's warning at Baker Street to permit no one entry. Surely a hearty breakfast would be welcome; I could almost taste the kippers and the toast and jam that Mrs. Hudson would have served us, had we been still in our home. But Holmes had been emphatic. What to do? What to do?

"We did not order breakfast." I spoke through the heavy oaken door.

"Courtesy of the management, guv."

Perhaps, I thought, I might admit a waiter bearing food. What harm could there be in that? I reached for the latch only to find my hand tugged away by another, that of Lady Fairclough. She had climbed from her bed and crossed the room, barefoot and clad only in her sleeping garment. She shook her head vigorously, drawing me away from the door, which remained latched against any entry. She pointed to me, pantomiming speech. Her message was clear.

"Leave our breakfast in the hall," I instructed the waiter. "We shall fetch it in ourselves shortly. We are not ready as yet."

"Can't do it, sir," the waiter insisted. "Please, sir, don't get me in trouble wif the management, guv'nor. I needs to roll my cart into your room and leave the tray. I'll get in trouble if I don't, guv'nor."

I was nearly persuaded by his plea, but Lady Fairclough had placed herself between me and the door, her arms crossed and a determined expression on her face. Once again she indicated that I should send the waiter away.

"I'm sorry, my man, but I must insist. Simply leave the tray outside our door. That is my final word."

The waiter said nothing more, but I thought I could hear his reluctantly retreating footsteps.

I retired to make my morning ablutions while Lady Fairclough dressed.

Shortly thereafter, there was another rapping at the door. Fearing the worst, I drew my revolver. Perhaps this was more than a misdirected order for room service. "I told you to go away," I commanded.

"Watson, old man, open up. It is I, Holmes."

The voice was unmistakable; I felt as though a weight of a hundred stone had been lifted from my shoulders. I undid the door latch and stood aside as the best and wisest man I have ever known entered the apartment. I peered out into the hall after he had passed through the doorway. There was no sign of a service cart or breakfast tray.

Holmes asked, "What are you looking for, Watson?"

I explained the incident of the room-service call.

"You did well, Watson," he congratulated me. "You may be certain that was no waiter, nor was his mission one of service to Lady Fairclough and yourself. I have spent the night consulting my files and certain other sources with regard to the odd institution known as the Wisdom Temple of the Dark Heavens, and I can tell you that we are sailing dangerous waters indeed."

He turned to Lady Fairclough. "You will please accompany Dr. Watson and myself to Marthyr Tydhl. We shall leave at once. There is a chance that we may yet save the life of your brother, but we have no time to waste."

Without hesitation, Lady Fairclough strode to the wardrobe, pinned her hat to her hair, and donned the same warm coat she had worn when first I laid eyes on her, mere hours before.

"But, Holmes," I protested, "Lady Fairclough and I have not broken our fast."

"Never mind your stomach, Watson. There is no time to lose. We can purchase sandwiches from a vendor at the station."

Almost sooner than I can tell, we were seated in a first-class compartment heading westward toward Wales. As good as his word, Holmes had seen to it that we were nourished, and I for one felt the better for having downed even a light and informal meal.

The storm had at last abated and a bright sun shone down from a sky of the most brilliant blue upon fields and hillsides covered with a spotless layer of purest white. Hardly could one doubt the benevolence of the universe; I felt almost like a schoolboy setting off on holiday, but Lady Fairclough s fears and Holmes's serious demeanor brought my soaring spirits back to earth.

"It is as I feared, Lady Fairclough," Holmes explained. "Both your brother and your husband have been ensnared in a wicked cult that threatens civilization itself if it is not stopped."

"A cult?" Lady Fairclough echoed.

"Indeed. You told me that Bishop Romanova was a representative of the Wisdom Temple of the Dark Heavens, did you not?"

"She so identified herself, Mr. Holmes."

"Yes. Nor would she have reason to lie, not that any denizen of this foul nest would hesitate to do so, should it aid their schemes. The Wisdom Temple is a little-known organization — I would hesitate to dignify them with the title religion — of ancient origins. They have maintained a secretive stance while awaiting some cosmic cataclysm which I fear is nearly upon us."

"Cosmic — cosmic cataclysm? I say, Holmes, isn't that a trifle melodramatic?" I asked.

"Indeed it is, Watson. But it is nonetheless so. They refer to a coming time 'when the stars are right.' Once that moment arrives, they intend to perform an unholy rite that will 'open the portal,' whatever that means, to admit their masters to the earth. The members of the Wisdom Temple will then become overseers and oppressors of all humankind, in the service of the dread masters whom they will have admitted to our world."

I shook my head in disbelief. Outside the windows of our compartment I could see that our train was approaching the trestle that would carry us across the River Severn. It would not be much longer before we should detrain at Marthyr Tydhl.

"Holmes," I said, "I would never doubt your word."

"I know that, old man," he replied. "But something is bothering you. Out with it!"

"Holmes, this is madness. Dread masters, opening portals, unholy rites — this is something out of the pages of a penny dreadful. Surely you don't expect Lady Fairclough and myself to believe all this."

"But I do, Watson. You must believe it, for it is all true, and deadly serious. Lady Fairclough — you have set out to save your brother and if possible your husband, but in fact you have set us in play in a game whose stakes are not one or two mere individuals, but the fate of our planet."

Lady Fairclough pulled a handkerchief from her wrist and dabbed at her eyes. "Mr. Holmes, I have seen that strange room at Llewellyn Hall at Pontefract, and I can believe your every word, for all that I agree with Dr. Watson as to the fantastic nature of what you say. Might I ask how you know of this?"

"Very well," Holmes assented, "You are entitled to that information. I told you before we left Claridge's that I had spent the night in research. There are many books in my library, most of which are open to my associate, Dr. Watson, and to other men of goodwill, as surely he is. But there are others which I keep under lock and key."

"I am aware of that, Holmes," I interjected, "and I will admit that I have been hurt by your unwillingness to share those volumes with me. Often have I wondered what they contain."

"Good Watson, it was for your own protection, I assure you. Watson, Lady Fairclough, those books include *De los Mundos Amenazantes y Sombriosos* of Carlos Alfredo de Torrijos, *Emmorragia Sante* of Luigi Humberto Rosso, and *Das Bestrafen von der Tugendhaft* of Heinrich Ludvig Georg von Feldenstein, as well as the works of the brilliant Mr. Arthur Machen, of whom you may have heard. These tomes, some of them well over a thousand years old and citing still more remote sources whose origins are lost in the mists of antiquity, are frighteningly consistent in their predictions. Further, several of them, Lady Fairclough, refer to a certain powerful and fearsome mystical gesture."

Although Holmes was addressing our feminine companion, I said, "Gesture, Holmes? Mystical gesture? What nonsense is this?"

"Not nonsense at all, Watson. You are doubtless aware of the movement that our Romish brethren refer to as 'crossing themselves.' The Hebrews have a gesture of cabalistic origin that is alleged to bring good luck, and the Gypsies make a sign to turn away the evil eye.

203

Several Asian races perform 'hand dances,' ceremonials of religious or magical significance, including the famous *hoo-la* known on the islands of Oahu and Maui in the Havai'ian archipelago."

"But these are all foolish superstitions, remnants of an earlier and more credulous age. Surely there is nothing to them, Holmes!"

"I wish I could have your assuredness, Watson. You are a man of science, for which I commend you, but 'There are more things in heaven and earth, Horatio, than are dreamed of in your philosophy'. Do not be too quick, Watson, to dismiss old beliefs. More often than not they have a basis in fact."

I shook my head and turned my eyes once more to the wintry countryside through which our conveyance was passing. Holmes addressed himself to our companion.

"Lady Fairclough, you mentioned a peculiar gesture that the dark stranger made at the conclusion of your brother's wedding ceremony."

"I did, yes. It was so strange, I felt almost as if I were being drawn into another world when he moved his hand. I tried to follow the movements, but I could not. And then he was gone."

Holmes nodded rapidly.

"The Voorish Sign, Lady Fairclough. The stranger was making the Voorish Sign. It is referred to in the works of Machen and others. It is a very powerful and a very evil gesture. You were fortunate that you were not drawn into that other world, fortunate indeed."

Before much longer we reached the rail terminus nearest to Marthyr Tydhl. We left our compartment and shortly were ensconced in a creaking trap whose driver whipped up his team and headed for the Anthracite Palace. It was obvious from his de-meanor that the manor was a familiar landmark in the region.

"We should be greeted by Mrs. Morrissey, our housekeeper, when we reach the manor," Lady Fairclough said. "It was she who notified me of my brother's straits. She is the last of our old family retainers to remain with the Llewellyns of Marthyr Tydhl. One by one the new lady of the manor has arranged their departure and replaced them with a swarthy crew of her own countrymen. Oh, Mr. Holmes, it is all so horrid!"

Holmes did his best to comfort the frightened woman.

Soon the Anthracite Palace hove into view. As its name would suggest, it was built of the local native coal. Architects and masons had carved the jet-black deposits into building blocks and created an edifice that stood like a black jewel against the white backing of snow, its battlements glittering in the wintry sunlight.

Our trap was met by a liveried servant who instructed lesser servants to carry our meager luggage into the manor. Lady Fairclough, Holmes, and I were ourselves conducted into the main hall.

The building was lit with oversized candles whose flames were so shielded as to prevent any danger of the coal walls catching fire. It struck me that the Anthracite Palace was one of the strangest architectural conceits I had ever encountered. "Not a place I would like to live in, eh, Holmes?" I was trying for a tone of levity, but must confess that I failed to achieve it.

We were left waiting for an excessive period of time, in my opinion, but at length a tall wooden door swung back and a woman of commanding presence, exotic in appearance with her swarthy complexion, flashing eyes, sable locks and shockingly red-dened lips, entered the hall. She nodded to Holmes and myself and exchanged a frigid semblance of a kiss with Lady Fairclough, whom she addressed as "sister."

Lady Fairclough demanded to see her brother, but Mrs. Llewellyn refused conversation until we were shown to our rooms and had time to refresh ourselves. We were summoned, in due course, to the dining hall. I was famished, and both relieved and my appetite further excited by the delicious odors that came to us as we were seated at the long, linen-covered table.

Only four persons were present. These were, of course, Holmes and myself, Lady Fairclough, and our hostess, Mrs. Llewellyn.

Lady Fairclough attempted once again to inquire as to the whereabouts of her brother, Philip.

Her sister-in-law replied only, "He is pursuing his devotions. We shall see him when the time comes round."

Failing to learn more about her brother, Lady Fairclough asked after the housekeeper, Mrs. Morrissey.

"I have sad news, sister dear," Mrs. Llewellyn said. "Mrs. Morrissey was taken ill very suddenly. Philip personally drove into Marthyr Tydhl to fetch a physician for her, but by the time they arrived, Mrs. Morrissey had expired. She was buried in the town cemetery. This all happened just last week. I knew that you were already en route from Canada, and it seemed best not to further distress you with this information."

"Oh no," Lady Fairclough gasped. "Not Mrs. Morrissey! She was like a mother to me. She was the kindest, dearest of women. She — " Lady Fairclough stopped, pressing her hand to her mouth. She inhaled deeply. "Very well, then." I could see a look of determination rising like a banked flame deep in her eye. "If she has died there is naught to be done for it."

There was a pillar of strength hidden within this seemingly weak female. I would not care to make an enemy of Lady Fairclough. I noted also that Mrs. Llewellyn spoke English fluently but with an accent that I found thoroughly unpleasant. It seemed to me that she, in turn, found the language distasteful. Clearly, these two were fated to clash. But the tension of the moment was broken by the arrival of our viands.

The repast was sumptuous in appearance, but every course, it seemed to me, had some flaw — an excessive use of spice, an overdone vegetable, an undercooked piece of meat or game, a fish that might have been kept a day too long before serving, a cream that had stood in a warm kitchen an hour longer than was wise. By the end of the meal my appetite had departed, but it was replaced by a sensation of queasiness and discomfort rather than satisfaction.

Servants brought cigars for Holmes and myself, an after-dinner brandy for the men, and sweet sherry for the women, but I put out my cigar after a single draft and noticed that Holmes did the same with his own. Even the beverage seemed in some subtle way to be faulty.

"Mrs. Llewellyn." Lady Fairclough addressed her sister-in-law when at last the latter seemed unable longer to delay confrontation. "I received a telegram via transatlantic cable concerning the disappearance of my brother. He failed to greet us upon our arrival, nor has there been any sign of his presence since then. I demand to know his whereabouts."

"Sister dear," replied Anastasia Romelly Llewellyn, "that telegram should never have been sent. Mrs. Morrissey transmitted it from Marthyr Tydhl while in town on an errand for the palace. When I learned of her presumption I determined to send her packing, I can assure you. It was only her unfortunate demise that prevented my doing so."

At this point my friend Holmes addressed our hostess.

"Madam, Lady Fairclough has journeyed from Canada to learn of her brother's circumstances. She has engaged me, along with my associate, Dr. Watson, to assist her in this enterprise. It is not my desire to make this affair any more unpleasant than is necessary, but I must insist upon your providing the information that Lady Fairclough is seeking."

I believe at this point that I observed a smirk, or at least the suggestion of one, pass across the face of Mrs. Llewellyn. But she quickly responded to Holmes's demand, her peculiar accent as pronounced and unpleasant as ever.

"We have planned a small religious service for this evening. You are all invited to attend, of course, even though I had expected only my dear sister-in-law to do so. However, the larger group will be accommodated."

"What is the nature of this religious service?" Lady Fairclough demanded.

Mrs. Llewellyn smiled. "It will be that of the Wisdom Temple, of course. The Wisdom Temple of the Dark Heavens. It is my hope that Bishop Romanova herself will preside, but absent her participation we can still conduct the service ourselves."

I reached for my pocket watch. "It's getting late, madam. Might I suggest that we get started, then!"

Mrs. Llewellyn turned her eyes upon me. In the flickering candlelight they seemed larger and darker than ever. "You do not understand, Dr. Watson. It is too early rather than too late to start our ceremony. We will proceed precisely at midnight. Until then, please feel free to enjoy the paintings and tapestries with which the Anthracite Palace is decorated, or pass the time in Mr. Llewellyn's library. Or, if you prefer, you may of course retire to your quarters and seek sleep."

Thus it was that we three separated temporarily, Lady Fairclough to pass some hours with her husband's chosen books, Holmes to an examination of the palace's art treasures, and I to bed.

I was awakened from a troubled slumber haunted by strange beings of nebulous form. Standing over my bed, shaking me by the shoulder, was my friend Sherlock Holmes. I could see a rim of snow adhering to the edges of his boots.

"Come, Watson," said he, "the game is truly afoot, and it is by far the strangest game we are ever likely to pursue."

Swiftly donning my attire, I accompanied Holmes as we made our way to Lady Fairclough's chamber. She had retired there after spending the hours since dinner in her brother's library, to refresh herself. She must have been awaiting our arrival, for she responded without delay to Holmes's knock and the sound of his voice.

Before we proceeded further Holmes drew me aside. He reached inside his vest and withdrew a small object which he held concealed in his hand. I could not see its shape, for he held it inside a clenched fist, but I could tell that it emitted a dark radiance, a faint suggestion of which I could see between his fingers.

"Watson," quoth he, "I am going to give you this. You must swear to me that you will not look at it, on pain of damage beyond anything you can so much as imagine. You must keep it upon your person, if possible in direct contact with your body, at all times. If all goes well this night, I will ask you to return it to me. If all does not go well, it may save your life."

I held my hand toward him.

Placing the object on my outstretched palm, Holmes closed my own fingers carefully around it. Surely this was the strangest object I had ever encountered. It was unpleasantly warm, its texture like that of an overcooked egg, and it seemed to squirm as if it were alive, or perhaps as if it contained something that lived and strove to escape an imprisoning integument.

"Do not look at it," Holmes repeated. "Keep it with you at all times. Promise me you will do these things, Watson!"

I assured him that I would do as he requested.

Momentarily we beheld Mrs. Llewellyn moving down the hallway toward us. Her stride was so smooth and her progress so steady that she seemed to be gliding rather than walking. She carried a kerosene lamp whose flame reflected from the polished blackness of the walls, casting ghostly shadows of us all.

Speaking not a word, she gestured to us, summoning us to follow her. We proceeded along a series of corridors and up and down staircases until, I warrant, I lost all sense of direction and of elevation. I could not tell whether we had climbed to a room in one of the battlements of the Anthracite Palace or descended to a dungeon beneath the Llewellyns' ancestral home. I had placed the object Holmes had entrusted to me inside my garments. I could feel it struggling to escape, but it was bound in place and could not do so.

"Where is this bishop you promised us?" I asked of Mrs. Llewellyn.

Our hostess turned toward me. She had replaced her colorful Gypsyish attire with a robe of dark purple. Its color reminded me of the emanations of the warm object concealed now within my own clothing. Her robe was marked with embroidery of a pattern that confused the eye so that I was unable to discern its nature.

"You misunderstood me, Doctor," she intoned in her unpleasant accent. "I stated merely that it was my hope that Bishop Romanova would preside at our service. Such is still the case. We shall see in due time."

We stood now before a heavy door bound with rough iron bands. Mrs. Llewellyn lifted a key which hung suspended about her neck on a ribbon of crimson hue. She inserted it into the lock and turned it. She then requested Holmes and myself to apply our combined strength to opening the door. As we did so, pressing our shoulders against it, my impression was that the resistance came from some willful reluctance rather than a mere matter of weight or decay.

No light preceded us into the room, but Mrs. Llewellyn strode through the doorway carrying her kerosene lamp before her. Its rays now reflected off the walls of the chamber. The room was as Lady Fairclough had described the sealed room in her erstwhile home at Pontefract. The configuration and even the number of surfaces that surrounded us seemed unstable. I was unable even to count them. The very angles at which they met defied my every attempt to comprehend.

An altar of polished anthracite was the sole furnishing of this hideous, irrational chamber.

Mrs. Llewellyn placed her kerosene lamp upon the altar. She turned then, and indicated with a peculiar gesture of her hand that we were to kneel as if participants in a more conventional religious ceremony.

I was reluctant to comply with her silent command, but Holmes nodded to me, indicating that he wished me to do so. I lowered myself, noting that Lady Fairclough and Holmes himself emulated my act.

Before us, and facing the black altar, Mrs. Llewellyn also knelt. She raised her face as if seeking supernatural guidance from above, causing me to remember that the full name of her peculiar sect was the Wisdom

Temple of the Dark Heavens. She commenced a weird chanting in a language such as I had never heard, not in all my travels. There was a suggestion of the argot of the dervishes of Afghanistan, something of the Buddhist monks of Tibet, and a hint of the remnant of the ancient Incan language still spoken by the remotest tribes of the high Choco plain of the Chilean Andes, but in fact the language was none of these and the few words that I was able to make out proved both puzzling and suggestive but never specific in their meaning.

As Mrs. Llewellyn continued her chanting, she slowly raised first one hand then the other above her head. Her fingers were moving in an intricate pattern. I tried to follow their progress but found my consciousness fading into a state of confusion. I could have sworn that her fingers twined and knotted like the tentacles of a jellyfish. Their colors, too, shifted: vermilion, scarlet, obsidian. They seemed, even, to disappear into and return from some concealed realm invisible to my fascinated eyes.

The object that Holmes had given me throbbed and squirmed against my body, its unpleasantly hot and squamous presence making me wish desperately to rid myself of it. It was only my pledge to Holmes that prevented me from doing so.

I clenched my teeth and squeezed my eyes shut, summoning up images from my youth and of my travels, holding my hand clasped over the object as I did so. Suddenly the tension was released. The object was still there, but as if it had a consciousness of its own, it seemed to grow calm. My own jaw relaxed and I opened my eyes to behold a surprising sight.

Before me there emerged another figure. As Mrs. Llewellyn was stocky and swarthy, of the model of Gypsy women, this person was tall and graceful. Swathed entirely in jet, with hair a seeming midnight blue and complexion as black as the darkest African, she defied my conventional ideas of beauty with a weird and exotic glamour of her own that defies description. Her features were as finely cut as those of the ancient Ethiopians are said to have been, her movements filled with a grace that would shame the pride of Covent Garden or the Bolshoi.

But whence had this apparition made her way? Still kneeling upon the ebon floor of the sealed room, I shook my head. She seemed to have emerged from the very angle between the walls.

She floated toward the altar, lifted the chimney from the kerosene lamp, and doused its flame with the palm of her bare hand.

Instantly the room was plunged into stygian darkness, but gradually a new light, if so I may describe it, replaced the flickering illumination of the kerosene lamp. It was a light of darkness, if you will, a glow of blackness deeper than the blackness which sur-rounded us, and yet by its light I could see my companions and my surroundings.

The tall woman smiled in benediction upon the four of us assembled, and gestured toward the angle between the walls. With infinite grace and seemingly glacial slowness she drifted toward the opening, through which I now perceived forms of such mad-deningly chaotic configuration that I can only hint at their nature by suggesting the weird paintings that decorate the crypts of the Pharaohs, the carved stele of the mysterious Mayans, the monoliths of Mauna Loa, and the demons of Tibetan sand paintings.

The black priestess — for so I had come to think of her — led our little procession calmly into her realm of chaos and darkness. She was followed by the Gypsy-like Mrs. Llewellyn, then by Lady Fairclough, whose manner appeared as that of a woman entranced.

My own knees, I confess, have begun to stiffen with age, and I was slow to rise to my feet. Holmes followed the procession of women, while I lagged behind. As he was about to enter the opening, Holmes turned suddenly, his eyes blazing. They transmitted to me a message as clear as any words.

This message was reinforced by a single gesture. I had used my hands, pressing against the black floor as I struggled to my feet. They were now at my sides. Fingers as stiff and powerful as a bobby's club jabbed at my waist. The object which Holmes had given me to hold for him was jolted against my flesh, where it created a weird mark which remains visible to this day.

In the moment I knew what I must do.

I wrapped my arms frantically around the black altar, watching with horrified eyes as Holmes and the others slipped from the sealed room into the realm of madness that lay beyond. I stood transfixed, gazing into the Seventh Circle of Dante's hell, into the very heart of Gehenna.

Flames crackled, tentacles writhed, claws rasped, and fangs ripped at suffering flesh. I saw the faces of men and women I had known, monsters and criminals whose deeds surpass my poor talent to record but who are known in the lowest realms of the planet's underworlds, screaming with glee and with agony.

There was a man whose features so resembled those of Lady Fairclough that I knew he must be her brother. Of her missing husband I know not.

Then, looming above them all, I saw a being that must be the supreme monarch of all monsters, a creature so alien as to resemble no organic thing that ever bestrode the earth, yet so familiar that I realized it was the very embodiment of the evil that lurks in the hearts of every living man.

Sherlock Holmes, the noblest human being I have ever encountered, Holmes alone dared to confront this monstrosity. He glowed in a hideous, hellish green flame, as if even great Holmes were possessed of the stains of sin, and they were being seared from within him in the face of this being.

As the monster reached for Holmes with its hideous mockery of limbs, Holmes turned and signaled to me.

I reached within my garment, removed the object that lay against my skin, pulsating with horrid life, drew back my arm, and with a murmured prayer made the strongest and most accurate throw I had made since my days on the cricket pitch of Jammu.

More quickly than it takes to describe, the object flew through the angle. It struck the monster squarely and clung to its body, extending a hideous network of webbing 'round and 'round and 'round.

The monster gave a single convulsive heave, striking Holmes and sending him flying through the air. With presence of mind such as only he, of all men I know, could claim. Holmes reached and grasped Lady Fairclough by one arm and her brother by the other. The force of the monstrous impact sent them back through the angle into the sealed room, where they crashed into me, sending us sprawling across the floor.

With a dreadful sound louder and more unexpected than the most powerful thunderclap, the angle between the walls slammed shut. The sealed room was plunged once again into darkness.

I drew a packet of lucifers from my pocket and lit one. To my surprise, Holmes reached into an inner pocket of his own and drew from it a stick of gelignite with a long fuse. He signaled to me and I handed him another lucifer. He used it to ignite the fuse of the gelignite bomb.

Striking another lucifer, I relit the kerosene lamp that Mrs. Llewellyn had left on the altar. Holmes nodded his approval, and with the great detective in the lead, the four of us — Lady Fairclough, Mr. Philip Llewellyn, Holmes himself, and I — made haste to find our way from the Anthracite Palace.

Even as we stumbled across the great hall toward the chief exit of the palace, there was a terrible rumbling that seemed to come simultaneously from the deepest basement of the building if not from the very center of the earth, and from the dark heavens above. We staggered from the palace — Holmes, Lady Fairclough, Philip Llewellyn, and I — through the howling wind and pelting snow of a renewed storm, through frigid drifts that rose higher than our boot tops, and turned about to see the great black edifice of the Anthracite Palace in flames.

NOTHING PERSONAL

The flashes on the surface of Yuggoth were so brilliant that they shorted out every bit of electronic equipment on *Beijing 11-11*. Dr. Chen Jing-quo was the sole occupant of the observation satellite at the time, and her own eyes were spared only through a lucky break. She had been showering when the flashes occurred, sealed off from the outer universe.

Still, she had a devil of time extricating herself from the shower-stall, now that the fractional horsepower motor that rolled the door open and shut as well as the touch-sensitive keypad that controlled the motor were dead.

Dr. Chen found the manual override control by touch, got the door open, slipped into a jumpsuit and made her way to one of *Beijing 11-11*'s visual ports. The series of flashes had jolted the ports' photosensitive intracoating to darken dramatically. Dr. Chen stared at Yuggoth, a pulsing, oblate globe that filled the sky above *Beijing 11-11*. Dr. Chen studied the planet's surface and the flashes briefly; she intuited that the observatory's electron telescopes would be useless. Fortunately the station was also fitted with an array of old-style optical telescopes. Dr. Chen made her way to one of these, a 500-millimeter Zeiss-Asahi model, and trained it upon the site of the most recent flashes.

The flashes continued. Dr. Chen, at first alarmed and confused by the unexpected events, was regaining her calm. She focused the Zeiss-Asahi on the apparent epicenter of the flashes and was rewarded by the sight of another flash. This time she observed a bright dot moving away from the surface of the planet. It flashed away into the black trans-Neptunian space, toward the tiny, distant jewel that she knew was the sun. She followed the brilliant dot as long as she could. When it disappeared from sight she set about repairing the assaulted electronics of *Beijing 11-11*.

As soon as she could do so she set up a hyper-light speed link with her superiors on Earth's moon. Even as she did so she trained one of *Beijing 11-11*'s powerful electron telescopes on Yuggoth's surface. She knew the planet's cities as well as — no, better than — she knew the cities of Earth. She had been born on the mother world but her recollections of the planet were only the vague images of a small child. Colors and sounds and odors. The feeling of her mother's arms, a flavor that she thought was that of her mother's milk. But she could not be sure.

She had been selected as a toddler and transported to the moon for two decades of training. She had emerged at the top of her class, triumphing in the final competitive examinations over a thousand young women and men who competed for positions in the world's ongoing scientific enterprises.

She had worked with joyous dedication on *Beijing 11-11* for the past decade, observing the enigmatic activities on Yuggoth. That huge planet and its four satellites, Nithan, Zaman, Thog and Thok, rolled eternally in a counterplanar orbit, crossing the plane of the solar ecliptic only once in a thousand years. No wonder it had gone undiscovered for so long, for Earthbound planetary astronomers had long concentrated their studies on the multi-billion-kiometer disk that surrounded Sol, containing the four rocky planets, the four gas giants, the asteroids and plutoids and the countless meteors and comets.

Barely a century ago Yuggoth and its moons had actually crossed the plane of the ecliptic, and thus it had been detected at last. The discovery of a new major planet had sent shockwaves through the scientific community of Earth. Probes had landed on the major solid bodies of the known solar system, the four rock planets and the solid moons of the four gas giants. The variety of worlds was incredible. There were the ice-covered bodies, the volcanoes, the nitrogen seas, the mountain ranges and deserts and canyon-like beds of ancient rivers, long run dry.

Above all, there was life and the evidence of past life. Exobiologists on Earth had long given hope of such discoveries. Their mantra: *Where life can exist, it does*! The flaw in their argument lay in the fact that they had only a single model from which to draw their conclusion. True, life flourished in the most astonishing of environments, in water close to boiling, in fissures deep within the Earth, on ocean floors where pressure reached tonnes per square centimeter and where neither sunlight nor oxygen could be detected. But it was possible — although it was vigorously debated — that life had originated but once upon Earth, and that all organisms, however varied their natures and locales, were descended from a single ancestor.

It took the exploration of dozens of moons to find jungles and prairies, natural gardens of unimaginable colors and forms, schools of swimming things that were surely not fish, and flocks of flying things that were anything but birds.

But no people. Not merely no humans like those whose robot explorers first landed on Calisto and Mimas, Miranda and Proteus and Galatea and all the others. The people of Earth both longed for and feared the discovery of alien intelligences, whether they looked like giant grasshoppers or self-conscious cabbages or whales with hands, whether they wrote epic treatises on the meaning of life or built machines to carry them across the dimensional barrier to other universes even stranger than the one from which they had come.

No people. No intelligent cabbages or whales with hands, no ancient cities to put the monuments of Thebes to shame and to make the mysteries of Rapa Nui and Stonehenge and the riddle of Linear B look like child's play.

Until Yuggoth.

Until the first robotic probe had circled Yuggoth sending back to Earth images of structures that were undoubtedly artificial, yet that resembled no city ever built upon Earth. They stretched for thousands of miles across the ruddy, pulsing surface of Yuggoth. They rose for hundreds miles into the roiling, cloudy atmosphere of the planet. At the poles of the monstrous globe, black, glossy areas that must be ice caps reflected the light of a billion distant stars.

At this distance from Yuggoth's sun the amount of heat and light from that star was infinitesimal. Clearly, Yuggoth's ruddy pulsations emanated from within the planet, whether the product of radioactivity, of tidal or magnetic forces, or of some other source of unfathomable nature.

Controllers on Earth — for this was before the construction and orbiting of Chen Jing-kuo's observation station — tried sending messages to the occupants of those cyclopean cities, relaying them from their own base of operations on Luna to the satellites orbiting the gigantic "new" planet. There was no response.

Were the Yuggothi extinct? Were their cities like the dead cities of Angkor Wat and Yucatan?

But the satellites detected movement on the surface of Yuggoth. Great creatures of alien configuration, beings like nothing encountered on

Earth or any other world of the solar system, moved between the buildings, between structures that had to be considered buildings, of those cities, which had to be considered cities.

Chen Jing-quo observed the Yuggothi with both electronic and optical instruments. They had heads and bodies and limbs. To that extent they resembled familiar species found both on Earth and elsewhere in the solar system. But where one might have expected to see facial features the Yuggothi showed clusters of waving, polypoidal tentacular growths. Their limbs were tipped with vicious-looking claws, and on their backs were what appeared to be vestigial, bat-like wings.

They were hairless, their skin of a scaly composition that suggested a onetime marine origin, and indeed Yuggoth was covered in part with dark regions that appeared to be composed of a black, viscid liquid. If these were the seas and oceans of Yuggoth, the winged creatures might have evolved in their depths, using their wings to "fly" through the seas as Earthly manta rays "flew" through the warm waters of the Caribbean Sea.

Once *Beijing 11-11* was launched from its construction site on Luna, it was piloted to the Oort Cloud by a two-member crew comprising Chen Jing-quo and Kimana Hasani. When *Beijing 11-11* settled into orbit around the ruddy pulsing oblate form of Yuggoth, Kimana Hasani informed Chen Jing-quo that he was going to take one of the station's EEPs for a closer look at the new planet.

Dr. Chen protested. *Beijing 11-11* carried only a limited number of EEPs — External Excursion Pods. They were meant to be used only in cases of extreme necessity. For servicing and repairs of the station, for transportation between space vehicles — although there were no other space vehicles within the better part of a two billion kilometers of *Beijing 11-11* — or as lifeboats. They were emphatically not intended for exploration.

But Kimana Hasani would not be deterred. He suited up in protective gear and entered the EEP. He promised Chen Jing-quo that he would maintain a continuous video and audio link with *Beijing 11-11* . Once he had climbed into the EEP he waited for the interlock to click green, hit the launch button and dropped away from *Beijing 11-11* .

Dr. Chen watched twin video screens. On one she followed the progress of her partner's EEP as it dropped away from *Beijing 11-11* and drifted down toward the atmosphere of Yuggoth. On the other she watched Kimana Hasani's face. He in turn concentrated on the instruments and controls of the pod.

As the tiny craft entered the atmosphere of the planet Chen Jing-quo heard her partner mutter something but this phase lasted only a few seconds. She thought she heard Kimana Hasani say something like *sizzling*, heard him speak part of her name. Then she observed a flash. The screen that had carried Kimana Hasani's image went blank. The screen that had carried an exterior image of the EEP flared a brilliant golden-orange. A shock wave spread visibly through the atmosphere where the EEP had been, then rippled outward and downward toward the surface of Yuggoth.

And upward, toward *Beijing 11-11*, where Dr. Chen cried out in startlement and grief at what she had seen, and at what she suspected was its meaning.

The only phenomenon that she could think of that would produce so violent a discharge was a nuclear explosion. She knew the design of the EEP as she knew every surface, every weld, every circuit on *Beijing 11 - 11*. She knew that Kimana Hasani's pod carried no fissile material. She inferred what had happened. The atmosphere of Yuggoth was composed of SeeTee matter.

SeeTee. CT. Contra-Terrene.

Antimatter.

She experienced a flash of recollection, of her school days, of a student joke: *What do you get if a normal matter boy makes it with an antimatter girl?*

Answer: *No matter.*

No matter. No matter, in truth. Just one hell of a release of pure energy.

Yuggoth was composed of SeeTee matter.

The mountains and plains of Yuggoth, its black, viscid seas, its ebony ice caps, its cyclopean cities with their towering, eye-wrenching structures, its monstrous inhabitants, all were composed of contraterrene matter.

Of antimatter.

Chen Jing-kuo returned to the electron telescope. She trained it upon the Yuggothian city directly below the point where Kimana Hasani's pod and Kimana Hasani himself had been converted to pure energy. The city lay in ruins. Titanic structures had been toppled, crushed to rubble. The inhabitants of the city had died by the millions, their terrible bodies torn and scattered hither and yon.

Shaking her head, Chen Jing-kuo wiped her tears. She turned from the telescope and opened a hyper-light speed link to Luna. The communications operator who received her call was a onetime classmate, Matyah Melajitm. For a moment Melajitm's smile filled Dr. Chen's screen. Then the comm-op saw the expression on Chen Jing-quo's face.

"What's the matter? Something's happened. What is it?"

"Get Dr. Jerom. Kimana is dead. We seem — I think we've started a war. The first interplanetary war!"

It seemed to take hours — more likely less than two minutes — for Harleyann Jerom to replace Matyah Melajitm at the Luna comm-link.

"Dr. Chen, tell me."

Chen Jing-quo gave her a quick summary of the event.

Harleyann Jerom groaned. "All right, Chen. Do nothing now. Better yet, batten down *Beijing 11-11*. Not that I imagine you can do much to defend the station if the Yuggothi choose to counterattack. They're likely to interpret the explosion as an attack. They surely will if they're anything like us."

"There was no way. I mean, how could Kimana ever imagine ..." Dr. Chen's voice trailed away.

"Never mind blame," Jerom responded. "There will be plenty of time for that later on. Or maybe not. But not now, that's for sure. Keep the link open."

Chen Jing-quo saw Harleyann Jerom turn away, heard her give instructions to Matyah Melajitm. Chen knew that Jerom was going to talk with Earth, get a quick decision from the politicians who ran planetary affairs.

A quick decision.

Fat chance.

Jerom reappeared on *Beijing 11-11's* comm screen. "Chen, was there ever — ever — any indication that the Yuggothi were even aware of *Beijing 11-11*?"

Chen Jing-quo shook her head. "No. That's what was so — we tried — we tried to establish communication with them. They ignored us. Or — it wasn't even that. It was as if they were completely unaware of us. As if were bacteria, viruses, and they were humans. Or mammoths. How many bacteria does such a beast crush with every step? To the Yuggothi we were bacteria. Or less. They never even noticed us. Until Kimana hit their atmosphere. Then ..." She spread her hands, helpless to continue.

Harleyann Jerom nodded. "An apt simile. They probably won't be angry with us. A mersa bacterium doesn't hate its host and a human doesn't hate a bacterium. They're just two kinds of organism, and one will kill the other in order to preserve itself and perpetuate its kind. The infection will kill the host or the host will kill the infection."

"Right." Chen Jing-kuo reacted with a manic grin.

Jerom's voice was harsh. "Get a grip!"

"Nothing personal," Dr. Chen went on.

"I said, *Get a grip*! This is a crisis that could make all the wars in human history look like playground squabbles."

"I'm sorry," Chen said. She was calmer now. Her nerves were jumping. She could feel her heart pounding in her chest. It must be beating close to two hundred beats a minute. Her breath was coming in desperate gasps.

She recognized the phenomena. Some ancestor was reaching down to her, reaching through the genetic matter that carried ancient reflexes. Her body sensed her desperation, prepared itself for combat or for flight. Appropriate reactions for a Cro-Magnon, for Pithecanthropus Erectus, for an ancestor even more ancient. But hardly apt for Homo Interplanetarius.

She was in control of herself. "What are my instructions, Dr. Jerom?"

"For now, observe and report. What do you see on Yuggoth?"

Chen returned to the telescopes. She activated a third screen, one for an electron image, one for an optical image, one for a superimposed combination.

"It's daytime down there. You know, it's always daytime on Yuggoth. The planet rotates but its light comes from its core so it doesn't really matter. The city that was destroyed by the shock wave — I see Yuggothi arriving from all directions. I suppose they're rescue crews. The devastation is terrible. The casualties — I can't even guess at the number. Some of them are still alive, though. I see Yuggothi crawling through the ruins. Some with dreadful injuries. Some are just — just — it looks as if their body parts, when they were ripped off by the shock wave, some of them didn't die and now they're flopping around, moving like torn starfish. And — and — I can't go on, Harleyann. I can't."

"That's all right, Jing-kuo. You've done what you can. And we're getting feeds from *Beijing 11-11's* instruments."

There was a pause, then Harleyann Jerom resumed. "You're convinced that Kimana Hasani's EEP set off the explosion on Yuggoth?"

Dr. Chen's eyes were still focused on the screens showing conditions on the surface of Yuggoth. "I'm certain, Harleyann. The only explanation — I'm convinced it's the only explanation, the only way that little EEP could cause the devastation — the only explanation is that Yuggoth is composed of antimatter. Once Kimana's EEP hit the atmosphere that was all it took. The EEP and Kimana himself were cancelled out. Converted to pure energy, along with an equivalent mass of Yuggothi atmosphere. He — "

Her words were cut off by a gasp from Harleyann Jerom. Then the voice of the woman on Luna said, "They're here!"

"Who? What are you saying, Harleyann?"

"The Yuggothi."

"Impossible. I just saw them leave their planet."

"They're here. They're circling overhead. Their ships are unlike anything else I've ever seen. They look like — like cyborgs. They're monsters, something like bats, something like octopuses, something like humans. And machines. They're machines, too."

"But — they can't have traveled that far in a few minutes."

"They can, Jing-kuo. They must have — I don't know — we manage to skip message through wormholes or subspace or however our system works. We don't really understand, do we, we just know that it works. And they've found a way to travel, oh, not through space. Between space. Whatever. And they're heading toward Earth, Jing-kuo. I can see. I can see waves of blackness sweeping across the planet. The atmosphere is burning, the oceans, forests, ice caps. Oh, my God, my God, my God. It's worse than — "

The transmission ended.

Chen Jing-kuo studied the surface of Yuggoth, pulsing red, filling the sky above *Beijing 11-11*.

The virus doesn't hate its host, she thought, and the host doesn't really hate the virus. There is nothing personal about it. Nothing personal. If the host doesn't destroy the virus in time, the virus will kill the host. But even if that happens, once the host is dead, the virus also will die.

Chen Jing-kuo turned the telescope toward Earth. The image was magnified until it filled a screen. As she watched, bits of black appeared on the blue-and-white disk. They spread from points to irregular blots. More of them appeared, and more, until they began to run together.

For a moment the planet disappeared against the solid black background of space. Then points appeared again, became blots, multiplied and grew until Earth was a red disk. Like Yuggoth, it began to pulse, to pulse like a malevolent heart. Now Chen Jing-kuo understood what she was seeing. The Yuggothi, she realized, had devised a means to convert the normal matter of Earth, contact with which would have been instantly, disastrously fatal to them, into contraterrene matter. Antimatter.

Now they could live in Earth, and now there remained no other life to compete with them.

But Yuggoth itself was also contraterrene. The Yuggothi had erected no shield against a potential plunging space station of terrene matter. For all Chen Jing-kuo could tell, the Yuggothi were as unaware of the station as a human would be of a single fatal bacterium.

Earth was dead. Chen Jing-kuo knew that now. The Yuggothi had simply fired uncounted bombs of solid contraterrene matter into Earth's atmosphere until there remained nothing of the world that had lived for billions of years. They had wiped it clean. The atmosphere was gone. The oceans, the forests. The ice caps were gone. The planet had been wiped clean. It now had new owners. Octopus-bat-man-machine *things* that even now were walking or slithering or flying across the black, dead surface of the once blue-green, beautiful world. The black surface that was now pulsing with a red, evil rhythm.

Even so, there was no way that Yuggothi could, themselves, land upon that murdered world. Unless they had devised a means to convert their own bodies to terrene matter — or the very Earth to contraterrene.

The oblate globe of Yuggoth spun beneath *Beijing 11-11*. Chen Jing-kuo set the controls, activated the verniers, sent *Beijing 11-11* plunging away from Yuggoth, away from Earth and Earth's sun, out into the arm of Earth's galactic womb.

Chen Jing-kuo fully expected to die in *Beijing 11-11*.

The odds of reaching an inhabitable world, no less meeting friendly aliens, were astronomical. Chen Jing-kuo laughed. Truly the odds were astronomical. But some day, some day a thousand years hence or a billion, some unimaginably strange creatures would find *Beijing 11-11* and know that a species with hands and feet and minds had lived. That they were not alone in the cold universe.

Made in the USA
Columbia, SC
24 July 2018